PRESCIENT SPIRIT

SUZI BAMBLETT

Broodleroo

 Created with Vellum

For my grandchildren.

PROLOGUE

High above us, a black crow swoops and circles around towering gothic chimneys. Shielding my eyes from the sun, I gaze up at the red brick façade, all but camouflaged by ivy.

Mark admires the structure. 'Look at the crenelations.'

'It's not a castle,' I tease.

I survey the old house from the weedy gravel drive. On each corner of the roofline, just below the parapet, open-mouthed gargoyles spew down evil curses. Between them, perhaps a metre apart, their closed-mouthed brothers proffer menacing glares.

The crow caws in disdain as the sun disappears behind a cloud, creating eerie images. I shiver.

Mark reaches for my hand. 'Come on. Let's go inside.' He leads me up stone steps to an impressive oak door. 'Smythe said he'd leave it unlocked.' As Mark lifts the rusty iron latch, the door swings open with a spine-chilling creak.

'Sounds like the house is auditioning for a Hammer Horror movie,' I say as we venture inside.

We're greeted by a vast hallway of checkerboard tiles and, pièce de resistance, an imperial staircase.

'Wow,' I say, relieved that the interior is far more promising. My gaze travels up to the half landing where the stairs divide into two. Although the carpet is long gone, the treads look solid while an oak banister exudes potential.

'See?' Mark beams with pleasure. 'I told you.' He opens the first door on the left. 'Bit musty in there.' He pinches his nose.

Unperturbed, I take a peek. Perhaps once a library or study, the room is dwarfed by an oversized marble fireplace. Dust sheets cover the furniture and I wonder if the foul smell lurks there too.

'Now this is more like it,' calls Mark.

I catch up with him in the next room. 'Oh, yes.' The kitchen's beautiful - high ceilinged and flooded with light and, although the cupboards are dated and the spaces where stand-alone units have been removed thick with grease, there's an impressive old range.

'This room's amazing.' Mark waves his arms expansively. 'Look at the size of it. You can design your dream kitchen. Anything you like.'

I stand in the middle of the room taking it all in. At the back, a stable door leads out onto a patio area beyond, while the other end is taken up by an enormous refectory table. I can almost visualise monks gathering for communal meals.

We head back out to the hallway. The remaining half of the downstairs is barricaded with warning signs: 'Keep out – structure unsafe', so we continue our viewing upstairs. Only the rooms on the east of the building are habitable. The staircase leading to the west wing is roped off, as is a narrow flight of stairs leading up to the second floor.

'Smythe said not to venture past the ropes,' says Mark. 'The floorboards are iffy. I'll come back with the surveyor tomorrow.'

We descend to the half landing where Mark takes my hands in his. 'So?'

I chew my lip. 'There's a lot to do. Can we afford it?'

Mark grins. 'That's the great thing about the legacy. We don't have to buy it and we get to live in it rent free. All we do is pay for renovations. I've got about thirty grand of equity in my apartment. We can use that for essentials, and get the business up and running as soon as possible.'

'There's also the money from the sale of my flat.' I offer.

Mark shakes his head. 'That's your money. And anyway,' – he grins – 'you might want to use that for your dream kitchen.'

I stare at my husband. He's such a good doctor, but the past two years working in A&E almost destroyed him. The legacy really is a godsend, and will enable him to set up a respite facility and conference centre. But, for his dream to be realised, we both need to commit one hundred percent.

I smile. 'Let's do it.'

CHAPTER ONE

Emerging from the trees, I lift my hood and make a dash for it. Hurrying past broken and boarded windows, I leap a puddle and race round the corner of the dilapidated west wing. Swerving to avoid two urns, bare but for the remains of last year's geraniums, I run up the wide stone steps, pausing with my hand on the cast iron latch of the oak front door. Five years, and yet it's still hard to believe *The Sanctuary* is ours.

As the door creaks open, I can't resist admiring the double staircase rising majestically from the hallway. Oak banisters, now stripped and revarnished, have come up a treat. I turn left into the tiny boot room, hang up my wet coat and tug off my wellies, replacing them with fluffy socks to keep me warm from the cold black-and-white tiled floor.

Rejuvenated by my unexpectedly wet walk, I head across the hallway to the kitchen. Good. My four-year old son, Ike, is with Nana Vita, ensconced in her apartment. After checking there's water in the kettle, I flick the switch. Hopefully I've enough time for a cuppa before they come in for lunch. Waiting for the kettle to boil, I lean against the drying rail attached to the old range.

'That thing?' Mark had scoffed when I suggested keeping it. 'We'll replace it with something swanky when we fit the new kitchen.'

But that was before the builders condemned the central heating and hot water systems, and the ring-fenced funding for my dream kitchen had to be diverted. Even so, I'm grateful. I'm very fond of this old Aga.

The kettle turns itself off. I make a peppermint tea and carry it across to the old wooden carver. I lean back against the multi-coloured, hand-knitted throw, and as I sip my drink, cast an affectionate eye around the room. The kitchen units may be tired and the stand-alone white goods eclectic, but I can't help a self-satisfied smile. Hours spent scrubbing and bleaching the scratched surface of the old table have paid off, giving it a rustic look. The brown pottery bowl of fruit finishes it off nicely. My gaze takes in the ancient American fridge, backdrop to Ike's artwork, while the repainted pine dresser houses an ever-expanding collection of charity shop-sourced china plates and mugs. I love it all.

The French doors swing open and Ike trots in, closely followed by my mother-in-law.

'I'm starving,' whines my son, widening his eyes and rubbing his belly for effect.

Vita lifts him up to the table. 'You sit there my boy, and Nana will fix some lunch.'

'There's pasta in the fridge,' I say.

Vita opens the fridge door and locates the plastic container. She peels off the lid, sniffs and pulls a face, before tipping its entire contents into the bin.

'Hey, that was fine,' I say.

'You know, Hanna, that I don't hold with reheating food in the microwave.' Vita smiles at Ike. 'Nana will fix you some eggs.' Breaking two eggs into a bowl, she whisks them ferociously with a fork. 'Ike likes Nana's eggs, doesn't he?'

Ike, the traitor, grins back with adoration.

Jenna, our office manager, strides into the kitchen. 'Hi all.'

'Cool trousers,' I say. 'They new?'

She thrusts her thumbs in her hip-pockets and strikes a boyish pose. 'Thanks. ASOS.'

I wince. 'It'll be a while before I can fit into anything like that.'

Jenna laughs and gestures towards my mug. 'Kettle just boiled?'

'Sorry,' I say. 'Think I used the last of the water.'

'No worries.' Jenna fills the kettle and flicks the switch again. She takes two mugs down from the dresser. 'Can I tempt anyone else?'

Vita continues to stir Ike's scrambled eggs. Her silence is palpable.

Jenna turns to me. 'Why don't you put your feet up for five minutes?'

'Thanks. I think I will.' I carry my tea through to the snug and sink into the couch. I love this room too. With floor-to-ceiling bookcases, it's the nearest I'll ever get to a library.

A few minutes later, Jenna joins me and places a plate with two chocolate digestives down on the side table. 'Thought you might need sugar. So, what's going on between you two now?'

'Bloody Vita,' I grumble. 'Always has to know best.'

Jenna perches on the arm of the couch. 'Spill.'

I sigh. 'She's so teacherly and yet Ike worships the ground she walks on.'

Jenna's eyebrow raises. 'Are you jealous?'

'No.' I lean my head back and close my eyes. 'Perhaps…
I don't know. Ike definitely loves her more than me.'

'You do know how ridiculous you sound?'

I open my eyes to stare at her. 'Sometimes I think he
hates me.'

Jenna laughs. 'Isn't that what parents are for? And moth-
ers-in-law, well…' She winks. 'Bane of your life.'

Despite myself, I smile. 'How come you're so wise when
you haven't even got kids?'

'And won't have if I get a say in the matter. I'm not cut
out for motherhood. But look at you. A four-year-old and
another on the way. Earth mother if ever I saw one.'

I punch her arm.

'Ow.' Jenna affects mock pain. 'Anyway, I'd better get
back before the boss comes looking for me.' She stands up.
'It suits you, you know?'

'What?'

'Pregnancy. You're beautiful.'

'Rubbish,' I scoff.

Left on my own again, I sip my tea. Jenna and I had met
at sixth form college, but it wasn't until Mark took her on to
cover my maternity leave that I realised how efficient she
was. It was fortuitous that she'd just been made redundant, as
we couldn't really afford her but, after a recent relationship
break up, she agreed to work for a pittance if we threw in free
board and lodgings. The plan was to job share while I showed
her the ropes, but she had everything under control after just a
week. Earlier than anticipated, I found myself idle for the first
time in years. I should be bitter, but I'm not. Jenna's so easy
going and makes my paranoid hormonal rants appear funny
rather than crazy.

I haven't the energy to put myself back in the fray with
Vita. Instead, I finish my drink and demolish both biscuits

before moving to the desk to carry on with work. I'm researching the history of *The Sanctuary* as a surprise for Mark. I thought if I found out some interesting facts, I could update the marketing publicity on the website to see if we can attract a few more corporate clients.

Mark always works hard. We barely saw each other for the first two years of our marriage. On his thirty-third birthday, when his godfather, Stefan, advised Mark of the legacy, we jumped at it. How was I to know, five years on, he'd revert to being a workaholic?

For the next couple of hours, I lose myself in research, chuckling as I read the words of an old monk who lived in *The Sanctuary* in the nineteenth century. 'May God's wrath fall on anyone who writes of me.' Strange words for someone purporting to be holier than thou. And yet, from what I've already discovered about Father Eduardo, perhaps it's not so strange. He was a bit of an eccentric, styling himself on St Frances of Assisi. From the many animal statues and shrines dotted around the gardens, he certainly appeared to favour creatures over humans. Anyway, it's not him I'm researching, it's the house.

I rub the small of my back. It always aches when I sit too long. Glancing at the clock on the mantlepiece I note it's three-fifteen already. The winter sun has shifted over to the other side of the building, leaving the snug chilled. I should light the fire.

Kneeling in front of the hearth, I build a criss-cross of kindling. Screwing up twists of newspaper from the rack beside the grate, I tuck them around, adding a few pieces of coal from the scuttle. When it's ready, I reach up to the mantlepiece. Damn, no matches.

I haul myself up and head for the messy drawer in the oak sideboard, where potentially dangerous things are stored away from Ike's prying fingers. As I rummage through for matches, my gaze is drawn to a shelf of books in the glass cabinet above. They don't look as if they've been touched in years, but their leather-bound spines have that enticing look of all old books. I drag a dining chair across to the sideboard and clamber up. The glass doors have done their job, as the books are relatively dust free. I run fingertips across the spines, reading the faded titles: *The Gardeners' Almanac; An English Flower Garden; The Garden Path.* I must let Norris, our gardener, know they're here. Perhaps the books will provide advice on when to cut back the older shrubs and bushes. Norris's mad axeman approach has resulted in one or two gardening disasters. Further along, other titles suggest themes more relevant to my research: *Foundations to Dissolution; Churchyard Monuments.* Mmm, that might be interesting. Standing on tiptoe, I reach a little further…

'Hanna, what on earth are you doing?'

I spin around to spot Jenna standing in the doorway. As I pivot, my socked foot slides on the polished seat of the dining chair, causing the chair to tilt and me to lose my balance. I make a grab for the open glass door. Luckily Jenna catches me.

'Are you completely mad?' she yells, helping me down. Her tone softens when she sees my pained expression. 'Are you all right?'

'I'm fine,' I yelp, holding out my finger. The nail's bent right back where I caught it on the glass door.

'Ouch.' Jenna rights the chair and lowers me onto it. 'I'm calling Mark.'

'No, really, I'm fine. He's so busy.'

'You can't go standing on chairs in your condition.'

'I'd have been all right if you hadn't made me jump.' I flinch as I push my nail back down.

'Are you sure?'

'Yes, I just scared myself.' I rub my stomach gently. 'I'll sit for a moment. It's not like I actually fell.'

Jenna perches on the arm of the couch. 'So, what were you trying to do?'

'Reach a book.' I point to the top shelf.

Jenna jumps up. 'Let me get it.'

'No, I've gone off the idea now.' I move across to the couch and examine my legs for bruises. 'I was doing research. I thought it might be good to have some history about the old place. It was once a Franciscan Monastery you know?'

'Yeah, the stained-glass windows in the chapel are a bit of a giveaway.'

'We had planned to rent the chapel out as a yoga studio. Offer classes for residents and non-residents, to stoke up a bit more business until the corporate bookings get going. But I never got around to sourcing a yoga teacher.'

'That's not a bad idea, I'll look into it.' Jenna folds her arms. 'It's freezing in here. Shall I light the fire?'

'Yes please.' I gesture towards the messy drawer. 'I was searching for the matches before I got distracted.'

Jenna locates the matches in the drawer and kneels in front of the grate. While she coaxes the fire to life, I practise my deep breathing. I'm rubbing my stomach, but my finger's giving me more pain than anything. I hold it up to examine it.

After placing the guard in front of the fire, Jenna glances at me. She wanders back to the messy drawer, pulls out a pair of nail clippers and comes over to sit next to me. 'Here. Let me.' She takes my hand.

I rest my head back while she gently tidies up my fingernail. 'There, that's better.'

'Thanks. Where are Vita and Ike?'

'Still in the kitchen as far as I know.'

I sigh. 'I shouldn't complain. It's just…'

'What?'

I grimace. 'Vita bought Ike this book explaining about having a new brother or sister. Before she started reading it to him, I don't think he'd noticed I was getting bigger. Now he's more aware. Sometimes I catch him staring at my belly and giving it evils.'

'That's natural, so I've been told.'

"Also, it's raising questions we're not quite ready for."

'What does Mark say?'

I sniff. 'He leaves that sort of thing to me.'

'Hey.' Jenna pulls a tissue from her pocket and passes it to me. 'Hormones.'

'I know.' I dab my eyes. 'I need a glass of wine.'

'Well, only a couple of months to go now.'

'Not if I'm breastfeeding.'

'Oh, yeah. Well, I'll have to drink it for you.' She laughs.

'No change there then.' I rest my fingers on her arm. 'Jenna, please don't mention what happened just now to Mark. The snagging list on Caleb block is giving him enough to worry about.'

'Okay.' Jenna gets up. 'Want me to get that book down before I go?'

'No. Leave the damn thing where it is. It's the curse of Father Eduardo.'

CHAPTER TWO

Unable to put dinner off any longer, I head back to the kitchen. I take a prepared vegetable lasagne from the fridge and slide it into the range. 'Dinner in half an hour.'

Vita and Ike are sitting at the table surrounded by colouring pens and paper. I move closer. 'What are you guys up to anyway?'

'I'm drawing,' says Ike, without looking up.

Spying a page filled with the letter d he's copied so diligently, I groan. 'Preschool say they don't want us to teach him letters.'

Vita glances up. 'What harm can it do?' She returns her attention to Ike. 'That's right, round the dinosaur's big bottom, up his long neck and down to his feet.'

'But they teach phonetically.' Wearily, I move back to the worktop and begin slicing carrots on the chopping board. 'They say it will confuse him.'

'It's good to have a head start. Ike can write his name already.'

I tip the carrots into a pan and take a pack of frozen peas from the freezer. 'But he doesn't understand what he's writing. He's just copying.' I rip open the bag and peas spill across the floor. 'Bugger.'

'Come on, sausage.' Vita gathers everything up from the table. 'Let's leave Mummy to her cooking.'

Why does she always have to make me feel so inadequate? I sweep spilled peas into a dustpan. It's not like I haven't done the research; honed my child-rearing philosophies. A child should understand what he's reading or writing… Vita, in contrast, holds the old-school view that a child learns by rote. I sigh. Annoyingly, Ike absorbs everything like a sponge.

———

As we finish our meal, Ike puts his knife and fork neatly together on his plate and looks up at Mark. 'Please may I get down from the table, Daddy?'

'Yes, buddy.' Mark turns to me. 'Did you hear that? Mum's such a good influence.'

Vita's cheeks flush. 'I'll take Ike up for his bath. I can put him to bed if you like and read a story?'

'Thanks, Mum.' Mark winks at her.

'Don't forget his Ruxolitinib cream…' I say, but Vita's already taken Ike's hand and is leading him away.

Jenna gets up from the table too. 'Sorry, I need to dash. I'm meeting a mate for drinks. Do you mind?'

I shake my head. 'It's fine.' Stacking the dishes, I carry them over to the dishwasher. I ram the plates into the rack and drop cutlery into the wire basket.

'Hey, careful,' says Mark. 'That's one of Mum's dishes.'

'Oh, and we mustn't damage Mummy's precious dishes,' I mutter.

'What's got your goat?'

I spin around to face him. 'Didn't you hear her over dinner?'

'She's just trying to be helpful.'

'No, she isn't, Mark. She undermines me with every bloody comment she makes.'

'You're being ridiculous.'

'Am I?' I slam the dishwasher door. 'Every time she opens her mouth it's to criticise me. It's that quizzical, sarky little flick at the end. "Is that what we're having for supper? Is that what you're wearing?" She drives me mad.'

'But everyone loves Mum.'

I glare at him.

Mark raises his hands. 'I'll give you some space to calm down.' He leaves the room.

Leaning against the kitchen island, I cover my face with my hands. Is Mark right? Am I overreacting by taking it as personal criticism when Vita picks up Ike on his Ps and Qs? I tear off a piece of kitchen roll and blow my nose. Everyone loves Vita, Ike most of all. I don't know why though. She's so strict, never lets him watch cartoons and everything they do has to be educational. But instead of seeing Nana as a miserable old cow, Ike simply adores her.

CHAPTER THREE

Loosening my bathrobe, I squirt a blob of moisturiser onto my upper thighs and rub in circular motions. Ooh, that's cold. This pregnancy is taking a toll on my thirty-three-year-old body, but it's worth it. I so want to be a good wife and mother.

I wipe my hands on a towel. The timing's not brilliant, of course, as the business has hit a plateau and we could do without the additional expense of my maternity cover.

I stroke my belly. It won't be long now. I can do this. After all, I'm already Mum to Ike. And yet, sometimes it feels like I'm play acting. I give myself a little shake. Don't be silly, everything's going to be fine. Once this one's here, we'll be the perfect family.

My baby kicks against my hand. I love her already. But suppose I love her more than Ike? Will he be able to tell? How does a mother share her love with more than one child?

Discarding my robe, I struggle into pregnancy underwear. I've attended natural childbirth classes, even persuaded Mark to come with me a few times. We haven't had to buy much, we still have all Ike's stuff and, if it's a girl – and the twenty-week scan says it is – we'll buy extra girlie clothes. I won't do that before she arrives, in case I tempt fate. Because what I really want is a daughter. It's what I've always wanted. I gulp down a sob. I miss having a mum. 'You can share my mum,' Mark had said on more than one occasion. As if that would be the same.

I pull my maternity smock over my head and the baby kicks again. I'm excited to meet her, but the closer the due date, the more I worry. Suppose my little girl rejects me, too?

'I'm going for a walk,' I say as I step into the kitchen. 'Do you want to come, Ike?'

Ike's up on a chair, a tea towel around his waist and a mixing bowl in front of him. 'Nana and me are making cookies.'

I glance across at the ingredients set out on the worktop like an episode of *Saturday Kitchen*. 'All right. I'll go on my own.'

I hurry out to the boot room and pull on my jacket and boots, wrapping a scarf around my neck. Turning right at the foot of the steps, I saunter across the lawn. Dew lingers, and the last of this year's snowdrops nod droopy heads. I feel a little guilty about the pleasure of walking alone, but I enjoy the solitude and I'm grateful the residents stick to the arboretum at the front of the house.

Heading across the car park between Aaron and Bartholomew blocks, I pass through a gate marked 'Private,' into an orchard of gnarled fruit trees extending clawing limbs. The trees are old and despite heavy pruning, unlikely to yield a good crop of apples and pears this year. As I enter the woods, calmness seeps over me. I stop to admire purple-streaked wood anemones hidden in the dappled shade, while sunshine-yellow heads of coltsfoot bring me joy. A squirrel runs back and forth between two trees, and I laugh when I spot a female blackbird wrestling with a worm.

The baby flips in my belly and I feel a familiar shiver of anticipation. Externally I'm going through the motions, attending appointments, making a note of changes to my body, but sometimes it's like I'm watching someone else. As if I'm not really connected. Out here, during daily walks, equilibrium returns.

I reach the small clearing dotted with statues. My favourite is the small boy curled up with a rather scary dog – or is it a wolf? – watching over him. He reminds me of Mowgli from *The Jungle Book*. I'm amused by the proximity of a deer and a rabbit to the big wolf dog. They must trust her – I always think of the dog as "her". I shudder as an alternative interpretation pops into my mind. Could she be sizing the child up for her supper?

I sit down on a large stone. It was probably once another animal statue, but it's so worn the figure can't be made out. What's wrong with me? Why do I feel so detached? It's Vita's fault. What was it someone once said? 'There are three of us in this marriage.' Bloody Vita.

It was two years ago when Mark suggested Vita move in with us. We were driving home after visiting her in Cambridge. 'She's not getting any younger,' he argued.

I stared out through the windscreen at the driving rain. 'She'll live for years.'

'You don't know that.'

'Oh, but I do. She'll do it out of spite.'

Mark changed gear to navigate a roundabout. 'Sometimes you act as if you hate her,' he said as he accelerated away again.

'I don't hate her, but no-one will ever be good enough for her precious son.'

'That's not true. It's just… Mum depends on me.'

'She doesn't depend on anyone.' I was being a bitch and I knew it.

'She's just lonely.'

I reached forward to adjust the air con. It was getting a bit steamy. 'Your mother is bearable in small doses, but to live with us?'

'She wouldn't be living with us. She'd have her own apartment. We have residents living at *The Sanctuary.* None of them bother you.'

I snorted. 'That's true.'

'You know we need Mum's financial investment to turn the place around. We've been losing money for months.'

I helped myself to a Werther's, unwrapped it and popped it in my mouth. Mark's idea to market *The Sanctuary* for corporate events was proving slow to take off. You couldn't blame the punters. Who in their right mind wants to book a training event in a home for crazy people? Despite all attempts to rebrand as a private rehabilitation unit, locals still affectionately refer to *The Sanctuary* as the nut house.

'If Mum moved in,' Mark continued, 'she'd put the proceeds from her house into the business. It would be in all our interests. What's the alternative? Hand *The Sanctuary* over to the bank and become homeless?'

I sucked my sweet thoughtfully. 'What if it isn't enough?'

'What?'

'Her money. What if it isn't enough? *The Sanctuary* is a

money pit. Suppose in a couple of years' time we're in the same position?'

'We won't be.'

'Okay,' I said. It seemed I didn't have a choice.

So, Vita moved in and, for a few months her money eased things. Mark got the creditors off his back and for a while everything went in the right direction. We were operating on a much smaller staff than the house could cater for and most of our specialist team – doctors and consultants – were free-lance or part time, living off site. But Vita drove me nuts.

A twig snaps and I turn to see our gardener approaching, with an axe over his shoulder.

I smile. 'Hello Norris.'

'Mrs Konteh.' Norris grunts. He stops and surveys the statues before scratching his head, tutting, and walking on through the trees.

I consider calling him back to chat about the gardening books, but perhaps it's best if I let Mark talk to him? I don't want Norris thinking I'm complaining about his work. A replacement head gardener would do nothing to help our finances and Norris does his best. He also takes care of household maintenance, liaising with Mark to get contractors in whenever it becomes completely necessary.

I get up, button my jacket and head home. The sun is hidden behind thick cloud and it's hard to tell whether it's yet reached the meridian. I tighten my scarf to protect myself from the cold wind. Emerging from the woods, I hurry back across the orchard. Blackthorn blossom gleams white in a leafless hedge and I make a mental note to return in autumn to gather sloes.

Arriving home, I'm greeted by a crash of pans coming

from the kitchen. Ike's playing drums again while Vita clears away debris from their bake-a-thon. Heading towards them, I take a deep breath, determined to be cordial. The heat from the Aga makes my cheeks glow. A wire rack on the central island is packed with cookies. The sweet smell of melted chocolate makes my tummy rumble.

'Mummy!' Ike runs towards me, clinging to my legs. 'Look what we made.'

'Wow.' I smile. 'Am I allowed to try one?'

Ike glances at his Nana. Vita nods. I try not to let the gesture spoil my good humour as I pick a cookie and seat myself in a chair in front of the Aga.

'Coffee?' asks Vita.

'Yes please.' I nibble the cookie. 'Ike, these are excellent.'

After lunch, I take a pile of clean washing upstairs. I cross our bedroom to the nursery, the tiny space created in the turret linked to our room, and place the freshly washed matinee jackets carefully in the drawer below the cot. As I slide the drawer closed, an aroma of fabric softener wafts up, tickling my nostrils. Ike was too big to take advantage of the newborn trousseau amassed over the years. This time they'll be used.

My baby kicks. 'Not long now,' I whisper. Placing my hands on the small of my back, I stretch. Movement catches my eye. I pad towards the window and glance across the sloping roof to the gardens below.

I scream and jump back as a bird flies into the window pane. Clutching a hand to my neck, I move forward and peer out at the bird's body, now lying motionless on the roof. A breeze ruffles its downy feathers. I hold my breath. Poor thing.

Perhaps it's stunned? After a few moments it seems to recover, lifting its head and flapping one wing. I cover my mouth to stifle a gag. Its neck is at a terrible angle. The poor creature is upright for a moment before tumbling over like prairie grass blowing across a desert landscape. In horror, I watch as it nears the gutter. At the last moment, it rises a few centimetres. I will the bird to flap its wings and fly away, but it drops like a stone.

My legs shake and I reach out, holding the window ledge for support. The millisecond before the bird hit the glass, our eyes had met. Unable to change its path, it recognised its fate. More than that, it was as if it had chosen it.

I stare down at splatters of crimson blood decorating the tiles where the bird had lain.

Charging from the nursery, I hurry across our bedroom and down two flights of stairs. Breathless, I peer through the French doors. The bird is lying on the paving stones.

I gasp as I spot Mr Biggles emerging from the kitchen garden. How is it that cats have a sixth sense? He can identify the opening of a tuna can from several hundred metres. Now he makes his way stealthily across the patio, like a lion stalking his prey.

'Shoo.' I bang on the glass doors. Grabbing a plastic bag from the basket below the sink, I unlock the French doors and head outside. 'Go away.' I yell.

I crouch to look at the bird's lifeless face. One eye stares up, glazed and accusing. Mr Biggles miaows, creeps closer, sniffing at droplets of blood.

'No.' I lift the bird by its feet and drop it into the supermarket bag. It seems disrespectful, but better than leaving it for the cat to consume before regurgitating it back onto the kitchen floor in an hour's time. I dispose of the bird in the dustbin. The bag lands with a thud.

The clock in the hallway chimes four o'clock. I grab my jacket and wander across to our day care centre. Ike goes there once a week with Vita when she plays piano for the older folk. Residents and day visitors enjoy nothing more than a singsong, and they love Ike. He's a solemn little boy, always polite and never complains when the old ladies make a fuss of him.

When I stroll into the room, I find Ike sitting quietly on a plastic chair beside Taiwo Ogola, one of the regular day visitors. Tai, as everyone calls him, is a likeable Nigerian chap around eighty, with black hair turning grey in small patches. Perhaps Ike is drawn to him because he too has skin depigmentation caused by an autoimmune disease. Ike's used to be mainly on his hands, but it's now starting to show around his eyes and mouth. Whatever commonality they share, Ike listens to every word Tai says.

'Come on, Ike,' I interrupt, worried he might be bothering the old man, but he refuses to budge, captivated by Tai's story.

Tai pats Ike's leg before glancing up at me. 'It's a grand boy you have here.'

I nod. 'Thank you. But the grand boy needs to come home for a bath and tea.'

'I can bring him home,' calls Vita.

'No, it's fine. Ike, come on please.'

Tai pats Ike's hand. 'I have enjoyed your company today, Ike. Daalu.'

'Daalu.' Ike slides reluctantly from the chair.

As I turn to go, Tai catches my arm. 'Angels watch over this boy.'

I smile and take Ike's hand. He probably does need angels watching over him, with a mother like me.

That night, I dream about the birth.

My contractions begin slowly and there's plenty of time to get to the hospital. Mark is with me – the Mark I married before The Sanctuary became a millstone and he turned into a workaholic.

My labour progresses exactly as planned. Contractions get stronger. Mark mops my brow with a cold flannel, breathing along with me.

The pain gets worse. The look on the midwife's face turns to alarm and a doctor is summoned. Mark is thrown out of the room. His protests echo along the corridor. My legs are in stirrups. The midwife and doctor are shouting, 'Push, push,' but I can't.

'If you don't push this baby out, it will die,' says the midwife.

I give one almighty push and the baby is out, but there's no crying. Just silence.

I wake tangled in a soggy, cold quilt. Feeling across the bed, I realise Mark's not there. My T-shirt's stuck to my skin. I clamber over to the drawer and pull out a fresh one. Heading into the ensuite, I wash my face before creeping downstairs. I follow the light to the snug and find Mark on the couch with his mobile phone, staring into space.

'Mark?' I say.

He doesn't respond.

I nudge his shoulder. 'Mark?' I repeat softly.

He jerks, shakes his head and gazes at the screen on his phone.

'What is it?'

'It's Dad. He's had a heart attack.'

CHAPTER FOUR

Vita sits staring into her second cup of coffee.

Ike frowns. 'What's wrong with Nana?'

'Nothing, honey.' I tousle his hair. 'She's just worried about someone who's feeling poorly. What do you want for breakfast?'

'Peanut butter on toast.'

The thought of it makes me gag, but I'm in charge this morning. I toast a slice of bread, trying not to inhale as I spread it with peanut butter. I'm way past the morning sickness stage, but I've never been able to stomach the stuff.

Mark strides in, mobile phone in hand. 'That was Temi.'

His casual mention of the name puts me on edge. 'What did he say?'

'Doesn't sound good. He thinks I should fly out as soon as possible.'

Vita tops up her mug from the cafetiere. 'I'll not be coming.'

'No one expects you to.' Mark sits down at the table.

I place a plate of toast and marmalade in front of him.

'Try to eat something.' I squeeze his shoulder. 'You've been up half the night.'

He rubs his eyes. 'I know it shouldn't matter, but this is such bad timing. I've a meeting with the contractor and the surveyor today.'

Ike licks peanut butter from his toast soldiers while Vita gazes into the distance.

'Give it another few hours,' I say. 'See what the day brings.'

'I need to book flights.' Mark opens his MacBook.

'Sit down for a moment,' I say. 'You've had a shock.' It's minutes since he received the call to say his father had passed.

'No, I need to get on it. Hopefully we'll get one tomorrow.'

We? 'Mmm. I'm not sure I'm allowed to fly…' I stroke my belly. 'Is it even safe for the baby?'

Mark Googles. 'It says here you can still travel on scheduled flights with a doctor's note.'

My heart beats fast. 'How long is the flight?'

'If we get a direct one from Heathrow to Lagos, six-and-a-half hours.'

Six-and-a-half hours? I gulp. 'I'm worried I might be more of a hindrance…'

'It's okay. I understand if you don't want to come.' Mark taps his details onto the screen. 'It's just… I could really do with your support.'

I feel sick. I can't leave Ike. But, while a small voice in my head whispers, 'Don't go', another hisses, 'You're such a bad wife'. Wasn't it me who persuaded Mark to wait? Why didn't I encourage him to fly out sooner?

Mark slides his credit card from his wallet.

It's unlikely Mark would have got there in time, even if he'd left this morning. But I know he'd have felt better if he was already in transit when he got the news. I rub my forehead. I should go. Ike will be perfectly fine with Vita, and it's my fault, after all. 'Okay, I'll come,' I say.

Mark gets up and gives me a hug. 'Thanks, Hanna. It means a lot. He returns to the computer, picks up his credit card and enters the details.

It's still dark when I wake. I check the time on my mobile. Not yet six, but I get up anyway and add the last few bits to my suitcase – wash bag, phone charger, hair straighteners. I creep around as Mark's still asleep. A short stroll will settle my nerves.

I head across the kitchen garden and into the woods. The wind blusters and leaves swirl about. A murmuration of starlings explodes from the trees, dispersing across the dawn sky. The sky turns dark as wind whistles through treetops. Perhaps this wasn't such a good idea.

As I retrace my steps, malicious beech trees either side of me sway. I shiver, imagining them trying to crush me. A crow swoops low, its caw slicing the air. He lands on the path, puffs out his chest and swaggers. Cocking his shiny head, he stares with beady, intelligent eyes.

I give him a wide berth and battle on down the path. The howl of the wind is deafening. Above, branches creak and groan. I want to run, but it's no good. Instead, I take shelter under a big oak. An almighty crack causes me to glance up at a silver birch, just as one of its limbs tumbles slowly, bouncing against other trees and bringing smaller branches and twigs with it. I cover my head with my hands and close my eyes.

When everything's still, I open them. A fallen bough blocks my way. Thank goodness I didn't continue along the path. Brushing leaves from my hair, I bow my head against the driving rain and run.

On reaching the house, I bound up the steps to the front door. The wind is so fierce that I struggle to close it once I'm inside.

'What the devil were you doing out in this?' yells Mark from the stairs. 'Don't you think I've enough on my plate without having to worry about you?'

The flight attendant smiles. 'Tea? Coffee?'

'Could I get some water, please?' I reply.

'And I'll take a coffee,' says Mark. 'Strong as you like.'

As she pours the drinks, I loosen my seat belt and wriggle around.

We'd hardly spoken on the way to the airport and now Mark sighs. 'What's the matter?'

'These seats are not exactly comfortable when you've an extra little person on board.' I offer a smile, not wanting to prolong his bad mood.

His face is sullen as he adds two sachets of sugar to his drink.

'I hope Vita will be okay with Ike,' I say.

He tastes his drink and pulls a face. 'She'll be fine. Ike gave her the perfect excuse not to come.' Catching the flight attendant's eye, he gives a thumb's up. 'Keep 'em coming.'

While Mark downs endless refills, I pull the blanket up around my chin and close my eyes. Despite my experience in the woods, I'm feeling calm. It's no longer a case of getting there before Mark's dad passes, because the worst has already happened.

I doze fitfully, to be woken by the captain. 'Good afternoon, ladies and gentlemen. We will shortly be preparing for landing. Please ensure your seat belts are secured and seats are in the upright position.'

We pass uneventfully through Lagos customs and head out to the concourse. I try to follow Mark's gaze as he scans the crowds. I've never met Temi, although he's had such an impact on our family.

'There he is.' Mark pushes ahead while I follow in his wake.

Temi, about Mark's age, is tall and good-looking. His multi-coloured shirt and chinos look smart and cool in contrast to our dishevelled state.

The men embrace like long lost brothers. After a few moments, Temi pulls away, turning to me with a broad smile. 'Hi, you must be Hanna.' He shakes my hand enthusiastically. 'It is good to finally meet you.'

'Hello.' I smooth down my messy hair.

'Come.' He grabs my carry-on case. 'I have a car waiting.'

The limo is sleek and air-conditioned. I gaze out at lanes heavy with traffic as impatient drivers hoot and rev engines. White, red-roofed houses line both sides of the concrete road, interspersed with the occasional tropical tree. Ahead, the skyline is broken by giant billboards and tangles of overhead cables, while intermittent cranes tower over half-finished four-storey new builds.

During the journey the men catch up, their voices becoming a distant hum as I struggle to keep my eyes open.

The car slows smoothly to a halt, and I jolt awake. We've pulled up outside the glass-fronted façade of *The Hotel International*.

Mark steps out and holds the door for me.

'Get some rest.' Temi waves a hand. 'We'll meet tomorrow at your father's apartment. I'll send a car.'

CHAPTER FIVE

I stare at the pictures, all inexplicably turned to face the wall.

'Nigerian custom,' explains Temi. 'You will note the mirrors are also covered.'

Mark wanders through his father's small apartment, picking things up and setting them back down, while I hover awkwardly. My maternity top is sticky, and I tug at it to prevent it accentuating my bump. 'It's so hot.' I fan my face with my hand.

Temi raises his hands skyward. 'The rain will come soon.' Despite the heat, he looks ridiculously cool and handsome, in a thin linen shirt and dark glasses.

Should I say something? Thank him for what he did?

Temi moves into the kitchenette, retrieves a bottle of water from the fridge and hands it to me.

'Thanks.' I unscrew the lid and take a long slug. Wandering into the bathroom, I find Mark poking through his father's shaving kit.

'What did you want to do about Nduka's possessions?' calls Temi.

'I don't know.' Mark ambles back into the living room. I follow and see him rifling through his father's vinyl collection. 'Wow, some classics here.' He pulls out a couple of albums. '*Sgt Pepper's*, Bowie's *Hunky Dory*. These might be worth a listen.'

'Shame we've nothing to play them on,' I murmur.

'*Led Zeppelin 111*, *The Doors 13*. I'd no idea Dad was into this stuff.'

Mark moves into the bedroom and once again I follow. He opens the wardrobe. Jackets, shirts and trousers all hang in orderly fashion. On the shelf below, three pairs of shoes are lined up neatly.

Mark reaches for a shoe box from the top shelf.

'Anything interesting?' I ask as he peers inside.

'Old photographs.' Mark closes the box and tucks it under his arm. 'I'll go through them later.' He turns to Temi. 'We'll take the albums, but you can get rid of the rest. There's nothing else I want.'

'Arrangements have been made for the funeral.' Temi clasps his hands together. 'Nduka organised everything. Even prepaid the funeral director.'

Mark rubs his chin. 'Will many attend?'

'Quite a few from the hospital. Your father was well respected.'

'What about afterwards?' I ask. 'Should we offer refreshments?'

'All arranged. My sister is hosting the wake.'

'That's good of her.' Mark pats Temi on the shoulder. 'We'll reimburse you, of course.'

Temi shrugs. 'No need. All covered by donations from work colleagues. There's nothing for you to do apart from turn up.'

Mark glances around the apartment. 'Are you sure you're okay dealing with this lot?'

'No problem. As I said, Nduka was well respected. Several colleagues have asked if there's anything they can do. They'll help me bag everything up and we'll donate it to a good cause.'

Mark exhales slowly. 'Not much to show for thirty-four years.'

'Your father didn't really have a personal life. This place was a base for when he wasn't on shift. In fact, he often slept at the hospital. He's got a locker there. I'll have it emptied before you head home.' Temi glances at his watch. 'Why don't we grab lunch? There's a café nearby.'

Mark and Temi eat heartily, but I have little appetite. Afterwards, we linger under the shade of an orange sailcloth canopy. They discuss Nduka's work while I, having nothing useful to contribute, sip my diet coke and watch the hustle and bustle of the market stalls around us. My legs are fidgety; they need exercise.

Mark glances my way. 'All right? We'll be a bit longer yet.'

I smile, grateful he's noticed my discomfort. 'I think I'll take a wander around the stalls,' I say.

'Don't go far.'

'Okay.'

As I get up, Temi stands. Flustered, I kiss Mark's cheek and move away. I've barely gone three steps before Temi's taken his seat and resumed their conversation.

Aware it will be easy to get lost, I treat the market as a

grid. If I walk up and down the rows, I'll be able to find my way back. The stalls are stocked with colourful fruit and vegetables I've never seen before – tamarind, agbalumo and tropical almonds. Spices heaped up like giant artist palettes make those silly little jars you buy in the supermarket seem ridiculously small. Shoes, shoes and more shoes – ironic as most people are wearing sandals or tatty trainers. Mountains of clothes, some new, some old. Rolls of fabric – beautiful silks and tie-dye cottons.

Traders call out, shouting and smiling while money exchanges hands. Punters haggle furiously in arguments that seem destined to end in a physical fight, until both parties abruptly smile and the deal is done.

A jewellery stall ahead catches my eye. I peruse the wares, admiring a pretty necklace very like one I have at home. Perhaps I should take something back for Jenna? The market trader shows me a bloodstone bracelet and points out a turquoise ring, but I smile, shake my head and move on.

I'm browsing a craft stall, considering purchasing some carved wooden animals for Ike when someone shouts. Seconds later, a goat hurtles down the gap between the tables, closely followed by two young boys. People laugh as they jostle to get out of the way. The crowd becomes a fast-flowing current and I find myself moving with it.

Once the commotion settles, I spot the fabric stall that I saw when I first came into the market. I make my way over, only to discover that it's not the same one. I spin around trying to get my bearings, but in every direction the stalls repeat themselves in an endless pattern – fruit and veg, shoes, spices, fabrics… I'm lost. I have no idea which is the way back.

I hurry in one direction and then, when things don't seem

familiar, try another. This is ridiculous – I haven't gone far. I must be able to get back to the café. I should ring Mark, but I don't want to be a nuisance and I'll look such a fool in front of Temi. Why does that bother me? Anyway, how will I describe where I am? I make a decision to head in one direction and keep going until I reach the edge of the market. Then I can either try to walk the perimeter or at least find a landmark that will help Mark locate me.

Pushing my way through an even busier crowd, I head off purposefully. I cover my belly to protect my baby from swinging shopping bags and sharp protruding elbows. I'm gasping for a drink. Why didn't I bring my bottle of water? Stupidly, I left it in my rucksack back at the table.

Eventually, I find myself at the edge of the market, but it's no help. I stare at a warren of narrow streets without any cafés or bars. I keep going a little way along one street, hoping to find a landmark and ring Mark. I'm so hot and thirsty. I can't go much further. I'm a complete idiot and need to be found.

A woman sweeps outside her house. A dog pants in the shade under a colourful line of washing strung across the street. Somewhere far away, another dog yaps repeatedly in the tiresome heat.

I'm being watched. Two girls sit on a step, looking like any other pair of school-age friends except both are heavily pregnant. They whisper together. Are they commenting on my own bump? I quicken my pace, attempting to divert my eyes but, as I pass, curiosity causes me to glance through the open doorway behind them. Standing in the shadows, staring out, is a matronly woman.

I realise I've stopped walking. I try to smile, but my mouth won't work. As I raise a hand to my forehead, everything goes blurry and my legs buckle beneath me.

. . .

I open my eyes. I'm in the street seated on a broken plastic chair. An old woman's face is close, her voice raised as she speaks rapidly. A skinny girl comes out with a plastic cup and I realise where I am. The woman grabs the cup from the girl and puts it to my mouth, but I close my lips. I don't want to drink. It might not be safe. Warm liquid spills down my chin.

The old woman mutters something, probably a swear word. She straightens up, a hand on the small of her back and hands the cup back. The skinny girl stares. Her gaze travels to my shoulder bag. I draw it close.

Reaching down into the pocket of her skirt, the old woman pulls out a knife.

I gasp. Am I going to die in this dirty, smelly street? Images of Mark, Ike and my little girl whirl about in my head as the blade glints in the bright sunlight.

My mouth's dry. I can't speak. Does she intend to slit my throat? Cut my baby from my womb? Wrapping my arms protectively around my belly, I back away.

The woman shouts something. The girl runs into the house.

My heart beats fast, or is it the beat of my unborn child? I must protect my daughter. Steadily strength returns. I glare at the woman.

The girl returns, holding out her hand. An orange. The old woman takes the proffered fruit, cuts it into quarters and offers it to me.

I exhale. She's trying to help. I'm perfectly safe.

My hand is shaking as I take a piece of orange and raise it to my parched lips. Juice trickles down my throat and I nod gratefully. 'Thank you.'

The old woman's speaking again. I've no idea what she's

saying. She gestures to my belly, repeating words – *Omo? Kun* something?

'She says you have boy child,' translates the young girl.

'No,' I stammer. 'It's a girl.'

The old woman wipes the sticky knife on her skirt and drops it back into her pocket. She reaches out and touches my shoulder bag, before raising a gnarled fist to her ear.

I shake my head, then I understand. My phone! Fumbling with the catch of my bag, I retrieve my mobile. Three missed calls.

I press a button and Mark answers immediately. 'Where the hell are you?'

It takes a moment to find my voice. 'I… I'm sorry… I…'

The old woman gestures frantically.

'What?' I say to her. 'Oh…' Meekly I hand over my mobile.

'I'll order us some tea.' Mark turns the air conditioning on full blast before picking up the phone. He presses a button. 'Hello? Room Service? Yes, a pot of tea, please. Room 312.' Hanging up, he makes his way over to the bed and sits beside me. 'You had me worried.'

'I'm sorry.' I smooth the duvet over my belly. 'I got lost. I was so hot. I panicked and the next thing I blacked out. It's not unusual for pregnant women to faint.'

'I still think you should let Temi examine you.'

'No.' My cheeks burn. I'm embarrassed by my attitude to the old lady. Why did I overreact? I'm married to a black man, how can I be prejudiced? I swallow. Was it unconscious bias? I search my soul and find shame.

There's a knock at the door. Mark opens it. The waiter

sets a tea tray down on the dressing table. Mark tips him before he leaves.

'When you didn't answer your phone…' Mark pours and passes me a cup. 'And then when you did call back, all I could hear was breathing and a woman shouting. I didn't know what was going on.'

My hands shake and the cup rattles in the saucer. 'I'm sorry.'

Mark takes the tea and sets it down on the bedside table. 'I imagined you'd been mugged, kidnapped or worse. Thank goodness Temi was there. I don't know what we'd have done without him.'

'I'm fine.' I wipe my eyes with the back of my hand. 'We're both fine.'

Mark gets up from the bed. 'I'm sorry for shouting. It's the funeral and everything… Anyway. You have a rest while I check my emails. Later, if you feel up to it, we can go down for dinner. Or we can order room service again if you prefer.' He settles himself at a small table by the window and opens his iPad, his mind already focused on work matters.

I wake gasping for breath and soaked in sweat. What was I dreaming about? All I can remember is Temi being there.

Mark is by my side. 'Hanna, are you all right?'

'Yes, just a bad dream.'

'Why don't I run you a bath?'

'Thanks.'

As he runs the water, I get out of bed and head into the bathroom. I'm touched to see him pour in bubble bath and swish the water.

He dries his hands on a towel. 'I'll leave you to it.'

I slip off my T-shirt and underwear, and step into the

warm, soapy water. I lay back and close my eyes. My dream haunts me. Temi carrying a baby under his arm… I jolt, open my eyes. Those poor girls. What will happen to them and their babies? I think about Ike, tucked up in bed at *The Sanctuary*. I want to pull him into my arms and protect him.

CHAPTER SIX

The alarm on my mobile wakes me. I reach for it and turn it off. Rubbing my eyes, I haul myself out of bed. We're due to leave within the hour. In the bathroom, Mark's taking a shower. I can't let him attend his father's funeral alone.

Once we're ready, Mark and I head down to reception. A white limo is waiting outside. We step out of the hotel and climb into the vehicle. As it pulls away, I gaze out of the windows at the colours and sights. Small stalls line either side of the road and whenever the car slows down, children rush over and tap on the window, offering us slices of watermelon and pawpaw.

I shake my head, but when that fails to discourage them, I copy Mark and stare straight in front of me. I keep thinking about those girls at the house yesterday. Do they bang on car windows trying to sell something in order to feed themselves?

The car pulls to a halt as we reach a procession blocking the street.

'I think this is it.' Mark opens the door and gets out, pushing his way around the car to open mine. As I step out of the air-conditioned limo, I'm overwhelmed by intense heat. A jazz band plays trumpets and drums. Men and women strut past, dressed in white and clapping to the beat. Two women carry wreaths of flowers.

Mark guides me through the bustling crowd. Ahead, I spot six men carrying the coffin on their shoulders. Rather than the sober walk of pall bearers at home, they take a few steps forward and a few back as they swing and sway to the music. The tune reminds me of *When the saints go marching in.*

We're jostled from all sides when Temi appears. 'This way,' he says. The crowds part as he leads the way through until we're head of the procession. Men – I assume they are Nduka's work colleagues – crane their necks, keen to catch sight of his only son.

Temi guides us along the street and through a grassy area to the rear of a large building. 'Training wing of the hospital,' he explains. 'Nduka is to be buried here in the Garden of Remembrance.' He stops beside a huge hole, big enough for four coffins.

Beside the grave stands a man in a black suit finished with a colourful hat. 'Gather around,' he says.

Several of Nduka's work colleagues make tributes, some in English. Even those I can't understand seem respectful, sad to lose such a hardworking and gifted colleague.

White from the men's suits blinds me in the glaring sun. I feel faint and lean against Mark for support.

'Sure you don't want to say anything?' Temi whispers to Mark.

He shakes his head.

Silence descends as the coffin is lowered into the grave. After a few moments, Temi touches Mark's arm and leads us away.

The limo pulls up outside a villa. The journey was short and I'm reluctant to leave the comfort of the air conditioning.

We're greeted by a large woman in her early forties who introduces herself as Lebe, Temi's sister. 'I am sorry for your loss.'

Mark puts a hand on my arm. 'I need to find Temi.'

As he hurries away, Lebe turns to me. 'Come, come. You must be exhausted.'

I give a weak smile. 'It's the heat. Bit of a contrast to February in the UK.'

Lebe raises her hands. 'Rains come soon.' She guides me to an area covered by a purple and white canopy.

'Thank you.' I lower myself into a plastic chair and admire the beautiful red and magenta blooms around me. 'Your garden is lovely. Is this Bougainvillea?'

Lebe smiles. 'Yes, and this one is Hibiscus – we call it Zobo. I have many varieties of lilies.' She points to an exquisite funnel-shaped flower. 'This is Calla lily, one of my favourites.'

Nearby is a trestle table loaded with food, while two men in white kaftans offer champagne from their trays. Lebe says something to a young girl causing her to rush away, returning moments later with a glass of orange juice. She proffers it with a small bow.

I take the glass. 'Thank you.'

The rest of the entourage arrive, most having walked from the burial site. Mark beckons me and I haul myself from the chair to join him. We're evidently supposed to greet the guests. Mark, who has done nothing in terms of the funeral arrangements, plays the dutiful son, while Temi, who has coordinated everything, stands at a respectful distance. The queue seems endless, but finally the guests all have a drink in their hand.

I notice no-one has touched the buffet. As if on cue, a giant platter is carried from the house. As it passes, a waft of gamey meat fills my nostrils, making me gag.

'Goat,' explains Temi as the plate is set down in the centre of the trestle table. 'It is African tradition to sacrifice a goat on such occasions.'

'Excuse me.' I cover my mouth. 'The loo?'

Lebe takes my arm and shows me to the bathroom. After retching in the toilet, I put down the seat and sit on it, wondering how long I can enjoy the air conditioning before someone comes to find me.

Moments later, someone rattles the door handle. Reluctantly, I flush the loo and go back outside to seek a shady place away from the food. Mark is engrossed in conversation with Nduka's colleagues and I can't see Temi. His sister is busy managing the catering staff. Feeling useless and unnecessary, I head away from the crowd to a spot under a tree.

An elderly, wizen woman approaches. As she smiles, her gummy mouth dribbles greasy fat and I try not to gag again. She's speaking, but I have no idea what she's saying. I nod politely and avoid staring at her chin.

Temi hurries to my side. 'Ada's one of the workers at the hospital,' he explains.

'Isn't she a bit old?' I whisper.

He laughs. 'If people manage to get a job here, they tend to keep it until they drop. Ada used to look after your father-in-law. She would make up Nduka's bed when he stayed at the hospital, change and wash his sheets, empty the bins in his office, that sort of thing.'

'What's she saying?' I ask.

Ada continues to smile and nod.

'She's saying what a good man Nduka was.'

Ada's face takes on a look of urgency. Her bony fingers grip my arm as she speaks. Finally letting go, she stares long and hard, before turning and hobbling away.

'What was that about?' I ask.

'She reminded you that this is only the first funeral. In Nigeria, it is customary to have a second one a few months later.'

'Whatever for?'

'Your father-in-law is now in *ita okazi* – the period of torment. When you have the second funeral, a celebration of his life, his spirit will be released into peace.' Temi smiles as if something amuses him.

'What?'

'The belief is that if you don't hold a second funeral, the dead come back to haunt you.'

I shiver, like someone walked over my grave. 'Excuse me.' Leaving Temi, I go in search of Mark. He's still talking to his father's colleagues. As I approach, he sees me and takes my arm. 'You haven't been properly introduced. Everyone, this is Hanna, my wife. Hanna, this is Yas and Oti and…'

I don't take in the names. The men nod and smile in acknowledgement, before continuing their conversation. They're discussing Nduka's great contribution to the hospital, to research and the training school. At their centre, a woman holds court. I know it's rude to stare, but I can't help myself. Tall and slim, with auburn hair and creamy skin peppered with attractive freckles. No wonder she has everyone's attention.

Tearing my eyes away, I look at the ground. When I feel

it's safe, I glance up to find her piercing green eyes trained upon me. 'Your father-in-law was a gifted man,' she says in a husky voice. 'He motivated many young people to follow in his footsteps.'

I realise everyone's waiting for me to respond, but I can't think what to say… 'He earned his place in the G-garden of Remembrance then,' I stammer.

'Yes indeed.'

I feel my cheeks burning.

Mark turns to me. 'Darling, you're exhausted.' He addresses Nduka's colleagues. 'Forgive me, I must take my wife back to the hotel. Thank you for your kind words.'

'It was nice to meet you.' The redhead leans forward and embraces Mark. After releasing him, she moves to me. 'Both of you.' As she enfolds me in a hug and bestows air kisses, I'm enveloped in an earthy, musky aroma.

We leave the group and find our hosts. Mark shakes Temi's hand. 'Thank you for all you've done. We'll be happy to reciprocate by offering accommodation and introducing you to useful contacts when you come to the UK.' He kisses Lebe's cheek. 'And thank you for offering up your home and garden for the wake.'

Lebe smiles. 'You are welcome. It was nice to finally meet you both, despite the circumstances.'

Back in the limo, I place a hand on Mark's arm. 'Temi's coming to the UK?'

'Yes, didn't you hear him say yesterday? I said we'd put him up. We've plenty of room.'

I fiddle with the buckle on my clutch bag. 'And who was that woman? The one with the red hair?'

'I don't know. A colleague of Dad's, I think.' He stares out of the window.

I kick off my shoes. Mark unzips my dress. 'Why don't you have a lie down for a while?' He tugs off his tie. 'I might go down to the bar for a beer. You don't mind, do you?'

'No, that's fine.' I slip off my dress, lay down and close my eyes.

I wake disorientated, rubbing at goosebumps on my arms. I'm freezing. The air con must be too low. As I try to sit up, I realise the bedsheet's soaking wet.

I reach for the light switch and grab my phone from the bedside table. 'Mark, you need to come back. My waters have broken.'

By the time he hurries into the room, I'm curled into a ball. Pain comes fast and furious. My jaw is clenched, my eyes squeezed closed.

He calls reception. 'We need an ambulance. Now. It's my wife…'

I'm aware of being carried through the hotel reception on a stretcher. Strangers stare and step aside as paramedics load me into an ambulance.

I gaze around, searching for Mark, but I can't see him. Tears pour down my cheeks. My belly hurts, but there's something else, something doesn't feel right. A paramedic leans in close and I taste rubber as he positions a mask over my nose and mouth. And, all the time, that hideous siren. *Wiu – Wiu, Wiu – Wiu…*

The vehicle halts abruptly and doors swing open. As they

slide the stretcher out, I'm terrified they'll pitch me off. They race me down endless corridors. Ceiling strip lighting flashes bright and white. Finally, the trolley crashes against double doors and I glimpse a bare, sterile room. I'm surrounded by people in pale blue.

'Just a scratch,' says a nurse, before I slip further and further away…

CHAPTER SEVEN

I'm travelling along a white line, in the distance a sharp U-turn. It comes closer and closer until I reach the hairpin. I'm stuck. Ripped in two. Back the way I've come or forward into a black hole. I have no physical body. The agony is both momentary and infinite.

Where am I? The room is empty. White. Nothing. No table, chair, window, not even a door. Just flickering lights. Who am I? I exist in spirit, not in form. What am I?

My energy circles for means of escape. I am spectre, I can squeeze through the smallest of gaps. But someone has sealed the edges. Not a chink of an opening anywhere. My shadow sinks to the floor. Curls into a tiny ball.

I've forgotten something... but what? I have no body, no need of physical things... but the nagging thought persists. I must go back.

Distant voices. One speaking in English, his tone soothing. 'Everything's going to be okay.'

I open my eyes.

'Hey,' he says.

Do I know him?

'It's all right.' Another voice this time. 'She's bound to be fuzzy. She's been out for eight hours.'

Out where? Who are they talking about?

I blink a couple of times. The man is holding my hand. Am I ill? My other hand rests on my belly… then I remember. 'My baby. Where's my baby?'

'It's okay,' the man says. 'Our baby is fine.'

———————

A sweet, citrus fragrance tickles my nose. I open my eyes. A huge vase overflowing with yellow roses on the bedside cabinet, a few petals scattered on my bed. I blink and glance across the room.

'Hi.' The man who is my husband smiles.

I smile back.

'Would you like to meet our baby?' He moves towards the door.

A buxom nurse enters carrying a swaddled infant. She places the child in my arms. I gaze down into the pretty face of our daughter – long lashes fringing closed lids, a rosebud mouth pursing and frowning.

'Hello, beautiful.' I barely recognise the voice as my own. I take her tiny hand in mine and her fingers open and close like a star. I feel something rough on the back of her hand – a tiny heart-shaped birth mark.

———————

A clatter of cutlery echoes as a trolley is pushed along the corridor. I open my eyes and gaze about me. I've been moved to a small ward. Two women in the beds opposite cradle their babies.

I raise my head from the pillow and call out. 'Hello?'

A nurse hurries over. 'You back. You been out a long time. How you feel now?' She sticks a thermometer in my mouth and wraps a band around my arm to test my blood pressure. She checks the IV fluids being pumped into my system. 'That all good.' She nods before moving away from my bed.

'Please,' I call after her. 'Can I have my baby?'

'Yes. Baby due feed anyway.'

As she leaves the room, I pull myself up to sitting, anxious to see my baby's beautiful face again.

The nurse returns moments later and places a swaddled baby in my arms.

Lowering the shawl, I stare down at a screwed-up face with wide indignant eyes. 'No.' I hold the child out to the nurse. 'This is someone else's baby.'

Frowning, she takes the infant. 'This your baby, ma'am.' She pulls the shawl away from its angry little face. 'See his little nose? Just like his mammy's.'

My heart races. 'No.' I try to remain calm. 'This is not my baby.'

She backs away while the women opposite watch.

Blood pounds in my ears. 'Mark, Mark.' Everyone's staring. 'Where's my baby?' I scream. 'WHERE IS MY BABY?'

Mark rushes into the ward, water sloshing from a paper cup. 'What's the matter, what's happened?'

The nurse shakes her head.

Mark comes closer. He cradles me in his arms.

'My baby,' I sob. 'My baby…'

I feel a scratch on my arm.

Mark is by my side, snoozing in a chair. I'm back in a single room. At the foot of the bed is a plastic cot. Phew. It must've been a bad dream.

I touch Mark's hand. 'Can I see our daughter?'

Mark jolts. 'What?' He rubs his eyes. 'Oh, sure.' He stretches his arms, gets up and moves over to the cot. 'Hello, little one.' He picks up the baby and places it in my waiting arms.

I glance down at the chubby face, closed lids and short, stubby lashes.

'No, Mark' – I shake my head – 'this isn't our baby. Look, it's not our little girl.'

Mark lays the swaddled baby on the bed, unwraps the shawl and lifts the baby out. He unbuttons the white babygro and peels it off. The baby stirs, but doesn't wake as Mark removes its nappy.

He holds up the naked child like Simba in *The Lion King*. 'This is our baby. I saw him delivered. This is our son.'

CHAPTER EIGHT

Mark passes the child to me. 'Just hold him, Hanna.'

'No.' I pull back, shaking my head.

Mark reaches forward, his fingers hover at the bodice of my hospital gown. 'What about trying skin-to-skin?'

I remember discussing this at Natural Childbirth classes. It's supposed to help the mother and baby bond. I'd been all for it. 'No, Mark.' I brush his hand away.

Mark rings the call bell.

A nurse hurries in. Briskly she dresses the infant. 'Does Mammy want to nurse him?'

Ignoring her, I face the wall.

'I give him bottle.' She whisks the child away.

I turn back to Mark. Is he really my husband? Or is it me I don't recognise?

'You've been through quite the ordeal.' He sinks into the chair. 'I came up to our room and found you lying in a pool of blood. The doctor said it was a placental abruption. The hospital staff have been amazing.' He strokes my cheek. 'If we hadn't been so near, I don't know what would have happened.'

It's as if he's recounting a story about someone else.

'Temi met us at the hospital,' Mark continues. 'Pulled strings to get you the top surgeon.'

Temi again, always there…

'They had to carry out an emergency caesarean. I know how much you wanted a natural delivery, but there was no option. For a while it looked like I might lose you both.' Mark rubs his cheeks. 'They let me watch from the observation room. I saw them lift the little chap from your belly before rushing him off to be checked out by neonatal.'

I grab his hand. 'That's it! That's when they switched them. You've got to find out where they've taken our daughter.'

Mark ignores me. 'Later they brought him back and allowed me a cuddle. I told him what a beautiful mummy he had and how she was dying to meet him. Sorry.' He looks away.

Is he crying? I feel no compassion. He watched them deliver our daughter and let them switch her for an impostor. But no, that can't be right… 'I saw her,' I say.

He stares at me.

'I saw her. When I was in the room with the yellow roses. They let me hold her.'

His face pales. 'I'll get you roses, as many as you like. They didn't allow them in intensive care. Some regulation…'

'You're not listening.'

'It must have been a dream. You've been through the mill. We'll get you strong again and then we can all go home. You, me and our beautiful baby boy.'

'I need the bathroom.'

Mark rings the bell for the nurse.

The nurse tries to persuade me to use a bed pan, but I'm not having it. After she's disconnected me from the drip,

Mark takes my arm. I shuffle along the corridor with him holding me up. I'm exhausted. I feel as if my hand on my belly is holding everything together.

I sit on the loo for a while until I manage to wee. Hauling myself up, I stagger to the basin and lather my hands with soap. My hands don't seem to belong to me. I gaze into the mirror, but a stranger looks back. Her features are familiar, like someone I see every day, a neighbour or work colleague, but I feel no connection. She's not a relative, not even a good friend. I don't care about her. I don't care about the man waiting outside the toilet cubicle, or the baby in the room along the corridor. I don't care about anything.

Temi perches on the plastic chair beside my bed. 'How are you, Hanna?'

'How do you think? I've been stuck in here for over a week.' I wriggle my bottom. 'This bed is like something from a *Carry On* film.'

He winces. 'You're not getting much sleep, then?'

'Fat chance.' I snort. 'Nurses, day and night, checking my temperature, blood pressure, giving me injections and pills.'

'Hmm.' He hesitates a moment. 'Mark says you've shown no enthusiasm for the baby.'

'Why should I? It's not mine.' I rub at a stain on my blanket. 'Doctors keep coming and going, asking me so many questions. "Do I know who I am? Where I am? Why I'm here?" I'm not sure my answers are what they want to hear.'

Temi leans in closer. 'It might be better if you provided the medical team with the answers they seek.'

I purse my lips. 'Why should I do anything they want?'

'Hanna, I know how things work out here. If you show no

sign of improvement, they may not let you leave.' He stands up. 'Is there anything you need?'

'No.' I gesture to my overcrowded bedside cabinet. 'Mark's supplied flowers, fruit and magazines. Even elastic socks to prevent blood clots.'

'I'll leave you to it then, but think about what I've said. I'm sure you don't wish to be detained for longer than is necessary.'

After he's gone, I mull over his words. What did he mean, "Detained"? Can they keep me here? I feel a jolt of alarm. No-one believes my daughter's missing, not even Mark. If I don't start cooperating, might they lock me up and throw away the key? Then I'll never find her. Perhaps it would be best to go home. Once back in the UK, I can contact the media, write to our local politician, even the Foreign Office... The thought of heading home without my daughter makes me feel sick, but what use am I here if they lock me up?

Provide them with the answers they seek, Temi had said.

When they next quiz me, I answer their questions as well as I can, while continuing to make excuses not to hold the child. I don't want to feed it, cuddle it, change its nappy. I've been ill. I'm still recovering. Why should I take on those responsibilities? But I won't give up on my little girl. Whatever it takes, I'll get her back.

I listen in on Mark's stilted phone conversations with people at home. 'Hold on a moment...' He holds his mobile out. 'It's Mum.'

I shake my head.

Mark's brow furrows. 'You do remember who Vita is?'

I glare at him. 'Yes, I remember who Vita is,' I hiss. 'And no, I have no desire to speak with her.'

'She keeps saying he's not hers...' Mark's on the phone again. There are gaps when someone else speaks. I pretend to be asleep and listen.

'Yes, I know...'

'I'm trying...'

I open my eyes, exaggerating a yawn.

'Hang on, she's waking up. Hanna?'

'Mmm?'

'It's Jenna.' He holds the mobile out to me. 'She's been pestering to speak to you for days.'

I take the phone. 'Hello?'

'Hi honey,' says Jenna. 'Congratulations. Mark told us you've had a beautiful baby boy. Such a surprise when you were so sure it was a girl... still, a brother for Ike. That's lovely.'

I don't say anything.

'Mark says you haven't decided on a name for him yet. Plenty of time. How are you feeling?'

I don't respond.

'Mark says you've really been through the wars, poor love. Such a stressful time for both of you. Anyway, we can't wait to have you home. Mark says, all being well, you'll fly back the day after tomorrow...'

I hold the phone out to Mark. 'Bad connection. I think she's gone.'

'Hello?' Mark steps away to get a better signal. 'Hey, Jenna? You still there. Sorry, we thought you'd been cut off. Yes, home on Thursday. Yes, I will. Bye for now.' He glances at me. 'I think the sooner we get home the better, don't you?'

We're taking far more home than we arrived with. Mark packs everything and Lebe steps in with baby stuff – milk, nappies, spare clothes – more than enough to last until we get home.

'Hope these are all right.' Mark lays some clothes on my bed. 'Everything else is packed.'

I eye the maternity jeans and loose top with distaste. 'Fine. My belly's so swollen, there's no way I'd fit into anything else.'

'I'll leave you to it, then.' He shuffles awkwardly. 'I've got to sign the discharge papers.'

After a week of bed baths, it's good to have a shower. I even wash my hair. After drying, I pull on my clothes. My belly hurts like someone sliced something away. Going home without my little girl is tearing me apart.

I chuck toiletries in the bag, trying hard to hold back tears. As I check around to make sure I haven't forgotten anything, I spot something yellow under the bad. Wincing, I lower myself down. A single petal from a rose. I tuck it in the side of my toiletries bag and wait on the bed for Mark.

'Ready?' He's at the door. 'I've been to the pharmacy.' He shakes a bag. 'The diazepam should help settle you for the flight. I might even take some myself.'

CHAPTER NINE

During our absence the daffodils have bloomed, golden heads swaying gently in the breeze as if trumpeting our arrival. Vita's waiting on the top step. 'Welcome home,' she says.

Mark gets out of the Range Rover and opens the back door to lift out the baby seat, a last-minute purchase at the airport. He carries the child up the steps. 'Hello Grandma.' He kisses Vita's cheek.

'Let me have a look at him, then,' she says.

Mark turns the baby seat around, allowing Vita the first glimpse of her grandchild.

'Oh, my precious prince.' She leans in and strokes the baby's cheek.

I watch the scene from the car as they croon over this child who's not mine. Temi breaks my thoughts when he opens my door. 'I can manage,' I snap.

'Okay.' He nods and makes his way round to the boot to unload our luggage.

What's he doing here anyway? I didn't even know he was flying back with us until he turned up at the airport clutching a cabin bag.

'It makes sense,' Mark explained. 'Temi can help us with our stuff.'

Grabbing the arm rest, I haul myself from the vehicle. Thanks to my sedation, the flight passed in a blur. Now, after the long car ride, my body has seized up. As I climb the steps to the house, I spot Ike hiding behind Vita's legs. I smile and wave. 'Hello.'

Ike buries his face in her skirt.

Temi strides past with two suitcases before returning to the car to retrieve the rest of the bags. Vita and Ike follow Mark indoors, leaving me to hobble slowly after them.

When I enter the kitchen, Vita's leaning over the car seat talking gobbledegook.

'Come and meet your new brother.' Mark holds out a hand to Ike.

Ike hangs back. Poor kid, it must be strange. Mummy and Daddy go away for two weeks and return with a baby. I smile at Ike, but he glares at me and runs from the room.

'Give him time.' Vita lifts the baby from the car seat. 'My new grandson. Aren't you gorgeous?' She turns to Mark. 'What are we going to call him?'

'We haven't decided yet.' He glances at me leaning against the door frame and extends a hand. 'Hey, come and sit down.'

'No thanks. If you don't mind, I'll go and take a bath.'

'Good idea,' says Vita. 'We can manage, can't we my precious?' She nuzzles the baby's face. At least I don't have to worry about the child being unloved.

Stepping back into the hallway, the long flight of stairs seems more like a mountain. I sigh, wondering how I'm going to make it up, when Temi appears with the last of the bags. 'Wait,' he says. 'I'll help you.'

'No, I'm…'

Dropping the cases, he offers me his arm. I lean on him for support as we make our way up the stairs.

He hesitates where the staircase divides, gesturing to the left. 'This way?'

'Yes, it's the second room along.'

By the time we arrive at my door, Mark and Vita's chatter down below has become a distant murmur.

'Thanks.' I feel my cheeks flush.

'You're welcome. I'll go back for your bag. Do you need anything else?'

'No, just leave it outside the door. I'm going straight to bed.'

I watch him run lightly down the stairs. Why does his presence make me feel so uncomfortable? Once he's out of sight, I make my way into the bedroom.

In the ensuite, I lock the door, turn on the taps and perch on the side of the bath. I'd hoped, once I got home, things would feel more normal, but everything is wrong.

I move over to the mirror and study the tired and washed-out stranger. 'Bath and bed,' I tell her. After a quick soak, I climb out, pat myself dry with a fluffy towel and pull a T-shirt over my head. Afterwards, I retrieve my bag from the landing and rummage for my medication. Filling a tumbler with water, I swallow two pills and lie down, willing my crazy mind to still.

CHAPTER TEN

Someone's in the room. It must be Mark. 'What time is it?' I murmur.

'Eight a.m.' he says. 'You slept right through.'

I attempt to lift my head from the pillow but it's pounding. 'Ouch.'

Mark touches my arm. 'There's no hurry.'

'What's going on? Am I ill?'

'Mum's holding the fort. I brought you a cuppa.' He slides his hand under my head and holds a cup to my mouth.

I sip the lukewarm tea. 'Thanks.' My chapped lips sting.

'You need to take these.'

I squint at two small capsules in his palm. 'I don't need them. I took some last night.'

'The doctor prescribed them to keep you calm.' He perches on the edge of the bed and pops one in my mouth. 'That's it. Now a sip of tea to wash it down.' He repeats the process with the second pill. 'Good girl.'

'What's wrong with me?'

As Mark leans over to adjust my pillows, I catch a waft of

lemony pepper aftershave and notice for the first time he's dressed. 'I didn't hear you get up.'

'I slept in the guest room. I thought it would be best.'

'Oh.' I close my eyes.

Mark's voice floats across from the direction of the door. 'We have everything under control. Why don't you sleep a little longer?'

The door opens and Vita enters carrying a tray. 'How are you feeling?'

'I'm not sure…' I put a hand to my forehead. 'I'm so tired.'

'That's to be expected.' She flicks on the bedside lamp and helps me to sit up before placing the tray on my lap. 'I thought you might manage some soup. Potato and onion.'

'Thank you.' I dip a spoon into the creamy chowder and raise it to my lips. 'Is it lunchtime?'

'A little after… Quarter past two.'

'I've slept all morning.'

'Mark said to let you rest. The midwife rang. She's calling in later. Finish that and I'll bring you a nice milky drink.'

Left alone, I sip the delicious soup, but every spoonful is an effort.

It's not long before Vita returns. Removing the tray, she hands me a mug. 'Here you are.'

'But I hadn't finished…'

'You need plenty of dairy to get your milk coming in.'

The baby… I glance across to the turret nursery. 'Where's my baby?'

'Downstairs. He's fine, but we need to get you well too.'

He? I clutch my swollen breasts. 'I'm not breastfeeding.'

'Let's not decide that right now. Drink up. Doctor's orders. I added cold milk, so it shouldn't be too hot.'

The hot chocolate is sweet, and I enjoy a few sips before leaning back on my pillow.

Vita takes the mug. 'That's it. You rest.'

'Knock, knock. Midwife calling.' A plump, rosy-cheeked woman bustles into the room. 'Hello, Mrs Konteh.' She sets her large bag down on the armchair. 'I hear you've had quite the time of it.' Unzipping the bag, she pulls out a plastic apron and gloves. 'Mind if I take a look at you?'

Self-consciously, I rub spittle from the side of my mouth. 'No, that's fine.' I struggle to sit up.

The midwife shakes her head. 'You stay where you are.' She lifts the duvet to examine me. 'Tummy's going down nicely, and the scar's healing well.'

'Should I be rubbing anything into it?'

'Avoid talc and anything perfumed. E45 cream would be all right. Some swear by Vitamin E.'

'Thanks.'

She covers me up. 'Well, everything seems in order. Are you still bleeding?'

'Just a bit…'

'That's completely normal.' Taking a small iPad from her bag, she makes a few notes. 'I just met your little man. He's doing splendidly. So nice you have your mum to lend a hand.'

'She's Mark's mother.'

The midwife purses her lips. 'I gather that you've chosen not to breastfeed?'

I feel my cheeks flush. It sounds like a criticism.

'I can give you something to suppress the milk but, if you haven't fed the child at all, I daresay it's no longer a problem.' She slides the iPad back into her bag. 'I've made an appointment with your GP for a six-week check. Your husband has the details. Don't hesitate to contact the surgery if anything should go awry.' She picks up the bag. 'Your mother-in-law seems eminently capable. I'm confident everything will be fine until then.'

Not long after she's left, Jenna pokes her head around the door. 'Can I come in?'

'Yes,' I reply.

She strides into the room. 'The midwife's gone so I thought I'd pop up to see how you're doing.'

'I'm exhausted. What time is it?'

'Nearly six.'

'Why am I so tired?'

'You obviously need to rest. It's fine.'

'It's those bloody pills.' I rub my forehead. 'They give me a terrible headache.'

'Mark says they relieve anxiety.'

'Well, maybe I shouldn't take any more.'

Jenna straightens my duvet. 'Hey, I don't think I told you. While you were away, I found a yoga teacher. A Buddhist. Bit of a hippy if you ask me, but we'll give him a shot. You might like to try a session when you're up and about.'

'Where is Mark?'

'In the office with Temi. And Vita's looking after the kids.'

I push back the duvet. 'I need to see my baby.'

Jenna touches my arm. 'Hanna, you need to stay calm.'

I stare at my belly, still round and stretched. A dragging

pain spreads across my lower abdomen and I wince. 'I'm going to be sick.' I cover my mouth and retch.

'I'll fetch Mark.' Jenna hurries from the room.

———

Next time I open my eyes, Jenna's on a chair by the window, engrossed with her mobile phone. I lay quietly trying to remember what happened. Wasn't there some sort of skirmish? Mark encouraging me to take more pills... Temi arguing with him... My daughter still missing...

Jenna looks up. 'You're awake. How are you feeling?'

'How do you think?'

She gets up and moves closer. 'You need to stay calm.'

'Why does everyone keep telling me to stay calm? What has Mark told you?'

'That you've been confused since the baby was born. It's hardly surprising with everything that happened.'

'It's more than that.' I rummage under my pillow for a tissue and blow my nose. Can I trust her? 'The baby's not mine.'

'I don't think it's unusual to experience a sense of disconnect when the baby's an emergency caesarean.' She grins. 'Okay, I Googled it. And with it all happening so far away...'

'Everyone's a bloody expert but no-one gets it. Why doesn't anyone believe me?'

Jenna takes a deep breath. 'Mark and I think it might help if you spoke with someone. Tom McCarthy can spare you an hour...'

Mark and I? When did they become a team? 'I don't need a bloody shrink.'

Jenna pales as she steps away from the bed. 'Okay, well, I just wanted to see how you were. I guess I'd better go.'

'Jenna?'

She stops in the doorway.

'Can you ask Mark where my mobile phone is?'

'Sure.'

Left alone, I mull things over. Jenna will report back to Mark. They're all in on this. What will their next move be if I don't cooperate? Tom McCarthy is the peripatetic psychologist we use for residents. He's a nice enough guy. Perhaps if I agree to see him it might buy me time. I need to alert the authorities and find my missing daughter. I yawn. Why am I so tired? Rolling onto my side, I drift back to sleep.

CHAPTER ELEVEN

'Come on, rise and shine.'

I roll over. Mark's pulling back the drapes. I squint as sunlight streams into the room. 'No.' I bury my face under the quilt.

'Uh-uh.' He hauls the bedclothes from the bed. 'I talked to Temi about the pills they dispensed in Lagos. He says Benzodiazepines should only be prescribed for short term use or can become addictive. We need to find another way to get you well.' He wrinkles his nose. 'It's stuffy in here. Not good to spend so much time cooped up.'

'Leave me alone.' I curl into a ball.

'I'm going nowhere until you're on the move.' Mark flings open the window.

The breeze is fresh, and I shiver as I slide my feet to the floor.

'Good girl. Now get dressed. Breakfast's waiting.'

After showering I feel more alive. I scrape up my shampooed hair with a claw clip, squeeze my post-baby belly into my biggest jeans and tug on a T-shirt and jumper.

Downstairs, I'm greeted by Vita at the kitchen island. She

has everything running with military efficiency. Ike and Temi are eating breakfast at the refectory table, while the baby's sleeping in a bassinet I haven't seen before.

'Is that new?' I ask.

The frying pan sizzles. 'Sit down,' Mark says. 'I've made pancakes.'

I lower myself onto a chair and he places a plate in front of me. 'Eat up.'

Temi winks at me as he passes the maple syrup. 'They're surprisingly good.' He turns back to Ike. 'Did you want me to cut those up for you, little man?'

Ike offers a huge smile and Temi slices a pancake into bite-sized pieces. He seems to have made a good impression on Ike, and it was he who told Mark I shouldn't stay on the medication. Perhaps he could be an ally?

The doorbell rings. Mark turns off the gas and disappears out of the kitchen to answer it. He returns with a brown box. 'Another Amazon parcel.'

Vita takes it from him, puts it on the table and slices the seal with a knife. 'No sign of a *JoJo Maman Bébé* delivery?'

'There's a package under the stairs that I took receipt of yesterday,' says Temi.

'At this rate we can open our own baby store.' Mark tops up his mug from the cafetiere. 'What is all this stuff anyway?'

Vita unpacks the box. 'Bottles and Aptamil. All necessities for your son.' She moves across to the worktop, fills a jug with water and pours it into the brand-new sterilising unit. 'Of course, if Hanna was to breastfeed…'

I glance up from my breakfast. 'The medication turned my milk bad.'

Mark slides onto the chair opposite. 'Jenna says she mentioned our idea about you speaking to Tom?'

Our idea? Still, I need to show I'm cooperating, so I attempt a smile. 'I don't suppose it would do any harm.'

'Great.' Mark beams.

I slice into my pancake. 'Mark, do you know where my mobile phone is? I haven't seen it since we got back.'

'No' – he flashes a quick glance at Temi – 'but I'm sure it will turn up. Shall I make you an appointment, then?'

I gulp. 'An appointment?'

'With Tom.'

'Soon.' I load my fork with another piece of pancake. 'I'm not ready yet.'

'It's just…' Mark wipes a damp cloth around the maple syrup lid. 'We need to find options other than pills.'

I drop my knife and fork. 'All right, Mark,' I snap. 'You don't need to go on about it.'

The room goes silent. Everyone stares at me. I push away my plate, get up and head for the boot room. Lowering myself down onto the bench, I lean forward and tug on my wellies.

'Hanna, wait.' Mark calls.

I grab my jacket, open the front door and step outside. The fresh air on my face is invigorating as I slip my arms into the sleeves of my jacket. I shouldn't go too far, but it's so good to be outside and alone. Taking cautious steps, I make my way across the gravel drive towards the trees. Everyone keeps saying I'm tired after my unexpected ordeal but I'm not tired, I'm grieving. Grieving for a daughter I only got to hold for a few precious moments before she was gone.

By the time I reach the gate I'm puffed. I lean on it to catch my breath. I don't even know if she's dead or alive. Pushing open the gate, I step into the woods. She could have been placed with a wealthy family but, with no-one on my side, I have little hope of finding her. Reaching down, I pick up a stick and swish it around, decapitating a small bunch of celandine poppies.

My heart's racing. Just breathe – in… out… in… out… I tell myself. After a few moments my pulse rate slows, and my temper abates. I need to keep my own counsel. If they knew what I was thinking, they'd keep me on medication. I can't stay in that fugue forever. I have to find out what happened to my daughter.

CHAPTER TWELVE

I'm woken by a knock. 'Come in.'

Vita pushes open my bedroom door. 'Have you forgotten Ike's phototherapy session?'

'Oh no!' I check the time on my alarm clock and sit up. 'Eight-fifteen, we'll never make it.'

'I'm happy to take him. He's already had breakfast.'

I lay back down, my head giddy. 'Would you mind?'

'No, it's fine. I'll get one of the care assistants to mind the baby.'

After a while I get dressed and wander down to the kitchen, hoping to have the place to myself.

Temi's there, his head behind a newspaper.

'Oh,' I say, 'I thought you'd be in the office with Mark?'

Temi glances up. 'He has a Zoom call this morning and the builders are re-plastering the communal area in my block, so I thought I'd make myself scarce. Am I in your way?'

'No, of course not. The contractors need to get Caleb finished before starting on Darius.' I make a mint tea and sit beside the range.

He gestures towards the window. 'It's a beautiful place you have here.'

I sip my drink. 'Yes, we're very lucky.'

He peruses the paper for a few moments before looking up again. 'How are you feeling now?'

'Much better, thanks.'

'Perhaps… no, it doesn't matter.'

'What?'

'Well, if you're not busy, I wondered if you might show me the grounds. After finishing your tea, of course.'

Perhaps I can get him on side? 'Okay.'

At the foot of the steps, we turn left. 'This is the proposed site for Darius.' I point out the footings. 'There's been a hold up at the planning office.'

'The new block will seriously increase capacity.' Temi's strides are long as we cross the parking area to join the footpath and I struggle to keep up. 'How did you and Mark meet?' he asks, opening a gate to the private woods.

I laugh. 'In a library.'

He raises an eyebrow.

'I was an assistant researcher at the University of Suffolk. One day I was helping on student reception when Mark came in. He had a right go at me about overdue charges.'

'Not the most auspicious of beginnings.' Temi offers me his hand as we navigate a muddy patch.

'Thanks. He returned next day with a bouquet of flowers and asked me out to dinner.'

'Ever the charmer…' Temi stops. Before him is a dense carpet of blue. Swathes of bluebells gently nodding heads under the trees. 'Wow!'

I smile. 'Impressive, huh?'

'I've never seen anything like it.' He strolls ahead along the woodland track.

I follow, intoxicated by the sweet fragrance of the flowers.

'So, you and Mark,' he continues. 'You're happily married?'

'Of course. What sort of question is that?'

'Sorry. It's just… you don't seem to have that much in common.'

'We love each other and balance each other. Mark's a risk taker, ambitious and driven, while I take on a more supportive role – wife, partner…'

Temi walks on while I dawdle behind. I've not been a great wife or partner lately…. 'Mark and I work well together. We're a team.'

Leaving the woods, we step onto a shingle beach. Temi pauses, admiring the view across the lake. 'Beautiful.' He wanders over to the boathouse. 'This yours, too?'

'Yes.'

He tries the door.

'We keep it locked.' Surreptitiously, I finger the key in my pocket, not comfortable to invite him inside. 'There's a bench over there.'

As we approach, we disturb a heron and it soars into the air like a prehistoric pterodactyl.

I take a deep breath as I sit down. 'I never did say thank you… for all you did.'

Temi shrugs. 'It was the right thing for both parties.'

'Yes.' I run my fingertips around a knot in the wooden seat.

'And now you're a family of four,' he says.

'Yes.'

'And business is good?'

'Pretty good,' I lie. 'Although it could be better. We've spent a fortune on renovations and constructing the resident blocks. Now we need corporate clients.'

'Mark tells me he hopes *The Sanctuary* will become a world-renowned conference venue.'

'That's the long-term plan. And when Darius is complete, we'll be able to offer accommodation on site.'

A silence falls between us. Eventually Temi continues. 'Mark has worked hard to make a success of the business.'

Worked hard is an understatement. Over the years he's become a complete workaholic. 'He always works hard.' I say, before getting up. 'Shall we head back?'

As we return through the woods, I wonder whether I've done enough to convince Temi I'm not crazy. I need him on side.

CHAPTER THIRTEEN

Mark raises his voice to be heard above the gurgles and whirs of the coffee machine as it runs through a self-clean programme. 'Did you manage to get hold of Tom yet?'

'He's busy,' I reply. 'He'll get back to me when he has a minute.'

'Hmm. He implied he'd be able to give you at least an hour this week.'

I pretend to read a copy of *Mother & Baby* while sitting at the table. Vita's taken to leaving the magazines around, probably hoping they'll ignite some sort of maternal response from me.

She's sitting in front of the range feeding the baby a bottle. I listen to him gulping down his milk and sneak surreptitious glances when no-one's looking. Despite my lack of bonding with the child, it hurts to see Vita taking everything in her stride. I'm pretty sure Mark has charged her not to leave me alone with Ike or the baby.

Once the bottle's empty, Vita lifts the baby onto her shoulder and pats his back to encourage wind. 'Have you thought any more about names?' she asks. 'I can't keep calling him little man.'

For Christ's sake… I flick over a page of the magazine. The baby's name is a conversation Mark and I should have alone.

'I've been thinking,' says Mark, buttering two slices of toast. 'What about naming him Nduka, after Dad?'

I shake my head. No way.

Vita humphs. 'You must make your own decision, of course, but I'm not sure it suits our little man. Do you definitely want a Nigerian name?'

'I think so,' says Mark. 'Especially as he was born there. And his brother has a Nigerian name.' He turns to me. 'What do you think, darling?'

Before I can offer an opinion, Temi strides into the kitchen. 'Good morning. How is everyone today?'

'Just fine, Temi.' Vita moves the baby onto her lap. 'We were just discussing names for this little prince.'

Temi moves closer and strokes the baby's head. 'He's beautiful. What about Kwami? It means born on a Saturday.'

I glare at him. What the hell business is it of his?

'Kwami,' repeats Mark thoughtfully. 'I like that.'

I close the magazine. Am I invisible?

'Kwami.' Vita nods. 'Yes, I like it too. Thank you, Temi.'

Mark pats Temi on the shoulder. 'Let's go along to the office. I want to show you the plans for Darius.'

I get up. 'I'm going for a walk.'

On my return, Jenna greets me at the door. She's sporting a new pixie crop. 'Good walk?' She hugs me but, when I fail to reciprocate, lets me go. 'How are you?' She pouts. 'We've barely spoken since you got back.'

We used to spend twenty minutes every morning putting the world to rights. Lately she's kept her distance and I'm glad. I don't trust her anymore. I've overheard them making excuses for me – "It must be baby blues; tiredness after the birth; she'll be fine once her body heals…"

'I'm okay.' I push past her and enter the boot room.

'Why don't we lunch together?' Without waiting for a reply, she heads into the kitchen where I hear her exchange a few words with Vita.

I'm still tugging off my boots when Jenna re-appears carrying a tray of sandwiches and two glasses of water. 'Come on.' She strides through to the snug.

It feels like a set-up but I follow anyway.

We sit in opposite armchairs beside the window. 'So' – she hands me a plate – 'how are you really?'

I sigh. 'What has Mark been saying?'

'He's worried about you. I've told him it's sure to be baby blues, but he's concerned it might be something more.'

Mark knows it's more. Didn't he witness first-hand when I insisted the baby wasn't ours and screamed for my phantom daughter?

Jenna switches to a different tack. 'How's Kwami?'

'That didn't take long,' I retort, my voice thick with sarcasm.

'What?'

'You do know I had nothing to do with naming the baby?'

Jenna gasps. 'I'm so sorry. I had no idea. Mark came into the office earlier and announced it was all sorted.'

I shrug. 'It doesn't matter. It's as good a name as any. I have nothing to add to the discussion.'

'Of course it matters. If you don't want to call the baby Kwami, you have every right to say so. He's your little boy.'

'Is he?' I stare at her.

'Look, I know this is hard, but it's not that unusual. What with the way the baby arrived early and so suddenly, it's only natural it will take time to bond.'

I snort. 'The baby has Vita bonding all over him.'

'This is crazy. You must talk to Mark about how you're feeling. If he knew Vita was making you feel left out…'

'It's fine,' I say. 'I really don't care.' Half-heartedly, I bite into my sandwich.

Jenna studies me, her own lunch untouched. 'Did you manage to make an appointment with Tom?'

I shoot her a look. 'Not yet. Why?'

She shrugs. 'I've heard he's a good listener.'

I put down my plate. 'Actually, can we do this another time?'

After pacing my bedroom for an hour, fluctuating between complete exhaustion and alertness, I go back downstairs for a glass of water. On finding Jenna in the kitchen, I sneak into the downstairs loo and wait until she goes back along to the office. I don't want to talk to her. She used to be my friend, but now she's on their side.

I tiptoe into the hallway, pausing when I hear voices in the snug. Creeping forward, I listen.

'You've become quite the expert,' I hear Temi say.

'Case of having to,' Mark answers. 'There, little guy. Now you'll be more comfortable.'

'Let me hold him,' says Temi. 'He's a fine boy. You should be proud.'

There's a pause.

'I'm sorry,' continues Temi. 'I didn't mean to imply…'

'It's okay,' says Mark. 'I'm sure Hanna will be proud too, someday. It's just hard right now. I don't know what I'd do if my mother wasn't here.'

'So, what's your next move?' asks Temi.

'I don't know,' says Mark. 'I've suggested she meet with our psychotherapist, but you heard how she reacted.'

'You need to insist.'

'I guess I was hoping things would settle down once we got home, but you're right. We can't carry on like this. I'm terrified of what she might do.'

'To herself or the baby?'

'Both.'

I run upstairs. How dare Temi interfere? First naming the baby and now suggesting I need psychiatric help. They're ganging up. They think I'm mad. Perhaps I should speak to Tom McCarthy? At least that way I'll appear to be going through the motions. If I'm not careful, they'll put me away.

CHAPTER FOURTEEN

The receptionist in the doctor's surgery looks up with a smile. 'The appointment before you has been cancelled so you can go right in, Mrs Konteh.'

'Thanks,' I say.

Mark picks up the baby seat. 'I'm coming with you.'

As we enter her office, the doctor bobs up from her seat. 'Mrs Konteh, Mr Konteh. Won't you sit down?'

Mark and I perch on two plastic chairs with Kwami in the baby seat on the floor between us.

The doctor peers at me over tortoise-shell glasses. 'I've just been reading through your notes. It sounds as if you had quite the adventure in Lagos. How are you, my dear?'

Mark speaks for me. 'We're doing well, thank you and, as you can see,' – he glances down at the baby – 'Kwami's thriving.'

'Well, let's take a look at your son first, shall we?' She nods towards a small examining table with a changing mat on the top. 'Please strip him down to his nappy.'

Mark unfastens Kwami, carries him to the table and strips off his outer layer, babygro and vest.

I remain seated, studying the poster on the wall behind the doctor's desk. *STROKE – If you act FAST, treatment is possible.*

The doctor punches a few keys before getting up. Positioning the ear tips of her stethoscope, she listens to the baby's heart and lungs before running her fingers down his spine. Removing the stethoscope, she leaves it dangling around her neck. 'Undo his nappy please.'

Mark does as she asks.

Gently she probes Kwami's genitals. 'Thank you.' She smiles at the baby before taking a multi-coloured block from the shelf and moving it slowly from left to right. Obligingly Kwami follows the block with his eyes.

'Good,' says the doctor. 'You can dress him again now.'

While Mark puts Kwami's vest and babygro back on, she returns to her desk and types rapidly on her keyboard.

Mark sits back down with the baby on his lap.

The doctor looks up. 'And how is Mum doing?'

Mark reaches for my hand. 'Hanna's fine, aren't you?' He glances at me 'She's getting lots of support.'

At least he didn't say I need psychiatric support. 'Yes, I'm fine,' I murmur.

'It would not be strange if you were to be finding the whole experience overwhelming, Mrs Konteh.' She studies me more closely. 'Your baby is completely healthy but' – she nods at Mark – 'perhaps you and your son could pop outside while I check everything is good with your wife. Give us ten minutes.'

I watch the muscle in Mark's cheek flex as he lifts Kwami onto his shoulder and steps into the waiting room.

The doctor nods towards a curtained area at the back of the room. 'Slip off your jeans and hop onto the examination table.'

Although it doesn't hurt, I wince as she prods my tummy and examines my caesarean scar.

'All good. It will be fine to resume sexual activity whenever you feel ready.' She peels off the latex gloves. 'Get yourself dressed.'

My legs shake as I pull up my jeans.

I've barely sat down when there's a knock at the door. Mark sticks his head in. 'All done?'

'Yes, Mr Konteh. You can come back now.'

Closing the door behind him, Mark settles Kwami in the baby seat.

The doctor completes her notes before turning to me. 'Any questions, my dear?'

'Was it the flight?' I ask.

'Sorry?'

'Is that why the baby came early? Because I took a long-haul flight?'

The doctor removes her glasses. 'Did no-one explain things to you in Lagos?

I shake my head.

'We know that it was a placental abruption,' interjects Mark.

'That's correct.' She clasps her hands. 'Placental abruptions occur in perhaps one percent of births.'

'But what caused it?' I ask.

The doctor shrugs her shoulders. 'Often we will never know, but it's likely it would have happened whether you were here or abroad.'

I exhale. So it wasn't my fault.

She waits a beat. 'This might have potential consequences for subsequent pregnancies. We'd have to monitor you closely, keep an eye on your blood pressure, that sort of thing.'

'So, it might happen again?' I ask.

'There's a fifteen percent chance of you having a placental abruption during your next pregnancy. Are you planning on having more children?'

'No,' says Mark.

CHAPTER FIFTEEN

Mark comes out of our bedroom with a pile of shirts draped over his arm.

'What are you doing?' I ask.

'Moving my stuff into the guest room.'

So much for resuming sexual activity. I'm hurt but, in a way, grateful to have the bedroom to myself. I'm not ready for love-making yet. I haven't tackled him about what he said at the doctor's yesterday, but I'm too weary to have it out with him now.

Mark's not coping well with a crazy wife and has been sleeping in the guest room since we got back from Lagos. 'So that you can rest,' was what he'd initially said, but this looks decidedly more permanent.

At least I won't need to worry about keeping him awake as I toss and turn, trying to figure out what happened. They told me the baby came suddenly, but I remember nothing of the actual birth. Was she stillborn? Did Mark find a replacement while I was out of it? Did Temi help? I know he's not averse to manipulating the system…

The shirts slip from Mark's grasp and he gathers them

into an untidy bundle. Now they'll need ironing. 'And what about the baby?' I ask.

'We've set up a cot in Ike's room. It'll be easier for Mum, given that she's seeing to him until you're feeling better.' He offers me a final glance before scurrying away along the corridor.

In our room – my room now – I flop down on the bed. I'm so tired. If only I could get some proper sleep. Although the tablets prescribed in Lagos knock me out, the downside is, next day I walk around in a fugue. But without them, all I do is doze and dream – nightmares about babies born dead or deformed. Perhaps Mark's right? I shouldn't have children.

I lie down and close my eyes. If I could just have an hour or two of dreamless sleep. Please God, don't let me have another nightmare…

I follow a man into a hut. Once inside, an old woman leads the way. First, we come to a kitchen where a young girl, heavily pregnant, stands at a table chopping vegetables. Then we come to a seating area with a battered sofa and a couple of white plastic garden chairs. Next comes a sleeping space, unoccupied and shabby - the sort of place the homeless or destitute might bed down. Dirty blankets are lined up dormitory-style along either side of the dark, airless room. The next room is the same, but with two occupants – one, a young girl, rolling and writhing as she clutches her belly; the other, a girl cross legged on the earth floor, using a rag to mop the brow of her friend in labour.

The man says something, but I don't understand his words.

On we go, to a final room where another girl sits, her back against the wall as she breastfeeds a child. The woman shouts. The girl pulls herself up to standing, her head hung low. Sullen faced, she follows the woman and the man as they return to the seating area. As they sit down, the man turns his head. I recognise Temi.

The girl stares at her feet, the baby still in her arms as the haggling begins. Just as in the market, faces turn ugly and, all the while, the girl hugs her baby tight. A deal is reached and money changes hands. The girl shows no emotion as she hands the baby over. Temi slings it under his arm as if it were a bundle of laundry. The woman berates the girl once more as he walks away with the child.

It's late afternoon when I venture downstairs. Everywhere is deserted, so I head to Mark's office and push open the door.

He looks up. 'All right?'

'I wondered if my phone had turned up yet?'

He scans the room as if the phone might materialise. 'No, it hasn't. Perhaps it was lost at the airport. I might have to order a new one.'

'Hmm.' I wander in and take a seat at Jenna's workstation. 'No Jenna?'

'Dental appointment.'

I run my hand across what was once my desk. I envy Jenna her carefree life. If only I could go back to before my maternity leave. I'd wanted a daughter so much, but now everything's gone wrong.

'You okay?' asks Mark.

'I suppose.'

'Did you manage to rest?'

'Not really.' I fiddle with the computer mouse. 'Where's Temi?'

'He gave Jenna a lift into Stowbury.'

'I was thinking…' I pick up a few paperclips and link them together. 'Perhaps I will chase Tom again. See when he can fit me in.'

Mark smiles. 'That's a really positive step.'

I jangle the small chain of paperclips. 'How long will Temi be staying?'

Mark turns back to his computer screen. 'A while yet, but he'll be to-ing and fro-ing. He's good at networking, so I'm having him scout around to find new clients to attend the conference. He's off to Oxford this evening.'

———

I'm feeding Mr Biggles when Temi strides into the kitchen and sets down an overnight holdall by the door. 'Is there hot water in the kettle?'

'You'd better see for yourself.' I move and sit at the table.

Temi lifts the kettle to check, tops it up with water and flicks the switch.

As I listen to the cat greedily gobbling biscuits, I sense Temi watching me.

'Are you all right?' he asks.

'Yep.' I stare out of the window and across the lawn.

'Did I do something wrong?'

'You tell me.' My voice is calm, but inside I'm seething.

He raises his hands in a gesture of confusion.

'You've got some bloody nerve,' I say. 'Pretending to be friendly…'

'I wasn't pretending…'

'Naming our child with no input from me.'

He puts a hand to his forehead. 'I had no idea that you didn't…'

I get up. 'Don't play games. I heard you advising my husband that I need psychiatric help.'

'I'm sorry, but in my professional opinion...'

'Who asked you? I'm going to see a perfectly good psychotherapist, thank you very much, and I'd appreciate it if you kept your bloody nose out of my business.'

He picks up the holdall. 'Perhaps I should skip coffee?'

'Perhaps you should.'

Mr Biggles has finished his food and is rubbing himself against my shins. As the front door slams, I bend down and lift the cat onto my lap. 'Good boy.' I stroke his ears, eliciting a loud purr. Outside, the rev of an engine is followed by a crunch of gravel as Temi's hire car sweeps away down the drive.

CHAPTER SIXTEEN

'I always enjoy coming here.' Tom gazes through the French doors. 'Such a lovely old place.'

'Yes.' I answer while pouring tea and adding a splash of milk. 'It has quite a history. Originally a monastery, then a hotel for a time before becoming a respite home for crazy people. Bit ironic really.'

He turns to face me. 'Why?'

'Well, I'm a bit bonkers, aren't I?' I hand him a cup and saucer. 'Why don't you sit down?'

'Thank you.' He seats himself in one of the armchairs. 'Do you think you're acting out of character, Hanna?'

'I don't accept my baby.' I sit down opposite. 'It's hardly normal, is it?'

'More normal than you might imagine.' He places his cup on the coffee table and smiles. 'Have you heard of post-partum depression?'

I scoff. 'It's not baby blues. I'm not depressed.'

Tom pushes his glasses up his nose, looking like a bewildered Clark Kent. I'd hoped this session might get Mark off my back, but how can this young guy possibly help me?

'This is confidential?' I clarify. 'You're here for me and everything we say stays between the two of us?'

'Of course. Any conversations are subject to normal doctor-patient confidentiality.'

I sip my drink as I study him.

'Tell me how you're feeling right now?' he asks.

'Right now?' I set down my cup and saucer. 'I'm trying to decide whether I can trust you.'

He continues to stare.

I tap fingers on the arm of the chair. 'How is it that I'm surrounded by people but, at the same time, completely alone?'

Tom leans forward. 'How so?'

I shrug. 'I don't know, I just feel so isolated. Sometimes it's as if I'm invisible. No one listens to a thing I say.'

'I'm listening.'

I give him a small smile.

'Hanna, I'd like permission to consult with your GP and get him to prescribe some new medication.'

I rise quickly. 'I'm not taking any more drugs. What's the point in meeting with you if I still have to take medication?'

'Please Hanna…'

I humph, but sit back down.

'What concerns you most about taking medication?'

'The pills they put me on in Lagos really knock me out.' I sigh. 'Even when I'm not asleep, it's like I'm walking underwater.'

'SSRIs are milder. They won't knock you out, but they should take the edge off. It also sounds as if you're feeling isolated. I'd like to try a technique called interpersonal psychotherapy. It's a talking therapy, focusing on improving the quality of your relationship patterns with others. Together we'll find ways for you to cope with feelings, set goals and respond to events in a more positive way. Does that sound acceptable?'

'I s'pose.'

'Good, but before we finish today, I need to ask one more question. Do you feel as though you might harm yourself? Or indeed anyone around you?'

I laugh. 'Right now, I don't have the energy to hurt myself or anyone else, even if I wanted to.'

———

Mark helps himself to vegetables. 'How did things go with Tom?'

'All right.' I lay down my knife and fork. 'I notice Jenna and Vita have made themselves scarce tonight. Was that your idea? So that you can grill me over supper?'

'Don't be ridiculous.'

I resume eating. 'Did you order me a new phone?'

'Yes. It should be here in a couple of days.'

'Thanks.'

Mark forks cottage pie into his mouth and chews thought-fully. He swallows. 'So, he's easy to talk to?'

'Tom? Yes.'

'And you're seeing him again?

I glare at him. 'I told you, it's confidential.'

'Okay, okay.' He holds up his hands. 'But it is a course of sessions, right?'

I get up and begin to clear the table. 'Look Mark, if this is going to work you've got to trust me. I can't share what I say to Tom.'

'No, of course. I just want you well again.'

CHAPTER SEVENTEEN

Perhaps the session with Tom did more good than anticipated, because next morning I sleep in. After dragging myself out of bed and into the ensuite, I stare into the mirror. What a sight. I turn on the shower and step under the hot spray. Reaching for the shampoo, I lather my hair. After towelling myself dry, I slip into joggers and a T-shirt. I can't be bothered to dry my hair, so I pull it into a ponytail, grab my cardigan and head down to the kitchen.

Mr Biggles miaows loudly when I walk in. 'You're pleased to see me, aren't you?' I fill his bowl with biscuits. Where is everyone? I glance at the clock: eleven-fifteen. I suppose they've had breakfast and are getting on with their day. I open the cupboard and stare at the packets of cereal before changing my mind. After making a cup of tea, I carry it over to the wooden chair in front of the range. As I sip the minty brew, I think about my session with Tom. I'm not fully convinced he can help me. More meds? I'm still trying to get the last lot out of my system.

Gazing about the room, I spot Mark's MacBook on the kitchen island. He must have been using it at breakfast. I get

up and move over to it. Shooting a quick glance at the door, I
grab the laptop and stow it under my cardigan.

My heart beats fast as I hurry from the kitchen and into
the snug, where I set the MacBook down on the desk and lift
the lid. It fires up immediately. I tap in Mark's passcode – his
birthday. Opening the search engine, I type, *My baby was
stolen in Nigeria.*

In moments, I'm scanning stories of children taken to
feed a thriving black market in Kenya. *BBC Africa Eye* have
an article detailing how they infiltrated trafficking rings
selling babies for as little as three hundred pound. My eyes
prick with tears. Mark said he saw our baby born. There's no
way he'd be in on this for a few hundred quid.

I read about a Zambian nurse who, before dying of
cancer, confessed to swapping five thousand newborn babies.
Five thousand? That must be fake news, it can't be true.
Another account tells of a Chilean mother tricked into
handing over her baby. She took him for a check-up where
she was told he'd been taken ill and died. When she kicked
up a fuss, they'd drugged her. I gulp back a sob. That sounds
scarily familiar. But they haven't just stolen my daughter,
they've switched her for another. Why would anyone do that?
It doesn't make sense.

I'm perusing a government website when soft footsteps
approach. I slam down the lid of the MacBook and snatch a
magazine from the coffee table.

The door swings open and Jenna enters. 'Hi Hanna. Mark
sent me to find his MacBook.' She spots the laptop on the
desk and tucks it under her arm. 'You okay?'

'What?' I glance up as if engrossed with my magazine.
'Yes, fine thanks.'

'All right. I'll leave you to it. Oh,' – she pauses in the

doorway – 'Mark says he's found you a replacement phone. He's left it in the hall.'

After she's gone, I hurry out to retrieve my new phone. On the side table is a battered cardboard box. I lift the flap. Rather than a new mobile, I find an old Nokia and charging lead. Seriously? Mark must have dug this one out of the loft. It doesn't even have WiFi. I pick it up, make my way back into the snug and plug the charger in the wall socket. I pace as I wait impatiently for the battery indicator to change from red to green. I'll have to work out how to use it later, but at least I can make an emergency call. The government website I'd been browsing suggested the first port of call was the police rather than an MP. As soon as the phone has sufficient charge, I tap in 999.

'Emergency. Which service?' asks the respondent.

'Police,' I whisper.

'Connecting you now…'

Another voice picks up the call. 'You're through to the police. What is the address or location of your emergency?'

'Hello, my name is Hanna Konteh and I live at *The Sanctuary*.' I give him our full address.

He repeats it back. 'Okay Hanna. What is the nature of your emergency?'

'My daughter's been abducted?'

'And how long has your daughter been missing?'

'Six weeks.'

'Six weeks?'

'Yes. It happened in Nigeria just after she was born.'

'Nigeria? And the abduction was reported to local police?'

'No.' I gulp. 'This is all a bit difficult. My husband doesn't believe she's been taken.'

'Is your husband with you now, Hanna?'

'Yes… no…' I glance at the door. 'Not exactly.'

'I see. Could your husband have anything to do with the abduction?'

'Well, yes… no… I don't know. I'm not sure I can trust him,' I whisper.

The door opens and Vita shuffles in.

'I'll have to call you back.' I press a button to end the call.

'Jenna said you were in here. I've brought you some tea.' Vita sets the tray down on the side table.

'Thanks.'

'I must say it's a help having Kwami in nursery three mornings a week.' She pours two cups from the pot and adds milk. 'How are you feeling?'

'A bit better thanks.' My hands shake as I take the cup and saucer.

Vita shows no sign of leaving as she settles herself in the armchair opposite. 'That's good. I hope your sessions with Tom are helping?'

The landline on the bureau rings. I ignore it.

Vita sips her drink. 'I expect Jenna will pick that up in the office.'

A few minutes later Mark sticks his head around the door. 'Everything okay in here?' He glances from Vita to me and back again.

'Yes.' I feel my cheeks burn.

'Right.' He closes the door.

Vita nods at the Nokia still attached to the charging lead. 'I see you've got a replacement phone.'

'Yes, but I can't use it until it's charged.'

Ten minutes later, the doorbell rings. Someone answers it because I hear voices in the hallway. Vita gives me a quizzical look as I set down my cup and tiptoe towards the door. As I ease it open, I see Mark showing two uniformed police officers along to the office. I feel a wave of nausea.

Vita's speaking. 'I was wondering if we should plant salad veg in the trug on the patio…'

I walk back to my armchair and ease myself down.

'It might be nice,' she continues, 'for Ike to watch them grow.'

I stop listening.

A few minutes later Mark comes into the snug. 'Mum,' he says, 'there are some police officers here who want a word with Hanna.'

My heart races.

Vita looks bewildered. 'Police officers?'

'Yes. Come out to the kitchen and I'll explain.'

Vita hauls herself up and follows Mark from the room.

I feel as if I might throw up.

There's a tap on the door and two police officers step into the snug. 'Hello Mrs Konteh. Would you mind if we had a word with you in private?'

'No, that's fine,' I murmur.

The female officer sits in the chair vacated by Vita while the male officer remains standing by the door.

The female officer smiles. 'Your husband tells us that you recently gave birth to a child in Lagos.'

'Yes.'

'That must have been quite traumatic. I understand he arrived a little early?'

'She,' I correct. 'Yes, that's right.'

'Mrs Konteh.' The female officer maintains eye contact. 'Your husband has shown us your son's birth certificate.'

'Yes,' I answer in a high-pitched voice, 'but that baby's not my child.'

'I see.' She glances at the other police officer before

returning attention to me. 'Mrs Konteh, do you feel safe in your home?'

'Yes, I…'

'Because we can escort you to a place of safety if you'd prefer?'

'No. I'm perfectly safe.'

'Your husband has told us you're receiving treatment for postpartum disorder.'

'Well, yes, I am, but I don't need it. I'm not crazy.'

The police officers exchange another glance.

'Right.' The female officer stands up. 'We'll follow things up with your husband in a week or two, Mrs Konteh.'

'But what about my daughter?'

Her look is sympathetic. 'We'll be in touch, Mrs Konteh.'

———

There's a rap on the door. 'Supper's ready,' calls Jenna.

I glance at the clock – six p.m. All afternoon I've been hiding in the snug. I watched from the window as Vita took the baby out in the pram with Ike trotting along beside her. Not missing me at all.

I follow Jenna into the kitchen and wash my hands before sitting down at the table. Everyone's acting as if everything's perfectly normal. As if we hadn't had a visit from the police that afternoon.

'This quiche is delicious, Vita.' Jenna pops a piece into her mouth.

'Thank you.' Vita smiles.

How the hell has she had time to make a quiche as well as minding the boys?

'Did you say you were going into Colchester tonight, Jenna?' Mark asks.

'Yeah, I'm meeting some mates.'

'Do you want a lift?'

'No, I'll order an Uber.'

I move food around my plate hoping no-one notices I'm not eating.

Vita stacks the dishes and moves them to the draining board. She picks up a serving spoon. 'Would anyone like apple crumble?'

She made dessert, too?

'Not for me, thanks.' Mark rubs his stomach. 'I'm full.'

'And I'm going to go and get ready.' Jenna gets up.

'That's fine, it'll keep for tomorrow.' Vita sets the pie dish on the worktop. 'Come on, Ike. Bath night.' She lifts the baby from the bassinet and heads for the door.

Ike looks at Mark. 'May I get down from the table, Daddy?'

'Yes, buddy.' Mark ruffles his son's hair.

Ike slides down from his chair and follows Vita, while Mark and I remain seated.

My heart's thumping. 'So, are we going to talk about what happened?'

Mark glares at me. 'What? About the police ringing before insisting on coming around to investigate whether I'd abducted one of our children?'

I feel my cheeks flush.

Mark gets up and loads the dishwasher. 'I knew it was a bad idea to replace your phone, but I thought once you started seeing Tom, things might settle down.'

I look at my hands.

'I really don't know what to say to you right now.' He slams the dishwasher door and reaches for a stack of paper-work on the dresser. 'Here's our son's birth certificate.' He throws it on the table. 'And here's your medical file from the hospital in Lagos.' He slams that down too. 'Honestly, Hanna, I don't know how to help.' He runs fingers through his hair

I feel like a kid getting a dressing down from a teacher.

He flops down on a chair. 'If you don't pull yourself together, I worry I won't be able to protect you.'

I stare at him. 'What do you mean, protect me?'

'I mean we might need to consider you spending some time in a specialist unit. If we don't sort this out, there's a serious risk we could lose custody of both children. Is that what you want?'

'No,' I murmur.

'What?'

'No,' I repeat a little louder.

'Right. Well, you need to talk this through with Tom. I also think you should go back on the medication.'

'But…'

'No buts.' He stands up again. 'Hanna, I'm at my wit's end.'

CHAPTER EIGHTEEN

Tom takes a paper bag from his satchel and sets it down on the side table. 'Your new medication. Hopefully serotonin won't knock you out like the other pills.'

I nod.

'I'd like to make a suggestion. I was wondering if you could keep a mood journal?'

'A mood journal?'

'Yes. Any notebook will do. Note down how you're feeling at different times of the day, along with any triggers. You should also record improvements or side effects from the new medication.'

'Okay.'

Tom sinks into the armchair. 'Mark told me what happened with the police.'

I squirm. 'Probably not my smartest move.'

Tom jots something in his notebook. 'Do you want to talk about it?'

'What? The police?' I swallow. 'Not really.'

He strokes his chin.

'I wanted to report that my baby had been abducted.'

'Abducted?'

I lean forward. 'The baby we brought home from Nigeria isn't mine.'

'I'm sorry, I don't understand. What makes you think that?'

'I've nothing against the child, but it's not mine. My baby's missing.'

'And what does Mark say about this?'

'He thinks I'm crazy. Says he saw the baby pulled from my womb during the caesarean.'

'And you don't believe him?'

'I believe that's what he thinks he saw. At least, most of the time that's what I think.'

'And the rest of the time?'

'The rest of the time I think he's in on it too.'

'In on it…' Tom repeats my words. Leaning forward, he takes a pad of A4 paper from his satchel. 'I'd like you to write down the names of the people in your social network.'

'Social network?'

'Family and friends.' He passes me a pencil. 'People you interact with on a daily basis.'

The list is short – Mark, Vita and Jenna.

Tom glances at what I've written. 'Good.' He tears off the page and draws a small circle on the next, then another circle around it and another around that. 'Now, where would you position these people – inner, middle or outer circle – based on how close you believe your interactions with them to be.'

'Mark in the inner circle, I guess.'

'Because he's your husband?'

'Yes, and my best friend.' I write Mark's name in the small circle, then pause, hovering the pencil above his name. 'Or he used to be.'

'Can you elaborate?'

I sigh. 'Mark's the only one who's shared life experiences with me. Important things, anyway.'

Tom nods.

I put Jenna in the next circle. 'She's a friend, but obviously not as close as Mark.'

'And Vita?'

I snort as I add her name to the outer circle. 'She should be further in, but she isn't.'

'And what about your children?'

My eyes widen. I'm such a bad mother. I haven't even considered Ike or the new baby. I write Ike in the middle circle and draw an arrow towards the outer circle.

'What does the arrow signify?' asks Tom.

'Ike's here, but Vita constantly pulls him into the outer circle with her.'

'And how does that make you feel?'

'Angry, jealous, completely inadequate.'

'And the baby?'

I write "The baby" in the space outside the outer circle. 'We have no interaction.'

Tom studies the diagram. 'This is a good start. Now, can you think of anyone that's missing? Or perhaps people who might be in circles further out?'

I tap the pencil on my hand. 'I don't think so.'

'No other family?'

'No.'

Tom leans back. 'Perhaps we could talk a bit about your parents?'

'Mum and Dad died when I was eight. After the accident, I was raised by Dad's sister, Auntie Brenda, but we didn't get on.'

'Why not?'

'She was very involved with the church. By thirteen, I

was a rebellious teenager. I suppose I was bitter and angry about losing my parents.' I squirm in my seat. 'I went a bit wild. Auntie Brenda and I were both relieved when it was time for me to go to Uni.'

'What did you study?'

'Literature to start with. Mum was a teacher and I hoped to follow in her footsteps.' I grimace. 'I soon realised I'd made a mistake and switched to History. That's where I get my love of research.'

'So, you graduated with a BA in Humanities?'

'No, I dropped out. Look, I'm not being funny, but is this relevant?'

'What would be relevant?'

I pull a thread on my cardigan sleeve. 'Sometimes I feel like I'm not really here.'

Tom adjusts his glasses. 'Can you explain what you mean?'

'It's since the baby was born.' The cuff of my sleeve is puckered, and I stretch it back into shape. 'I don't feel like me anymore. I go about my day, but I feel nothing. All that remains is a shell.' I sigh. 'Perhaps there's another part of me going absolutely mental, but it's as if she's been packed off somewhere. She probably got left in the white room.'

'The white room?'

'Yes, a place I remember… or perhaps it was a dream?'

'I wonder if some of these feelings could be down to loss of identity. You're transitioning from Mark's partner, both in terms of business and life, to… well…' He pauses. 'What do you see your role as now?'

'I don't have a role. I should be a loving wife and a good mother, but I'm failing on both counts.'

'I'd like you to try to focus on compassionate and constructive self-talk rather than the negative and critical.'

I glare at him. 'Jenna's got my job and Vita's taken over my role as mother. How am I supposed to turn that into a positive?'

'Have you talked to friends and family about this?'

I shake my head. 'I've got other things to deal with.'

'Other things?'

'Like tracking down my missing daughter.'

CHAPTER NINETEEN

The baby's crying. My body goes rigid. Since starting the new medication, I'm emerging from the fog, but with that comes new clarity. My senses are heightened.

'Now, now, little man.' Vita bends down to lift him up. 'What's all this fuss?'

The baby stops fretting and I breathe.

Mark drains his mug. 'I've got a consultation this morning about a new admittance.' He stands up and straightens his tie.

'Hope it goes well,' I say, trying to convey a sense of normality.

'It better. We can certainly do with the money now I'm having to fork out for private nursery for Kwami.' He strides out of the kitchen.

Vita's in my chair by the range, giving the baby a bottle while I pretend to peruse the newspaper.

'Please can I have more cereal, Nana?' asks Ike.

'Mummy will get you some,' says Vita.

I reach out and pour another helping of Cheerios into Ike's bowl before slopping in some milk.

'Thank you,' he whispers.

After a while, Vita shifts the baby onto her shoulder to bring up his wind while I do my best to ignore them.

The baby burps. 'Well done, little man.' Vita gets up and turns to me. 'I'll get the boys dressed.'

'Thanks.'

'Come on Ike.' Vita takes the boys through to her apartment while I resume reading the newspaper.

At ten past nine the doorbell rings. I'm heading to answer it when Jenna comes hurrying through in a grey jersey jumpsuit and high-heeled wedges. 'I'll get it.' She opens the front door. 'Mr and Mrs Jordan? Won't you come this way?'

I step back as Jenna leads the middle-aged couple across the hallway and through to Mark's office. Mr Jordan wears a grimace, while Mrs Jordan's face is pale. She looks on the verge of tears.

From along the corridor, I hear Mark greet them. 'Mr and Mrs Jordan? Please, take a seat.' The office door closes.

There was a time when I'd attend admittance consultations. I wait a few moments before tiptoeing along to stand outside the room.

From inside I hear Jenna ask the couple, 'Would you like a cup of tea?'

I take a step back. If she comes out now, she'll catch me. When the door doesn't open, I creep forward again.

Mr Jordan's speaking, 'Mr Konteh, we're desperate.'

'Go on,' says Mark.

'Our daughter, Sorrel, is sixteen and suffers from a form of epilepsy.'

'Petit mal,' says Mrs Jordan.

'Absence seizures are common among young people living with epilepsy,' says Mark.

There's a pause.

'To be frank,' continues Mr Jordan, 'we usually cope. But lately, well, Wendy could do with a break.'

'We both could,' says Mrs Jordan.

'That we can offer.' Mark reassures them. 'We provide respite care on a weekly basis. How long were you thinking Sorrel might stay?'

The Jordans don't respond.

'May I suggest,' Mark continues, 'that we review progress on a fortnightly basis?'

'I feel so guilty.' Mrs Jordan sniffles.

'Don't,' says Jenna. 'It's nothing to be ashamed of. We'll look after Sorrel while you go home and recharge your batteries. Then you'll be fresh and ready for when she returns home.'

'Jenna will show you around our facilities…' says Mark.

I hear movement as they ready themselves to leave, so I sprint quickly back to the kitchen.

Next morning. I pull on coat and boots and step out across the lawn. The grass is dewy underfoot and it feels good to be outside. Daily constitutionals have eased my post-caesarean stiffness and physically my body's recovering. The baby weight's shifting, too. I've scarcely eaten since we got home. I even squeezed into my old jeans this morning.

As I near Bartholomew block, Jenna steps out of the door with a young girl in tow. It seems the Jordan's didn't waste time before signing the paperwork for their daughter's respite care. They don't know how lucky they are. If I ever find my daughter, I'll never let her go.

Jenna introduces us with her 'welcome tour' voice. 'Hanna, this is Sorrel. Sorrel, this is Mark's wife, Hanna.'

I take in the teenager's blue-black hair, black lipstick and multiple piercings. Perhaps the goth phase contributed to the need of her parents for respite. 'Hello, Sorrel,' I say. 'Welcome to *The Sanctuary*.'

The girl stares sullenly before offering a reluctant, 'Hi.'

'Sorrel enjoys walking too,' says Jenna. 'You might bump into each other when you're out and about.'

'Hmm,' I murmur. I've no intention of allowing Goth Girl to intrude on my quiet time and, by the expression on her face, the feeling's mutual.

Jenna is unperturbed. 'I'm going to show Sorrel the chapel. Yoga classes will be starting soon.' She takes the girl's arm and leads her towards the main house.

I smile to myself. Jenna's got her work cut out with that one. Sorrel doesn't strike me as being the least bit interested in yoga.

Recently I've kept my walks short, staying within sight of the house, but today I feel the need to venture further. I stride out purposefully along the path bordering the car park when I almost trip. Bending down, I examine erosion caused by bulging tree roots. I must remember to tell Norris.

As I enter the woods, leaves and twigs crackle under foot. Arriving at the animal shrine, I perch on my usual stone. I'd been intending to sit quietly and plan the next move for tracking my daughter, but my attention's drawn by the earth around my feet. It looks as if it's been disturbed and there's a raised mound a little way from the other gravestones. Moles? Or has someone buried something?

There's a chill to the air and after a few moments I conclude I'm not going to find the stillness of mind I'd hoped for. I get up, emitting a small cry. Norris is right behind me. I hold a hand to my chest. 'You startled me.'

'Sorry, Mrs Konteh. I was waiting until you'd gone. Didn't want to intrude, like.'

'What are you doing here?' Is he hiding something? I glance at the freshly heaped earth and back at Norris.

He pulls a piece of wood from behind his back, holding it out for me to see. Scratched into the soft wood is a name. *FRED*. 'Was me old dog, Mrs Konteh. Passed while you were away. Sixteen he was. Had a good innings.'

My tone softens. 'I didn't know you had a dog.'

'No, well… he weren't able to come around the grounds with me. Emphysema. Poor old thing couldn't walk more 'n a few feet.'

'I'm sorry. You'll miss him.'

'Didn't seem right to replace him while he was still alive. Disloyal somehow. But Mr Konteh says he'll sort me out with another. Grateful I am. Can do with one, yer see, to keep down those blimmin' rabbits. Mr Konteh didn't tell yer?'

'No. Things have been a bit hectic.'

'Yes'm. What with the birth of the little one. Congratulations to you both. You and Mr Konteh.'

'Thank you.' I'm unsure how to bring the conversation to a close. Then I remember. 'I noticed some damage to the path.' I point back the way I came. 'If a resident should take a tumble…'

'Yes'm. I'll take me a look on the way back.' He holds out the piece of wood. 'I'll just be fixing this on 'is grave first, if that be all right with you?'

'Of course.'

'Not fancy like 'em others.' Norris bends down to fix the plaque. 'But this'll more 'n do for old Fred.'

That night I dream I'm back in Lagos.

From my bed in hospital, I hear a baby cry. I get up and go to the crib. My beautiful daughter's gone and in her place is a swaddled changeling. It looks up at me with evil red eyes and a horrid smirk on its face.

Outside the room, I hear laughter. Flinging open the door I find the old lady from the market. She's holding my daughter in her arms. Cackling, she lowers my beautiful baby into the pocket of her apron before charging off along the corridor at the speed of a roadrunner.

'Wait,' I yell. I try to follow but the corridor's never-ending, my legs heavy as lead. It's like wading through a swamp.

CHAPTER TWENTY

I wake sweaty and panicked, my heart beating so fast it might explode. Clambering out of bed, I make my way into the ensuite and splash my face with water before going downstairs.

Having screwed up any chance of the local police taking me seriously, the MP route is my only course of action. It's still early, so I'm not disturbed as I retrieve the baby's birth certificate from the dresser in the kitchen and creep along the corridor to Mark's office. I swiftly locate the MacBook and, after a quick Google search, establish that our local MP is James Hardcastle. Noting down his constituency email address, I type the email I've been composing in my head for the past few days.

Dear Mr Hardcastle,

I'm in desperate need of help. Eight weeks ago, while in Lagos, Nigeria, I gave birth to a child. She was a few weeks premature, but I saw her and held her in my arms. The next day, another child was substituted for my daughter. I don't know the reasons behind this or why no-one, including my husband, believes me, but research suggests this is not an uncommon occurrence in Nigeria and I beg you to investigate.

I'm attaching a scan of the birth certificate provided for the changeling child. This may help you find out what happened.

I'm also sending a copy of this email to the Foreign Secretary.

Please respond as soon as possible. I'm obviously beside myself with worry and fear for my daughter's safety.

I scan the birth certificate, attach it to the email and hit send. There. Now they can't ignore me.

Donning my jacket and boots, I head out for a walk. Hopefully I won't bump into Goth Girl at this early hour. I don't want to adjust my habits to avoid her. Entering the orchard, I turn right and make my way to my favourite thinking place.

The Italian Garden is out of bounds to residents, so I have the place to myself. The area is a little wild. Since we let the previous head gardener go, Norris, a groundsman by trade, struggles to maintain the former glory. Vintage roses, once prolific, have been cut back too hard and never quite recovered. A few hardy climbers remain and will be joined in a few months by purple buddleia and an abundance of butterflies. Part of me hopes one day we'll have the money to restore the gardens, while another part likes it just the way it is.

The long walk, two hundred metres in length, was used by monks for walking meditation. Columns line both sides and I imagine I'm wandering through a Greek temple, treading slowly up one side and down the other.

Between the paths lie squares of cultivated plants surrounded by low box hedging. At the far end, the land dips abruptly, creating an effect not unlike that of an infinity pool. It feels as if one might drop off the end of the world. On the ridge, a statue of a small boy looks out across open country-side. As I reach him, I follow his gaze across fields of sheep where a few lambs run and prance.

The birds begin their dawn chorus and, as I watch the sun rise, a sense of calm descends. I feel so much better now I've done something. A weight's been lifted from my shoulders. Someone will help me, I'm sure.

———

When I arrive back at the house, everything's quiet. Perhaps they're still in bed? I perch on the boot room bench and tug off my boots. As I pad through the hallway in my socks, Mark calls out. 'Hanna, can you come into the kitchen please?'

Pushing open the door, I find Mark, Jenna, Vita and Ike sitting at the table.

'Join us,' says Mark.

Vita lifts Kwami out of the bassinet. 'Come on, Ike. We'll get you dressed in Nana's room.'

My son slides down from the bench and she leads him through the French doors to her apartment while Mark and Jenna remain seated.

'Sit down,' says Mark.

'What's this?' I take the carver at the end of the table. 'Some sort of intervention?'

Jenna stares into her lap while Mark gestures towards the MacBook on the table. 'You tell me.'

My heart thumps, but I don't say a word.

A muscle in Mark's cheek pulses wildly. 'What the hell were you thinking?'

I swallow. 'I don't know what you're talking about.'

Mark sighs. 'Seriously? Are you going to play this game?'

Jenna reaches across and takes my hand. 'The email, Hanna.'

I snatch my hand away. 'You've been reading my emails?'

'Of course,' says Mark. 'After what happened with the police, I've been monitoring your computer and internet usage.'

'You have no right,' I yell.

Jenna shakes her head. 'Oh, Hanna.'

'Don't *Oh Hanna* me,' I scream.

Mark slams his palm down on the table, making Jenna and I jump. 'I think you'd better go to your room,' he says.

I laugh. 'Go to my room? What, am I grounded now?' I get up. 'I will go to my room, but only to get away from you two.'

I run upstairs and throw myself onto the bed. How dare Mark send me to my room when I'm the only one taking the disappearance of our daughter seriously?

I must have been lying there about half an hour when heavy footsteps echo along the landing. I sit up, expecting Mark to come in and have another go at me. Instead, the key turns in the lock. What the hell?

My legs shake as I swing my feet to the floor and stumble over to the door. Grasping the handle in both hands, I twist and turn, but it doesn't budge. Frantically I rattle the door-knob. 'Let me out.'

After a few minutes of no-one answering, I slide to the floor and dissolve into sobs.

Eventually, tears spent, I haul myself to standing and try the door again. The room is in darkness and the door's still locked. He can't keep me locked up. I bang on the door with my fist. 'Help. Let me out.' But no-one comes.

CHAPTER TWENTY-ONE

'Hanna?'

The overhead light dazzles me. I sit up as Mark approaches the bed. 'No.' I flail my arms and kick my legs.

He takes a few steps back. 'It's all right, I didn't mean to scare you.'

I shrink away.

'How are you feeling?'

'How do you think I'm feeling? I'm being held against my will.'

He rubs his face. 'I'm not proud of that, but you left me no choice.'

'No-one came when I shouted. Anything could have happened. I could have been dead on the floor. Where's my phone? I'm reporting you.'

'I don't think that's such a good idea.' Mark pulls a chair close to the bed. 'I've kept the police in the loop. If you contact them again, I'm afraid they'll have you sectioned.'

'Well, it will be your fault if I am.' I take a deep breath. 'I missed my meeting with Tom.'

'I told him you weren't feeling well.'

'You can't keep me locked up,' I plead. 'You have to let me out.'

'Not until I've talked some sense into you.' Mark shakes his head. 'Our M.P? The Foreign Secretary? What on earth were you thinking?'

I stare at my hands. 'I had to do something. No-one was listening.'

'You need to understand that you're ill. It's not your fault, it's the postpartum psychosis causing a chemical imbalance in your brain.'

'I am NOT ill.'

He swallows. 'You are ill, Hanna. And, as your husband, I need to take steps to protect you. What's the alternative? Section you myself?'

I feel sick. Would he do that?

'This is what's going to happen. You'll continue with your new medication. It's barely had time to kick in. And you'll meet daily with Tom. He's optimistic that he can help.' Mark rises from the chair. 'When you show signs of improvement, I'll look at relaxing things. Meanwhile, you'll take your meals up here.'

'Please, Mark…' I beg.

'You need to show me that I can trust you. Otherwise,' – he sighs – 'well, you know what the consequences will be.'

After he's gone, I wander into the turret room linked to my own. It was supposed to be my daughter's nursery, it shouldn't be empty. I gaze at the pretty white cot with lemon gingham bumpers and coverlet. The drawers underneath contain all the things I collected for her. Vita hasn't used them. Instead, she's set up a makeshift day nursery in the kitchen with a new bassinet from Mothercare. In fact, she's restocked everything – nappies, bottles, babygros and romper suits. At night, Kwami sleeps in a cot in Ike's room, while this tiny room remains unused.

I move towards the window and wipe a smudge from the glass. It looks like one of Ike's handprints, but it's on the outside. I gasp, recognising the imprint on the pane and remembering the bird that left its mark. Storms and rain have not washed it away. Perhaps the shadow will remain as a reminder each time I look out of the window?

As days go by, it becomes less and less likely that I'll find my daughter. Why won't anyone listen to me?

———

Someone's fumbling with the lock. With a hefty shove, Jenna opens the door. 'I've brought you supper.'

I sit up, glaring at her. 'Why am I still locked in?'

Avoiding eye contact, she sets the tray on my dressing table.

'Why are you letting him do this?' I continue. 'I thought you were my friend.'

She says nothing.

'What did I ever do to you?'

Finally, she looks up, her cheeks flushed. 'I'm sorry Hanna, but Mark says I have to help. He says if I don't, you'll end up being sectioned.'

I glance at the tray. 'No pills?' My voice is thick with sarcasm.

'Mark didn't say anything about medication.' She gestures to the sandwich. 'Please try and eat something.'

I shake my head. 'I don't want it.'

'Well, I'll leave it there anyway.' She moves towards the door. 'We just want you better, Hanna.'

I flop back down and turn my face to the wall.

Jenna sighs. 'You must keep up your strength. Mark says if you calm down, you can meet with Tom tomorrow.' As she leaves she turns the key in the lock.

CHAPTER TWENTY-TWO

Next morning, Mark brings a breakfast tray. He glances at the untouched plate on the dressing table. 'You didn't eat your supper.'

'I'm not eating anything you give me. It's probably drugged or poisoned.'

'Don't be silly.' Mark draws back the curtains. 'Tom's here. I thought you might like to freshen up before you see him.'

'Really?' I sit up and scramble off the bed, heading for the ensuite.

'I'll show him up in about ten minutes, shall I?'

I spin around. 'I'm meeting him up here?'

'Yes, for now. It's for the best.' Mark leaves the room, locking the door.

After using the bathroom, I pull on a clean T-shirt and drag a brush through my hair. Perhaps Tom can get me out of here?

Tom perches on the dressing table stool while I'm on the bed. 'How are you feeling, Hanna?'

'You do know I've been locked up for the past twenty-four hours?'

'Yes.' He shuffles uneasily. 'I told Mark it's completely inappropriate.'

'So, he's going to let me out?'

'I hope so. He mentioned something about you sending emails to members of Parliament?'

'That's my business.'

'Well, even so, there's no way you should be held against your will. How are you getting on with the new meds?'

I shrug. 'The pills don't knock me out like the last ones.'

'Good. You said you didn't like living in perpetual fog. Is there anything you'd like to share from your mood journal?'

I rub my fingers. 'I haven't got around to starting it yet.'

'That's okay.'

'I just feel so helpless.' I sigh. 'I suppose I'm grieving.'

Tom nods. 'For the daughter you were expecting?'

For the daughter who was spirited away. But no, I mustn't share those thoughts anymore. Not even with Tom.

'Depression can cause many feelings,' continues Tom.

'I told you, I'm not depressed.'

He tugs his ear lobe.

'I Googled postpartum depression. I don't have the symptoms.'

I'm on the bed, dressed and waiting, when Mark comes into the room.

'Tom says you seem quite calm,' he says.

'I'm completely calm.'

He paces up and down. 'If I let you out, you need to promise to behave.'

What am I? Ten? But I choke back anger and incline my head.

'No mobile phone, no computer, and you're to stay in the house where I can keep an eye on you.'

'Daily walks are part of my recovery,' I argue. 'Tom agrees I should have fresh air.'

'Let's take it one day at a time.' Mark opens the door. 'You know, Hanna, everything I do, I do because I love you.'

Downstairs, I settle myself in the snug. I don't want to mix with the others. Instead, I start my mood journal, venting anger at Mark, Jenna and Vita onto the page.

At lunchtime, Jenna brings me a sandwich. She places the tray on the coffee table and hovers.

'Thank you.' I avoid looking at her.

'You're welcome. Look, Hanna. I just wanted to say sorry for…'

'Locking me up?' I retort. 'Cheers.'

She stares for a few moments but, when I refuse to make eye contact, she leaves.

I spend the afternoon dozing on the couch. I'd be more comfortable upstairs, but I don't want to risk being locked up again.

At supper time, Mark brings me a portion of pasta bake.

I take the proffered bowl. 'Thanks. What about my pills?'

'Tom says I must trust you to take your own medication. He says autonomy is important for your recovery.'

I smile graciously. 'Am I seeing him again tomorrow?'

Mark returns my smile. 'Yes, I think that would be a good idea.'

CHAPTER TWENTY-THREE

During the night I'm unable to sleep. I keep getting up to check the door and make sure it's still unlocked. In the end, I pick up my mood journal. Despite initial reluctance, writing does seem to help. Soon outpourings of frustration are joined by passages of self-reflection. Could the first lot of drugs have caused such lucid hallucinations that I dreamt I had a daughter? Is it possible that Kwami is mine?

After a couple of hours and several pages written, I close the notebook. I take two serotonin, shower, dress and add a touch of make-up before heading downstairs.

It's not yet nine, but Tom's already in the kitchen. I make us both tea and lead him into the snug, where he settles himself in an armchair.

'How are you today?' he asks.

'A little brighter thanks.' I flop down on the couch. 'Perhaps the meds are kicking in?'

'I'm pleased to hear it.'

'Thank you for getting me out of the locked room.'

'You're welcome.'

I hold up my notebook. 'I've started a mood journal.'

'Good. Would you like to share anything?'

I flip through the pages. 'It's mostly rantings.' I close the journal with a sigh.

'Remember to focus on feelings, although it's fine to also note down triggers.' Tom opens his satchel and pulls out a notebook. Rifling through, he finds what he's looking for. 'You mentioned at a previous session that you studied humanities at university. Was that something you wanted to do for a career?'

I shrug. 'I don't know.'

'But you ended up partnering Mark in his business?'

'Yes.'

'And you found that rewarding?'

'I suppose. I liked knowing I was supporting him.'

'You also said Mark used to be your best friend? Past tense.'

I snort. 'Well, we're not exactly close now, are we!'

Tom waits for me to continue.

'Mark worked at the hospital when we were first married. He was run ragged. When he got this place, things changed. For the first time we were a proper team. But it's not been easy. Lately Mark's reverted to being a workaholic.'

'That can't be easy.'

'No.'

'We've discussed addressing your relationship with the boys by being more assertive with Vita. I think we should simultaneously address other aspects of your identity. Your work?'

'Jenna's doing much too good a job for Mark to let me have my old position back.'

'Have you discussed the possibility with him?'

'Not yet.'

Tom sits back. 'I'm wondering if it would be a good idea

to invite Mark along to one of our sessions?'

I stare at him aghast. 'Why?'

'So that you can put some of these things to him in a calm and constructive manner.'

I shake my head. 'No way.'

Tom examines the circle diagram again. 'Could you give me an example of a confrontation with Vita?'

I recount the incident about Kwami's name. How Mark, Vita and Temi decided on it without consulting me.

'And how did that make you feel?'

'Invisible, worthless, redundant.'

'Have you tried talking to Vita about this?'

I raise my eyebrows. 'Really?'

'Fair point.' He sits forward. 'Let's try some role play. I'll be you and you can be Vita.'

To my surprise, I throw myself into the game, cheerfully mimicking Vita. 'What's the matter my little cherub? Has silly Mummy forgotten to feed you again?' I hesitate, aware such an accusation might be justly deserved.

Tom uses his normal voice. 'Actually Vita, I've fed Kwami, and now I'm letting him self-settle.'

'Silly Mummy shouldn't leave you crying,' I mime, picking up the baby.

Tom holds up his hand in a stop gesture. 'I'd prefer it Vita, if you didn't pick Kwami up when he's settling.'

I glance at Tom. 'That's all very well, but I can't stay calm like you. Vita knows how to press my buttons. I'll end up yelling at her or walking away.'

'I'd like you to try. Let me know next time how it goes.'

After Tom's gone, I wander through to the kitchen. Mr Biggles is curled in the chair by the range. At my arrival, he stretches, jumps down and slinks across to his bowl. He looks up plaintively and miaows. 'Okay, okay.' I tip biscuits in his bowl and he munches noisily, while I make myself a tea and take his vacated place in front of the range.

I'm deep in thought when Mark comes in. 'Tom agrees a daily walk would be good for you,' he says. 'But don't forget what I said. No funny business.'

'Thanks. Where is everybody?'

'Mum's minding the boys in her apartment and Jenna's in the office. She thinks you're mad at her.'

'I am.'

'Well, if you're going out for a walk, don't stray too far.'

As I approach the folly, I sense I'm not alone. My heart beats fast as I glance over my shoulder, but no-one's following. I move closer and peer through the stone archway. Damn it, Goth Girl is on my seat.

She looks up from her book unperturbed. 'Hey.'

'What are you doing here?'

'I like it. It's peaceful.'

'You know the Italian Gardens are off limits to residents?'

Ignoring me, she continues to read.

I sit on the seat beside her.

Sorrel strokes her belly in an absentminded gesture I recognise.

I stifle a gasp before blurting out, 'You're pregnant?'

She gives me a sideways glance. 'I didn't think it showed yet.'

Envy aches within me, but I force myself to ask. 'When's the baby due?'

'Mid-October.'

Sixteen, epileptic and pregnant. She's so young. I wonder about the baby's father.

'There is no father,' says Sorrel, as if I've spoken the words out loud. She rotates her ankles and I notice she's not wearing shoes. Her soles are stained green.

'Isn't the grass cold?' I ask.

'I like feeling earth under my feet.'

I gesture towards the cobbled paths running the length of the garden. 'This was where the monks did walking meditation. I come here to be alone,' I add, hoping she'll take the hint.

'I get it.' She closes her book. 'It's a place of reflection, but also of memories and shadows.'

I turn to her. 'What do you mean?'

'Can't you feel them?'

'Who?'

'The souls of those who've trodden this path before.' She gets up. 'I feel them, all around.'

I shiver.

'Oh no. They're not malevolent. This is a place of safety.' She picks up her boots. 'You don't need to fear them. I'll leave you to your contemplation.'

I watch her saunter away. Bloody weirdo. But there's no way stupid Goth Girl's going to freak me out. This is my special place and I'm reclaiming it.

When she's out of sight, I slip off my shoes and set my bare feet on the ground. It's freezing, but after a moment or two I grow acclimatised, treading up and down on the grass alongside the cobbled path. A robin lands close by, chirping as if pleased to see me. I close my eyes, listening to birdsong.

When the sun disappears behind a cloud, I find myself chilled. Going barefoot is ridiculous. I open my eyes, slip on my shoes and head for home.

CHAPTER TWENTY-FOUR

'It's a lovely day,' Tom says. 'Why don't we take this session outside.'

I get up. 'Sure.' I follow him out of the house. 'Which way shall we go?' I ask, as we head down the front steps.

Tom shrugs. 'You choose.'

'I'll show you the lake.' I head across the parking area and through the gate into the woods. Clusters of creamy primroses line the trail, while tiny insects buzz busily around yellow celandine.

Tom clears his throat. 'This made you a little uncomfortable a couple of sessions back, but I'd like to talk more about your family.'

'I wasn't uncomfortable. I just didn't think it was relevant.'

Although I'm not walking fast, Tom lags behind. 'Your relationship with your Aunt Brenda wasn't positive. Is she still part of your life?'

'No,' I call over my shoulder.

'Why? Oh blast.'

I turn around, stifling a giggle when I see he's snagged his jacket on a bramble. 'For all her supposed Christian charity and good works,' I say, as I walk back to Tom, 'Auntie Brenda was nothing but a hypocrite.' I release him from the spiteful thorns. 'She wasn't happy when I started dating Mark.'

'Why not?'

I move on again more slowly. 'Well, I'm not exactly labelling her racist, not that she'd admit it anyway, but she took great delight in pointing out all the problems we'd have as a mixed-race family. Raising a child together, that sort of thing.'

'So you didn't stay in touch?'

'She's a bigot. I cut her out of my life.' We arrive at the lake and I stop talking.

'Wow,' says Tom. It's often the reaction when people see the view for the first time. He gazes across the water. Ducks flap their wings before diving underwater. Dragonflies hover at the water's edge.

I lead the way to the bench beside the boathouse. 'We can sit here.'

Tom waits a beat. 'Can we talk about Ike?'

I turn to him in surprise. 'What's Mark said?'

'He told me some of the story. Perhaps you can fill in the gaps?'

'Hardly anyone knows.'

'I think it might help.'

I pluck bobbles from my jumper.

'I'd like to hear it from you,' he says.

'When Mark and I got married, we didn't try for a child straight away.' I feel like I'm describing someone else. 'Mark was given the opportunity to take on this place and the work consumed us both. When we did get around to thinking about starting a family, it just didn't happen.'

'That must have been hard.'

'It was. Mark and I both wanted kids. We had tests and found out there were potential problems on both sides. We discussed IVF but it's terribly expensive. Also, we'd watched friends go through it, trying for years before seeing their marriage destroyed as hope died.'

'So you looked into adoption?'

I wince. 'Mark was keen to give an unwanted kid a home.'

'And how did you feel about bringing up a child that wasn't your own?'

I shrug. 'I just wanted a baby. I researched, read all the official paperwork. There were no guarantees we'd get a child through UK systems, especially a baby.'

'And then Ike came along.'

I shoot Tom a look. 'Mark went out to Lagos to visit his father. While he was there, his father introduced him to Temi. As well as being a paediatrician, Temi works on community projects. He and Mark got on well. Mark shared our fertility issues and Temi told Mark about kids in Nigeria in need of help. Poor little mites with no future. Temi had contacts, knew whose palms to grease...' I pause.

'So, Mark brought Ike home?'

'He didn't even let me know, just turned up with him. And Ike wasn't the tiny baby I'd imagined. He was already ten months old.'

'How did you manage?'

'Not well. It wasn't like being pregnant and having time to get used to the idea. It wasn't even like starting with a newborn and learning as you go along. Ike was just there and very needy. He has a medical condition.' I take a deep breath. 'Ike requires regular sessions of ultraviolet light to stimulate growth in the skin and prevent the destruction of melanocytes.'

'That's hard.'

'You've no idea. I read medical journals and books on childcare. I did my best but, as time went on, I felt the distance between us grow. We never bonded like we should. Even before Vita arrived, we were struggling.'

'But Vita helped?'

I stare across the water. 'Vita seemed to know what to do. She and Ike have a great connection.'

'That must be difficult.'

'It is. I suppose I'm jealous. That's why, when I found out I was pregnant and having a baby of my own… well, I thought everything would be all right. This time would be different. I'd grow to love my baby while in the womb and, when she arrived, I'd know instinctively what to do.' I smile. 'I thought it might help my relationship with Ike, too. Once I knew how to be a proper mother, he'd also benefit.'

'How did you manage the legal side of things regarding Ike's adoption?'

'Mark and his father took care of that. And Temi, of course. Ike's ours now. It's all legit and above board.'

'Until Mark told me, I hadn't realised Ike was adopted.'

I grimace. 'I hate that word. Lots of people believe Ike's our natural child. Some even comment how alike he and Mark are.'

'Does Ike know?'

'No, and Mark doesn't want to tell him yet, but…'

'But what?'

'Sometimes I think Ike knows I'm not his real mum. I dread the day he turns on me, yelling, *You're not my mother.*'

'I wonder…'

'What?'

'If there's a small part of you that fears loving Ike. You worry that one day someone might turn up to reclaim him.' We sit in silence for a while before Tom gets up. 'Well, nice as this is, I need to be heading back.'

'I think I'll stay a little longer.'

Half an hour later, I'm retracing our steps when I spot Goth Girl on the path ahead of me. Damn it. I'd intended walking the long way home through the arboretum. Don't say she has the same idea. Avoiding Sorrel is easier said than done. She wanders freely through the grounds, blatantly ignoring rules about off-limit areas.

I continue along the track, slowing my pace so I don't have to walk with her. Every time I catch sight of her belly, I'm consumed with envy. What I'd give to go back to those early days of my pregnancy, when I'd been looking forward with hope still alive.

Sorrel heads through the ornamental trees and shrubs towards the boundary wall, while I keep my distance. Reaching a small clearing, she halts, glancing about as if to check she's alone.

I stop abruptly, taking cover behind the twisted trunk of a hornbeam. Sorrel approaches a silver birch growing so near the wall that several branches protrude across the lane.

Catkins dangle from a branch above me and I brush them from my hair. I don't know why I'm hiding and I'm about to step out when Sorrel reaches up into the silver birch. What the devil's she up to? After poking about for a few moments, she lowers her arms and shoves her hands into her pockets. Hunkering down in her scarf, she hurries back the way she came.

CHAPTER TWENTY-FIVE

Something wakes me. My eyes jolt open. '*Hush little nightjar.*' A child's voice?

I check the time on my alarm clock. Ten past one. Yawning, I haul myself up, pull on my dressing gown and tiptoe along the landing. I open Ike's bedroom door and move across to his bed. He's sound asleep. I watch him for a few moments but he doesn't stir. Was he talking in his sleep? Closing the door softly, I head back to my room.

On the way, I hear the voice again, louder this time. '*'Tis time to sleep.*' The tune is *Rockabye Baby,* but the lyrics are wrong. It's coming from below. Holding onto the banister, I creep downstairs. In the hallway I pause to listen. '*You made a promise…*'

Now it's coming from the back of the house. I pad across the black and white tiles, but as I step onto the red carpet, the words stop. I tiptoe on, heart thumping, fingertips brushing lightly against the wooden panelling. On reaching Mark's office, I turn and retrace my steps. Nothing. I can't have imagined it…

I'm now wide awake. I need something to get back to

sleep but I don't want pills. Perhaps hot chocolate will help? I make my way to the kitchen, turn on the light and flick the switch on the kettle. While it boils, I take a mug down from cupboard and blend chocolate powder with a little coconut milk.

Curled up on the chair by the range, Mr Biggles half opens his eyes before closing them again. 'Wish I could go back to sleep as easily as you,' I murmur.

A beam of light outside the window catches my eye. Is it a torch? Abandoning the drink, I hurry through to the boot rack, slip my bare feet into wellies, unlock the front door and step outside. The cold wind is biting. I hug my dressing gown around me and peer across the gravel driveway.

Something is there, near the trees.

As I jog towards the source, apprehension creeps in. It could be a burglar. Why didn't I wake Mark?

On reaching the gate marked private, I pause and look around. The moon is high and stars twinkle in the dark sky. Straight ahead the light bobs, appearing then disappearing. Leave it, I tell myself. Call Mark. Then that tune again. Soft, like a sigh on the wind. *'Secrets to keep.'*

I retie my dressing gown belt and open the gate. As I enter the woods, it's as though I'm under a spell. Each time I think of turning back, the tune calls me on. *'You made a promise…'*

Ten minutes later, I arrive at the lake. I step onto the shingle beach as the words fade away. I tiptoe around the boathouse. Is someone inside? I try the door, but it's locked. I'd have brought the key if I'd known where I was heading. Stepping away, I gaze across the water. The moonlight gives a clear view right across to the other side. Tiny black waves ripple black and white, lapping against the water's edge.

What's that? Something propped against the jetty. Is it a

body? I run into ankle-deep water, my dressing gown growing sodden as I wade closer.

Sorrel's leaning against the timbered structure, her feet and ankles submerged.

I crouch down. 'Sorrel?'

She stares across the water, her face pale in the moonlight. Is she dead? I place two fingers on her neck to check for a pulse. Her skin's cold, but she's alive. Sliding my arms under her armpits, I drag her up the shingle beach until her feet are clear of the water and we both collapse on the ground. I adjust my posture to rest her head and upper body against my knees. Her clothes are damp but not wet.

'Sorrel?'

She blinks.

'What are you doing out here?' My tone sounds crosser than intended.

'I don't know, I was just...' Her gaze shifts uneasily about.

'Did you have a seizure?'

She doesn't reply.

As we sit there, hairs on the back of my neck rise. Is someone watching us? 'Come on. We need to get you back.' I put my arms around her and help her to her feet.

'Why did you come?' she asks, as we stumble through the trees.

'I heard something.'

'What?'

'I'm not sure. Let's get you to your room.'

I run Sorrel a bath. While she soaks, I switch on the kettle in the kitchenette area and open her wall cupboard. The contents are typical teenage fare – Pot Noodles, baked beans, chocolate Hobnobs and a giant bar of Cadbury's Dairy Milk. At the back of the worktop, hidden behind half a loaf of sliced bread, I spot the complimentary tea caddy supplied to our residents and locate a couple of mugs.

She comes out of the bathroom wrapped in a fluffy white towel.

'How are you feeling?' I ask.

'All right.'

'I've made tea.'

She eyes the mug with suspicion. 'I don't drink tea.'

'It's sweet and hot. Good for shock.'

Reluctantly, she accepts it.

'We need to get you and the baby checked out.'

Her eyes flash with alarm. 'No. I'm fine.'

'You might have had a seizure. I should do an accident report at least.'

She grabs my arm. 'Please, don't.' Moving towards the bed, she sets the untouched mug down on the bedside table. Her eyes hold mine as she slips under the quilt. 'Will you stay until I'm asleep?'

CHAPTER TWENTY-SIX

Someone taps on the kitchen window. I put the cheese grater down and glance up at Sorrel peering through. She waves and gestures towards the door.

I open it. 'Sorrel?'

'Mrs Konteh…' She glances away before continuing. 'I just wanted to say thank you for…'

'You're welcome,' I interrupt. 'And call me Hanna.'

'I suppose I need to explain what happened.'

'When you're ready.'

'You didn't tell anyone?'

'No, but I haven't decided yet if that's the right course of action. Are you sure you're okay?'

'Yes.' She glances down at her black-painted fingernails. 'I was wondering if you might lend me a book to read? I've just about finished everything I brought with me.'

I'd already observed that Sorrel is not the sort to be permanently glued to a mobile phone or iPod. 'Yes,' I say, 'but don't you have a Kindle?'

'No, I prefer holding a book in my hand. Makes it more real.'

'I know what you mean. Come on in and we'll take a look.'

Sorrel slips off her boots, leaving them on the doormat. Abandoning lunch preparations, I lead the way into the snug where she pores through shelves of self-help and well-being books. 'You've a good selection. Can I borrow a couple?'

'Of course. You'll find the novels over here.' I take a favourite from the shelf. 'Have you read Carlos Ruiz Zafon?'

'No, but I've heard of him.'

After settling on three books, she moves across to the sideboard and picks up a photo in a silver frame. 'Is this your little boy?'

'Yes.' I smile. 'Ike.'

'You've a baby too, haven't you?'

'That's right.' I take the frame from her and place it back.

'Okay.' She holds up the books. 'Thanks for these. I'll take good care of them.'

She follows me back to the kitchen.

'Jenna says you like to walk,' I say, as she re-laces her boots. 'We could walk together sometime if you like?'

Sorrel glances up and smiles. 'Sure.'

She heads back through the private gate to Bartholomew block. While standing on the patio, I catch high-pitched wails coming from Vita's apartment. Kwami sounds really worked up. No wonder they're late coming over for lunch. I step towards Vita's door and cautiously push it open. 'Hello? Everything okay?'

Vita's pacing the room with Kwami on her shoulder. 'Shh, shh, little man,' she coos.

Ike's sitting at her tiny kitchen table with hands over his ears making an odd growling noise.

I can do without this.

Vita catches sight of me just as I'm about to duck out. 'Here's Mummy, Ike. Perhaps she can help you?'

Reluctantly, I enter the apartment. 'Help with what?'

Ike's bottom lip protrudes in a pout. 'Nana said she'd help with my picture.'

I move towards him.

He kicks his feet against the leg of the table. 'No, I want Nana.'

Vita sighs. 'I did promise, but Kwami won't settle. The only thing that calms him when he gets in this state is a quick turn about the garden.'

I take a deep breath. 'I suppose I could take him?'

Vita raises an eyebrow.

'Just around the lawn, right?'

Vita glances from me to Ike and I'm convinced Mark's told her not to leave me alone with the boys.

'You don't need to go far.' She retrieves a quilted pram suit from the shopping tray of the Silver Cross. Kwami wriggles and writhes as she zips him into the suit and lays him, still screaming, in the pram. 'Just a few circuits of the lawn should do. He drops off as soon as he feels the motion.'

I hesitate. Can I do this?

Ike slams the table-top with open palms and resumes his growling. Perhaps Kwami's the lesser of two evils. I step forward and grasp the handle of the pram. Vita opens the door and I'm alone on the patio with a screaming infant.

Cautiously I manoeuvre the pram down the step and onto the perimeter path. As soon as the wheels begin to roll, Kwami's sobs morph into hiccups. The pram is huge and bounces gently. We haven't gone far when the hiccups stop. Is he still breathing? I peek under the hood. His eyes are half-closed, arms flung above his head.

Scared he might wake, I march on, beginning a second

circuit when I arrive back at the patio. I'm in a rhythm. Birds sing in the trees and the fresh breeze on my face is invigorating. Before I know it, I've completed a third circuit.

I pull the pram back onto the patio, parking it near the French doors. Pressing the brake pedal with my foot, I enter the kitchen. Vita and Ike are at the table with heads together as they crayon.

Vita glances up. 'All right?' she mouths.

I nod.

She gives me a thumbs up.

I resume lunch preparations. As I set three slices of bread and cheese under the grill, I realise I'm smiling.

CHAPTER TWENTY-SEVEN

'Tom's here,' says Jenna. 'Go on in. I'll bring you some tea.'

Heading into the snug, I find Tom seated in one of the armchairs. 'Hi.' I sink down on the couch.

'Hello.' Tom begins with the usual question. 'How are you feeling today?'

'A little brighter. I've been taking my meds, going for daily walks, writing in my journal.'

'That's good. You're looking better.'

I finger a lock of my hair. At least this week I got around to washing it.

'Here you go,' says Jenna as she comes in and sets a tray on the coffee table.

Those boot-leg trousers really show off her tiny waist, I muse.

'Thank you.' Tom adjusts his glasses.

Jenna pauses in the doorway. 'I'll leave you to it, then.'

Tom's cheeks flush darkest red and I realise he fancies her. Composing himself, he consults his notes. 'A few sessions ago you described feelings of dissociation.'

'That's right.' I smile. 'But I'm feeling more like myself now.'

'No longer in the white room?'

'No, all present and correct.'

'No hallucinations or feelings of paranoia?'

I lean forward and pour the tea. 'Milk and one sugar, isn't it?'

'Hanna?'

I sigh. 'Well, I did hear singing. Does that count?'

'What sort of singing?'

'It sounds silly… it was like a nursery rhyme. Is that classed as hallucination?'

Tom picks up his cup. 'It depends.'

'Perhaps I was mistaken.'

'This is an old house. I'm sure it makes many mysterious sounds – wind rattling down the chimney, water pipes expanding and contracting… but if it should happen again, note it down in your journal and we'll discuss it.' He sips his drink. 'What about Kwami?'

I adjust my cushion. 'What about him?'

'How are your feelings towards him?'

'I'm a terrible mother, aren't I? It's not that I don't care. I wouldn't let anything happen to him.'

'But you're not feeling any bond as yet?'

'Not really.' I cover my face. 'I'm such a failure.'

'Not at all. The next step is to identify how your interactions with other people affect your attitude and behaviour towards Kwami.'

'Aren't I already doing that in my journal?'

'Yes, but you're working towards recognising what's happening and when, to enable you to break the negative pattern.'

'I did take Kwami for a walk in his pram yesterday.'

'Well done. That's a huge step.'

I hunch my shoulders, embarrassed by the praise. 'It was only a couple of circuits of the lawn. Vita was struggling. I took him to help her out.'

'It's a great start. You're developing positive skills and activities. Practise them when you're in a good place and they'll come more naturally when you're not.'

When I knock on her door, Sorrel opens it a crack and peers out. 'Hold on.'

I huddle outside waiting. It's a cold one this morning. After at least five minutes she finally strides out in a chunky jacket and hood, slamming the door behind her.

'Where shall we go?' I ask.

She pulls on knitted mittens. 'I don't mind.'

'We'll do the short circular then.' I lead the way across the main driveway and around the west side of the building. As we walk, I point out the newly dug footings. 'This is the site for Darius block. We're hoping to start building by the end of the year.'

She nods, but the proposed building seems of little interest. We head through the gate and turn left, passing Caleb block as we follow the perimeter path around the house.

I take a deep breath. 'Did you want to talk about what happened at the lake?'

She sighs. 'If we must.'

'You know you could have drowned?'

'It wasn't my time.'

'What were you doing out there?'

'I wasn't trying to kill myself, if that's what you're thinking.'

We walk on in silence, skirting the south side of the chapel.

'I was feeling lonely, I guess,' Sorrel continues. 'My parents won't let me have my mobile or internet access while I'm here, and your husband…' – she makes it sound as if I'm responsible for Mark's actions – 'is only too happy to go along with their wishes.'

'I'm sorry, that must be hard.'

'It is.' She adjusts her scarf. 'I went for a walk, sat on the beach and watched the sun set. I hadn't eaten anything all day. I suppose I must have had an episode.'

'Did you take anything? Pills or something?'

'You do know I have epilepsy?'

'Sorry, yes.' I gesture towards her baby bump. 'Does that create extra risks?'

Sorrel cradles her belly. 'It shouldn't harm the baby. Anyway, what about you? What were you doing there?'

'I couldn't sleep.'

'And happened to walk all the way to the lake?'

I feel my cheeks flush. 'I heard something. It was like someone singing a nursery rhyme. Something about a nightjar.'

'Secrets to keep,' she murmurs.

'What?'

'It's getting chilly.' Sorrel quickens her pace as we pass the greenhouses. 'Let's head back.'

———

That night I dream again.

.   .   .

I'm pushing the pram through an avenue of trees. The sun shines through the leaves creating dappled patterns on the hood and apron. I gaze down at my beautiful sleeping daughter.

Suddenly the pram bounces erratically and my hands are jolted from the handle. In seconds, the pram races away from me.

'Stop,' I yell, running after it. The pram bounces along, eventually coming to a halt as it bumps into a silver birch blocking the path. As I race towards it, I hear my baby cry. I catch up and pull down the hood. Inside, a baby is bawling, but it's not my daughter. It's Kwami.

I stagger down to the kitchen later than intended.

Vita shoots me a knowing glance from across a pile of ironing. 'You look tired.'

I slump down at the table. 'I didn't sleep well.'

She places a mug in front of me and Mr Biggles jumps onto the table.

'Off.' I shoo, but stealthily he creeps onto my lap and curls into a ball. I stroke his soft fur, beginning to relax. It must be gone ten, because *Women's Hour* is on the radio. I yawn. 'Where is everybody?'

'Mark and Jenna are working, Ike's at preschool and Kwami's outside in the pram.'

Vita always insists children need a daily airing, regardless of the weather. She continues to iron while I sip tea, contemplating my dream. What did it mean? Is it time to give up on my daughter and accept Kwami is my baby?

When I've finished my drink, I ease the cat from my lap,

haul myself up and place my cup in the dishwasher. 'I'm going for a walk.'

———

I knock for Sorrel. 'Just a mo,' she says, grabbing her jacket.

'How are the books?' I ask, as we trek through the ornamental trees in front of the house.

'Good,' says Sorrel. 'I've started the Elizabeth Gilbert.'

'I love that one.'

'Have you read *Fragile Things* by Neil Gaiman?'

'No, but I liked *The Graveyard Book*.'

'Me too.'

I smile. It's fun to have someone to discuss books with. 'Perhaps they'll make it into a movie,' I suggest, 'like *Coraline*.'

Sorrel shrugs. 'I'm not that into films. Or TV come to that.'

I glance at her. Definitely not a typical teenager.

'I prefer experiencing the world around me,' she explains, as if responding to my unvoiced question. 'Dawn chorus, sunrise…' A gust of wind blows hair across her face and she brushes it away, laughing. 'Fresh breeze in my hair.'

As we approach a clearing, I ask, 'Would you like to visit your special tree?'

Sorrel stops in her tracks. 'Have you been following me?'

'Just the once. I didn't intend to, but you looked so furtive.'

She chews her lip. 'You had no right.'

'Sorrel, you can trust me. I won't tell anyone.'

She lowers herself down onto a fallen tree trunk. 'I was hoping to get a letter from Will.'

'Will?'

'My boyfriend. He's the only one who gets me.'

'Is he…?' I gesture to her stomach.

'Yes, but no one knows and I'd rather it stayed that way.'

'Why?'

'He's a bit…' She sighs. 'Oh, I don't know. Not what they deem suitable. It's not that he's trouble or anything. Not now, anyway.' She chuckles. 'He used to be, but he says I've mellowed him.'

'And he writes to you? That's quite retro, isn't it? Communicating by snail mail. Why not ring or text?'

She smiles self-consciously. 'We resorted to old fashioned methods because I didn't want my parents to know. They used to go through my mobile when I was at home.' She shoots me a look. 'You promise you won't tell?'

'I promise.'

She pulls a crumpled envelope from her coat pocket. 'He left this in my locker at school.'

'A love letter?'

Her cheeks flush. 'I don't know about that. Will's not the most romantic of boys. Hardly a boyfriend at all really, but we're soulmates.'

'He hides letters in a tree. That's pretty romantic.'

Sorrel hauls herself up. 'That's just it. Will said he'd leave a message in the nearest silver birch to the gates. It's been eight days and I've heard nothing.'

CHAPTER TWENTY-EIGHT

I wake early feeling more positive than I have in days. It's ridiculous, Sorrel's half my age, but we have a lot in common. After all, we're both considered to be a little crazy. I sit up and stretch. If Sorrel can cope with what the world's thrown at her, then I can too. It's time I started acting more normal. What is it they say? Fake it until you make it?

After a quick shower, I pull on jeans and one of my nicer T-shirts. I make my way to the boys' bedroom and gently ease open the door. Ike's still asleep, but Kwami stirs. I gaze down at him. His eyes are tightly closed as he screws up his little face and flexes clenched fists.

'Come on then.' I reach into the cot to pick him up and carry him over to the changing trolley. He's heavier than I remember. I unzip his sleep suit and unbutton his babygro. 'It's all right, I can do this,' I whisper, not sure which one of us I'm trying to reassure. All the while I'm changing his nappy, Kwami gazes up at me. 'There, that's better.' I button him back up.

Positioning him in the crook of my arm, I make my way downstairs to the kitchen. 'Right, let's see if we can work this out.' I rummage in the drawer for instructions for the bottle-making contraption. 'Okay.' Taking a bottle from the sterilising unit, I place it in the machine, press a button and a shot of hot water is dispensed. Still jiggling Kwami, I check the instructions on the formula packet. It's not easy scooping powder with one hand, but I manage. I screw a cap on the bottle and give it a good shake before taking the cap off again and placing the bottle back in the machine to top up with more water. I sniff the mixture. 'Mmm, smells like baby milk.'

Mr Biggles, who usually gives the baby a wide berth, circles my ankles. 'Go away,' I scold. I refit the cap with a sterilised teat and dribble a few drops onto my wrist. 'Seems to be about right.' I move across to the wooden chair and sit down, adjusting Kwami so he's resting against my left arm.

Trustingly, he latches onto the teat and sucks greedily. He fixes his eyes on me as he takes the feed.

'There.' I smile. 'This isn't so bad, is it?'

'You're up.'

I glance at Vita in the doorway. 'Yes, and Kwami's changed and fed.' Placing down the empty bottle, I shift Kwami onto my shoulder and pat his back. Obligingly he emits a loud burp.

She moves towards the steriliser unit.

'I'll do that,' I say. 'I'm going to make up his bottles for the day and put them in the fridge.'

She turns to me. 'Okay, good.'

'You could give Ike his breakfast if you like?' I wonder if I sound patronising.

'All right, and I'll get him dressed and drive him to preschool.'

'Thank you.'

. . .

After settling Kwami in his bassinet, I make up two more bottles and stow them in the fridge. By the time Vita returns, I've tidied the kitchen and emptied and reloaded the dishwasher.

Vita offers a tight smile as she sits at the table. 'You're obviously feeling better.'

'Yes.' I pour coffee into mugs. 'I'm sorry I've not been myself. Perhaps the medication's finally kicking in.'

'Your body's had a shock. Give yourself time to heal. When the body is healthy, the mind follows.'

We sip our drinks in rare companionable silence.

'If you're feeling better,' she says. 'I'd like to ask you about something.'

'Go on.'

'Well, I didn't want to worry you before, but it's about Ike.'

My stomach flips. What now?

Vita sets down her mug. 'Has Ike ever mentioned his imaginary friends?'

My drink goes the wrong way and I cough. Vita slaps me on the back.

'I'm all right.' I brush her away. 'Imaginary friends?' I croak.

'Are you sure you're ready to hear this?'

'Yes. What has Ike said?'

'Well.' She glances at me before continuing. 'I first became aware the day you came home with Kwami. I said something to Ike about how lovely it was to have a little brother, a new best friend, and Ike told me he had one already. I asked him who, expecting him to say Joe or Ethan from preschool. Ike said his friend was called Gainde.'

'Perhaps it's a new kid?'

'No, I asked. They don't have a child by that name.'

'Perhaps it's someone from the telly?'

'I don't think so. I limit Ike's television viewing to one hour a day and always watch with him. There's no character with that name.'

I try not to be irritated she's criticising my own lax attitude to the TV. 'I'm sure it's nothing to worry about. Lots of kids have imaginary friends.'

'Perhaps not.' She surveys the garden a little nervously. 'Do you know, I think I'll eat in my apartment tonight. I've a nice fish pie in the freezer that needs using up.'

I raise a quizzical eyebrow.

'You and Mark can have the place to yourselves.' She pats my hand. 'It will do you good to spend time together. Just the two of you.'

'All right,' I say. 'Thanks.'

She heads for the door before hesitating, her hand on the handle.

'What?' I ask.

She spins around. 'It's just… when I asked Ike what his friend looked like, he told me that Gainde was a big dog.'

———

Mark saunters into the kitchen and washes his hands. 'Just us?'

'Well, apart from Kwami.' I gesture towards the bassinet. 'It was your mum's idea actually.' I set the salad bowl on the table and take a margherita pizza from the oven. 'She thinks we need alone time.'

Mark pulls out a chair and sits down.

I serve him two slices of pizza.

'Thanks.' He helps himself to salad.

We eat in silence. Should I put the radio on? I don't want to wake Kwami...

'So,' he asks, between mouthfuls. 'Are you feeling better?'

'A bit.'

'The sessions with Tom help?'

'Yes, and my walks. And I'm sleeping better.'

I wonder for a moment if Mark's going to suggest moving back into our bed. When he doesn't, I'm oddly relieved. 'Is everything okay with the business?' I ask.

He nods. 'Jenna's a godsend.'

Of course she is.

'Temi's seminar in Leeds is proving productive. It's been a great opportunity to network with colleagues.'

'He's coming back?'

'Yes, he's proving to be a great asset to our conference plans.'

'Mark' – I push salad around my plate – 'could we talk about me returning to work?'

He finishes his mouthful before replying. 'It's way too soon. You're still on maternity leave and there's a baby to look after.'

So that's it? End of conversation? Perhaps I should have come at it from a different angle. I listen to the kitchen clock ticking and I can't think of anything else to say. When did Mark and I run out of things to talk about? 'Ike seems happy with the extra morning at preschool.'

Mark helps himself to another slice of pizza. 'It's the only option really, now Mum's looking after Kwami.'

Ouch. 'I'm sharing Kwami's care too.'

As if on cue, the baby stirs.

Mark shoves the last of the pizza in his mouth.

Kwami wails.

'There, there.' I pick him up, put him on my shoulder and sit back down. 'Vita says Ike has an imaginary friend.' I jiggle the baby, patting his bottom. 'He told her it's a dog.'

Mark pushes his plate away, muttering under his breath.

'What?'

'You don't think it's odd that our son has an imaginary friend?'

'No, I…'

'Well, I do.' Mark stands up so fast his chair tips over. 'Don't go encouraging Ike with your weird ideas.'

The disturbance causes Kwami to cry in earnest.

'Christ, don't you think I've got enough to deal with?' Righting his chair, Mark stomps out of the room.

CHAPTER TWENTY-NINE

Sorrel steps out of Bartholomew block. 'Hiya.'

I stop, my hands resting on the pram handle. 'Morning.'

She peeks under the hood. 'Cute. What's his name?'

'Kwami.'

She joins me and we perambulate the lawn.

'I have news,' she whispers, eyes sparkling as she taps her side.

My eyes are drawn to the corner of a blue envelope peeping out of her pocket. 'So, your rosy cheeks are not entirely due to the cold wind then?' I tease.

'No.' Her cheeks blush even pinker.

'Everything all right with Will?'

'Yeah, but we're keeping things quiet for now.'

As we walk side by side, I have a sudden urge to share. 'How are you getting on with Tom?'

Sorrel shoots me a look. 'Isn't that supposed to be confidential?'

'Yes, sorry.' I slow my pace. 'Look, I wasn't prying, it's just, I'm having sessions with Tom too.'

'You?'

I nod.

'Why?'

I glance into the pram. 'I'm having difficulty bonding with the baby.'

'Looks as if you're doing okay to me.'

'I'm trying.' I sigh. 'To be honest, I have difficulty bonding with both children.'

'Why?' she repeats.

'Ike's not the easiest to care for. He has a skin condition called vitiligo. It means he can't go out without sunscreen and has to have regular sessions of ultraviolet light.'

'Poor kid. I suppose that's why your mother's so hands-on with them?'

'Vita's my mother-in-law.'

'Bummer.' Sorrel laughs and I find myself joining in. I don't remember the last time I laughed.

'Has she got the other one now?' she asks.

'No, he's at preschool.'

'He's sweet. I spoke to him the other day when he was out with your mother-in-law. He wasn't at all shy, telling me all about his dog, Gainde.'

'Sorry,' I give an apologetic smile. 'Gainde is Ike's imaginary friend.'

'No, the dog that follows him about the garden.'

I scan the lawn as if an imaginary dog might bound towards us. 'Are you sure you saw a dog?'

'Yes. I was quite surprised you had such a big dog, what with having little kids.'

I park the pram on the patio and enter through the French doors.

Jenna greets me. 'Cuppa?'

'I'll have a mint tea.'

I move towards the kettle, but Jenna waves me away. 'Sit down. I'll do it.'

Before relaxing, I peep outside to check on Kwami. He's still asleep, so I leave the door ajar and take my favourite seat beside the range. Mr Biggles immediately jumps onto my lap, purring.

'Cold out there?' Jenna shoos the cat and hands me a mug.

'Yes, but the baby's well wrapped up,' I reply defensively, cradling the tea in my hands to warm my fingers.

'You were walking with Sorrel again.'

I glance up. 'And?'

Jenna picks up a cloth and wipes the already immaculate kitchen surface. 'Nothing. It's just… you two seem to spend quite a bit of time together.'

'Hmm.' I set my mug on the floor.

'What?'

'I'm wondering if Mark's put you up to this.'

Jenna throws the cloth in the sink. 'What do you mean?'

I get up from the chair. 'This sudden interest in who I'm friends with.'

She straightens the storage jars, avoiding eye contact. 'He did mention something about Ike and an imaginary friend.'

'What of it?'

'Well, you know Sorrel has mental health issues.'

I scoff. 'I didn't think you were supposed to share confidential client information with people who are not staff.'

Jenna sighs. 'Don't be like that.'

'Like what? You're the one with the problem. What's it to you if Sorrel and I are friends?'

'Mark and I think that…'

'Mark and I?' My voice is high pitched. 'When did you two become "Mark and I"?'

'Hanna, I didn't mean…'

Kwami wails.

'I need to see to the baby.' I move towards the door. 'Do you mind?'

'No, I'll leave you to it.'

———

'Tom's here.' Mark hands me a cup of tea.

'Already?' I check the clock on the wall. 'He's early.'

'He's fine. I've put him in the snug and made him coffee. He said not to rush.' Mark settles himself at the kitchen island with a plate of toast.

'Okay.' I help myself to a digestive from the biscuit tin.

'Actually, he's seeing Sorrel Jordan after your session. Best not keep him waiting.'

I carry my drink into the snug and greet Tom with a smile. 'Hi.'

'You look pleased with yourself.'

'I am. I took Kwami for another walk in his pram.'

'That's really good progress, Hanna. Well done.'

'Thanks. What didn't go so well was my conversation with Mark about me coming back to work. He says I'm not ready.'

'Well it's still early days and at least you've opened up the dialogue. How do you feel about Jenna still doing in effect what was your job?'

'It's fair enough, I suppose. She was taken on as cover for my maternity leave.'

Tom turns over a page in his notebook. 'So, if we go back to your goals – being a good mum and returning to work. Do you have any thoughts on how you might achieve these?'

I sigh. 'I started out with high aspirations, but now I'm not sure if it's possible to do both.'

Tom takes an A4 pad from his satchel. 'I'd like to get this down so that we can visualise it.' He turns to a clean page and draws a horizontal line. 'So, this is your timeline, and here's where there have been significant life changes.' He adds labels for the death of my parents, marriage and motherhood. 'Now, I'd like to focus on your goals. So, this point here' – he adds an asterisk – 'is before you had children, and this is after.'

'Okay.'

'So, aspirations before children...'

'To be a good business partner.'

'Yes, we'll note that down.' He writes, *Partner in The Sanctuary.* 'And what inspired you about this sort of work?'

'Wanting to help people.'

'Let's have that on the timeline too.' He jots down, *Helping others.* 'Okay, so looking at this, it doesn't mean you're unable to do what you dreamt about. You can still ultimately do both.'

'But I'm not achieving either right now.'

'Do you know what's stopping you?'

'I'm not sure I have the confidence or skills for work and I haven't sorted out my relationship with the boys yet.'

Tom scratches his chin. 'To be honest, I don't have answers for you, but I gather from what you've said that work is something you enjoy. You had to take a break because of your new priorities – family and children – but perhaps you need something other than the children to stimulate you? I'm not suggesting you go back to work full time, but I don't see why you couldn't have some involvement with the business even while on maternity leave. What do you think?'

'That if I don't try, I'll won't be happy. I want to stop feeling such a failure.'

CHAPTER THIRTY

As I amble through the woods, I turn over in my mind what Tom said. Will I regret it if I don't try? Everyone thinks they know what's best for me. Now even Jenna's getting involved. Picking up a stick, I swish angrily at the nettles. Bloody cheek, suggesting I shouldn't be friendly with Sorrel. All that stuff about her mental health… and yet, Sorrel did say she'd seen a dog with Ike. If Gainde's imaginary, she can't have seen him.

Arriving at the pet cemetery, I freeze. Something's been rooting around the gravestones: the ivy's torn away and small fragments of wood are scattered about. The grave marker on Fred's grave is smashed and there's a gaping hole where the mound once stood. I cover my mouth. The fragments are not wood, they're bones. With a gasp, I turn and run.

Jogging through the orchard, I hear crying. Is that a baby? I pass through the gate and onto the lawn, where Vita's put Kwami for his daily airing. My heart skips a beat. Beside the pram is an enormous dog. I stare in horror as it noses under the hood.

'Get away,' I scream.

The beast turns towards me.

'Get away from the baby.' I remember the stick in my hand and hurl it, but the dog doesn't flinch and the stick bounces off the side of the pram.

I move forward and a low growl resonates from deep within the canine's belly.

'Come on, boy.' Norris hauls himself up from where he's tidying the flowerbeds a few metres away.

The dog turns and trots obediently to his master.

'What the hell are you doing, letting your dog near the baby?' I rush over to the pram and gaze down at Kwami, but he's fast asleep. It wasn't him crying.

'Sorry, Mrs Konteh.' Norris pats the dog's head. 'But the dog won't hurt 'im. He was just keeping guard.'

'Guarding him from his mother?'

'Hasn't met you yet, Mrs Konteh.' Norris holds the dog's collar. 'Here, come and get acquainted.'

Shaking my head, I release the brake on the pram and wheel it away. 'If you see my mother-in-law,' I call over my shoulder, 'tell her I'm taking the baby home.'

———

At bath time, I rub corticosteroid cream into Ike's skin, before settling him in bed with his books while I bath Kwami. Cupping warm water in my hand, I trickle it over his little round tummy. He smiles up at me and my own belly does a flip. 'I suppose you are quite cute,' I whisper. 'We'll get to know each other, but we need to take small steps.'

After reading Ike a story, and feeding and settling Kwami, I head downstairs. Mark's in the snug and I join him on the couch, curling my legs underneath me.

He doesn't look up from his MacBook. 'How did bedtime go?'

'All right, actually,' I chuckle. 'But I think Vita's giving me a wide berth.'

He snorts. 'Probably enjoying a night off.'

Is that a dig? I won't rise to it. 'Fancy a glass of wine?'

He glances up. 'Should you be drinking? What with the medication…'

'I didn't say I was having one.'

'No, I'm all right thanks.' He returns to his work.

I drum my fingers on the arm of the couch. 'Why did you let Norris get that huge dog?'

'He needs something as a deterrent for the rabbits.'

'Couldn't he find another way of dealing with them?'

'Well.' He looks up again. 'I didn't want to tell you this, but Norris found rats around the bins.'

'Rats?' I shudder.

'I thought a bigger dog might keep them at bay,' Mark continues. 'It's an old house. We don't want vermin.'

'But why not encourage Norris to get a puppy? One he could train. I'm scared that big dog is not safe with the children.'

'I checked the dog out. He used to be on a farm until his master died and the farm was sold. It's not a pit bull for heaven's sake, just an Alsatian cross.' Mark sighs. 'They assured me the dog's fine with children. But if it makes you happier, I'll tell Norris not to let him near the house when the kids are around.'

'No. Better the dog gets to know them if it's going to be living in close proximity.'

Mark resumes rapid typing.

'I think,' I say, yawning as I get up, 'I'll head up to bed.' I move towards the door. 'Anyway, Ike's already made friends with the dog.'

'Ike?' Mark pauses, fingers suspended over the keys. 'Why do you say that?'

I hover in the doorway. 'What?'

'Ike's petrified of the bloody beast. Mum says he won't go anywhere near it.'

CHAPTER THIRTY-ONE

Norris heads towards the allotments, the dog pulling and straining on a long piece of rope.

'Norris.' I stop to speak to him.

'Yes, Mrs Konteh?' The dog tugs violently on the rope and, in the effort to yank him back, Norris drops his shovel. He cusses under his breath.

'I'm sorry. I overreacted yesterday. You don't have to keep your dog on a leash all the time. Perhaps just keep him tethered when the children are around? Until we all get used to each other.'

'Much obliged, Mrs Konteh.' He shortens the rope. 'Sit.' The dog complies.

'What's his name?'

'Arnie.' He pats the dog's head. 'He don't like being on a rope. Always ran free, see, at the last place.'

'Let him off then. I hate seeing an animal tied against his will.'

Norris slips the rope from the dog's neck. Arnie runs in a circle and shakes before sitting quietly beside his master.

I reach out my hand and Arnie licks it. He has kind eyes.

Sorrel and I take the woodland path towards the lake. When we arrive, we gaze across the water as if standing at the edge of an ocean.

'Let's rest awhile.' I make my way to the bench beside the boathouse and Sorrel joins me. 'Sorry I was a bit prickly about Ike's imaginary dog. Mark gets annoyed when I talk about it.'

'The dog I saw wasn't imaginary,' says Sorrel.

'I know. I've solved the mystery. It was the gardener's dog.'

'Oh, right.'

We stare out at the water for a while before Sorrel continues. 'I used to have imaginary friends.'

'Really?'

'Yes, only I'm not sure they were imaginary.' She gets up, picks a leaf from a nearby bush and shreds it. 'I had two friends when I was Ike's age. I thought everyone could see them.'

'Tell me about them.'

'Eleanor was my best friend.' Sorrel sits back down. 'I don't remember a time she wasn't there. She was fourteen.'

'That's quite an age difference.'

'Yes. I suppose that's why people thought it was odd. It didn't matter to us though. She was fun. We played this game where she'd say things and I copied her.' Sorrel smiles. 'We also played hide and seek, although I never did get the hang of hiding from her.'

'What else did you do?'

'She sang me to sleep every night. Sometimes she taught me nursery rhymes.'

The hairs on the back of my neck prickle. 'What rhymes?'

'One about a nightjar. That's why I freaked out the other day when you said you'd heard someone reciting a rhyme. Mum thought I'd learnt it at school, but when she checked, the teacher didn't know it.'

I shiver. 'Do you think Eleanor was a ghost?'

'She was real to me, but she always wore the same thing – a long dress with a crown of flowers in her hair. Sometimes I'd ask if I could wear the flowers and she would kneel so that I could lift the crown from her head and place it on my own. I really loved her.'

Sorrel's opened up more today than ever before. Should I push her further? 'You said you had two friends?'

'Yes. Henry came later. He always appeared beside the sitting room fireplace in bare feet, and he wore tatty trousers and a ragged shirt. Henry couldn't go anywhere else, whereas Eleanor roamed all over – upstairs, along the landing, into my bedroom. They never visited together. If Henry appeared, Eleanor vanished. Henry was cheeky. Sometimes he did naughty things like knocking things over. No-one was supposed to touch Mum's ornaments, but he'd clamber up the shelves, take them down and put them back in different places. Mum would get so cross. "You've been playing with my china again," she'd complain. "It wasn't me, it was Henry," I'd say, while Henry sat in the corner beside the fire-place, sniggering. Sometimes he stuck out his tongue and wiggled his fingers in his ears, and when I laughed, Mum would tut and tell me off for telling lies.'

'What happened to Eleanor and Henry?'

'When I was eight, we moved from the Old Rectory. I was sorry to lose my friends.' Sorrel pulls her coat around her. 'I don't make friends easily and the kids in my new school gave me a wide berth.'

'Why?'

'They called me a liar because I was always talking to people they couldn't see. It worried my teachers, so they spoke to Mum and Dad. Told them I was anti-social. When they mentioned me talking to people who weren't there, Mum said, "Oh, I thought she'd grown out of that." That's when I got referred to Mr Dimitri, the school psychologist.' Sorrel shivers. 'I'm getting cold. Shall we go back?'

We retrace our steps. On the way, we pass Norris returning to the shed with his tools. We stop and pet Arnie, before Norris walks on.

'He's behaving so much better off the rope,' I say, 'but there's one thing I don't understand. Mark says Ike's scared of Arnie and yet you saw them playing together.'

Sorrel stops. 'That dog? That's not the one Ike plays with. Ike's dog is bigger and darker in colour.'

Back at the house, I find Mark in his office on the computer. 'Has Norris got two dogs?'

'No, just Arnie.' Mark glances up. 'I thought you were okay about it now. I told Norris to keep the dog away from the kids.'

'Yes, I met Arnie. The dog's not a problem, but Sorrel says…'

'Sorrel? What are you doing getting friendly with a patient, Hanna? You know that's not ethical.'

'She's not my patient.'

'No, but you're…'

'What?'

He returns his attention to the screen. 'I just don't think it's a good idea.'

'Why?'

'Because Sorrel Jordan has serious psychological problems.'

'I know.' I mock. 'Her parents think she talks to dead people. Why can't you accept Sorrel is a brave, sensitive and intuitive young person with special abilities?'

'I think it's quite likely that Sorrel suffers from undiagnosed schizophrenia, and I'm concerned you may not be good for each other.'

'So, I can't have a friend now?' As I turn to leave, Jenna enters. 'Seeing as you've taken the last one away.'

CHAPTER THIRTY-TWO

Sorrel and I trek across the orchard on our early morning jaunt. 'I've got a session with Tom later,' I tell her.

'Lucky you.'

'How are you getting on with him?'

Sorrel shrugs. 'He's okay, I guess.'

'You said you'd seen psychologists before. How does Tom compare?'

She pulls a face. 'The school psychologists were hopeless. They encouraged me to talk about my *friends*, the invisible ones no-one else could see.' She laughs. 'Mr Dimitri was overly interested. "Are they here now?" he'd ask. As if I'd tell him, even if they were.'

'It must have been difficult.'

'It got worse. Sometimes my *friends* told me stuff that hadn't happened yet. Once I said to a girl in my class, "Sorry about your mum". Two weeks later her mum was diagnosed with cancer.'

I cover my mouth. 'Oh no.'

'Another time I told a boy his granny was calling him.

When he got home, he found out she'd had a heart attack that afternoon and died.'

'Was it just bad things you were able to predict?'

'Pretty much. The kids at school started a rumour that I was a witch. They kept their distance even more after that. The only time they pretended to be friendly was for a dare.'

I rub her arm. 'Poor you.'

Sorrel shrugs. 'It was okay. I used to walk home through the churchyard. I never felt alone there.'

'I suppose some would see it as a gift.'

She nods. 'It is. I read auras too and I can tell when someone is to be trusted or not. That's why I like talking to you.'

'How did you learn to read auras?'

'I taught myself. As I didn't have many friends, I spent a lot of time in the library. They called me a witch, so I thought I might as well live up to it, and began researching black and white magic.'

'From the school library?'

Sorrel laughs. 'No, the dark web. The school library wouldn't stock books on the occult.'

'Didn't they have internet blocks on subject matter like that?'

'Not if you know how to get around them. Will helped.'

'Ah, Will… the illusive letter writer.'

'He might be a bit of a geek, but he's a computer genius.' Her face glows with pride. 'He can get around any blocking systems schools and libraries put in.'

'Why are you so worried about your parents finding out Will's the father of your baby?' Something is niggling… 'Sorrel, your parents do know that you're pregnant?'

She chews her bottom lip.

'Oh my God!'

'You promised not to tell.'

'I said I wouldn't reveal who the father was. I didn't agree to collude in hiding the fact that you're having a baby. Oh, God. This is so bad!'

'Mum and Dad are religious. They forbade me to see Will or even speak with him.'

'But why?'

'He's different. He has long hair and paints his nails.' She sighs. 'He's been suspended a couple of times for accessing school records - exam papers and things.'

'You have to tell your parents that you're pregnant. I can't keep this to myself.'

'I will. I'll tell them next time they visit.' She grabs my arm. 'But you can't say anything. There's no way I'm dropping Will in the shit.'

'You said the other week that you didn't think Kwami was your son.'

We're in the snug. I get up and adjust the cushions, delaying my response.

Tom's persistent. 'Have your feelings changed?'

I flop down on the couch. 'They might have shifted a bit...'

'Could your previous concerns have been because you didn't see Kwami born?'

'Maybe. But also' – I lean forward – 'I saw my daughter.'

'You saw her?'

'Yes. I held her in my arms. She was beautiful.' I give myself a little shake. 'Everyone says it was a dream, a hallucination caused by the drugs.'

'You were unconscious for several hours?'

'Yes.'

'So, it's possible it was a reaction to drugs, combined with longing for a daughter.'

'I s'pose.'

'I have a suggestion.' Tom taps his pen against his chin. 'Have you thought about doing a DNA maternity test?'

'Do they do those for mothers?'

'Of course. Women who have IVF often need reassurance the egg fertilised in the lab is their own.'

I stare out of the window. What if the test comes back positive? Suppose I've been neglecting my own child for weeks? Will I feel better or worse?

'Do you think it would help?' Tom asks.

'I'm not sure, but it's worth a go.'

CHAPTER THIRTY-THREE

There's no one about when the package lands on the doormat a few days later. It had been surprisingly easy. Under cover of online grocery shopping, I Googled *Maternity DNA testing*, checked a box and inserted PayPal details before deleting everything from my search history. Ninety-nine pounds. Small price for certainty. I snatch up the padded envelope and hurry to my room.

Tearing it open, I read the instructions – fill in the forms, take a swab from my mouth and another from Kwami's, and post the samples for testing.

I bundle everything back into the envelope and hide it under a stack of jumpers in the wardrobe.

If only I could share this with someone. In the past it would have been Jenna. I sigh. I'm carrying too many secrets… It's ages since Jenna and I talked. Perhaps I should extend an olive branch?

Before I can change my mind, I hurry downstairs and along to the office to find her. But as I approach, I hear Mark's voice. Damn, I thought he was out. I peer around the door and spot Jenna at her workstation. Mark's standing behind, studying something on her computer screen. They look very cosy together.

Mark says something in a soft voice. It's too quiet for me to catch the words, but Jenna laughs, turning her face towards him.

Are they about to kiss? Covering my mouth, I race back along the corridor and upstairs to my room. Tearing into the bathroom, I kneel before the toilet bowl and retch. Was Mark coming on to Jenna? My heart pounds. All that stuff I've read about *Me Too*... is this sexual harassment? Hauling myself up from the floor, I cross to the basin and fill my toothbrush mug with water. Jenna didn't seem bothered. In fact, they looked comfortable, as if such intimacy was normal. As I sip water, I recall her words, *Mark and I*. Are they having an affair?

My world shifts as if built on sand. Everything I thought fixed becomes fluid. My head spins and I reach for the wall to steady myself. I can't pin anything down. I need something solid, an anchor...

I stagger into the bedroom and over to the wardrobe. Opening the door, I rummage through the jumpers and retrieve the DNA kit.

Vita's coming out of the kitchen with a pile of freshly laundered clothes loaded in her arms. 'I'm just taking this ironing upstairs.' She gestures towards the bassinet. 'Don't go picking Kwami up. It's taken an age to settle him.'

I stifle a giggle, thinking back to the role-play with Tom. Vita gives me a quizzical look, hesitating a moment before hurrying on her way.

As soon as she's gone, I take the plastic tube from my pocket and move towards the baby. My pulse quickens as I pop the swab in Kwami's mouth and rotate it three times before taking it out and sliding it carefully back into the tube.

Kwami whimpers. Guiltily, I shove the tube in my pocket and turn away. I pass Vita on the stairs but ignore her suspicious glance and hurry to my room, where I swab my own mouth before packaging everything up.

In the boot room, I grab my jacket and put on trainers before marching down the driveway and along the lane to the postbox. Without pausing to reconsider, I drop the package into the slit. Done. No turning back.

When I arrive back at *The Sanctuary*, I don't go straight inside. Instead, I take advantage of the fine weather, continuing past the house and through the kitchen gardens to my favourite thinking place.

In the Italian Gardens, I slip off my trainers and socks. The path is so familiar that I have no difficulty closing my eyes and taking tiny steps. Recreating the walking meditation of the monks, I breathe deeply and exhale. The leaflet said the results should be back in five days. I'll have to intercept the postman. Mark can't find out what I'm doing.

As I approach the folly, a gentle breeze touches my face and I'm drawn by a soft tinkling sound. I open my eyes, scanning the pathway, but there's no one there. Just an inquisitive robin hopping along beside me at a safe distance.

Silly, it must have been the bird. Walking slowly with my eyes open, I recall Sorrel's words. The spirits here are friendly. I chuckle. What nonsense.

But no, there's something ahead. Something yellow, an orb, ten centimetres in diameter, suspended in mid-air. Is that the source of the sound? A line from *Peter Pan* comes to mind – *Do you believe in fairies?*

I duck behind a column, although it does little to conceal me. 'For goodness' sake,' I chide. 'Probably just sunlight reflecting against a pillar.' Feeling foolish, I step into the open, blinking as sun and shadows play tricks. Is it a balloon?

Whatever it is floats a few metres ahead, weaving in and out of the columns and, like a game of hide and seek, I follow. I creep forward, peeking behind each pillar, but every time the orb darts away to appear somewhere else. The tinkling sound is playful, sometimes close, sometimes far away.

Rounding another column, I freeze.

A little girl grins and waves. I glimpse a birthmark on the back of her tiny hand. Then she's gone.

Heart racing, I circle the pillar but there's no one there. Hairs on the back of my neck prickle. Retrieving my trainers, I glance nervously over my shoulder as I hurry towards the house.

On reaching Bartholomew block, I take a detour.

'It was a child.' I tell Sorrel. 'Pretty and petite, no bigger than Ike.'

She nods. 'Probably his little friend.'

'What friend?'

'There was a little girl playing with Ike the other day. I saw them outside your mother-in-law's apartment.'

As I step into the kitchen, Ike covers his colouring with his arm. 'Don't look, Mummy.'

'I won't.'

Vita smiles. 'Why don't I give Ike tea at mine and see to

the boys' bedtimes? You and Mark might benefit from a date night.'

'Thanks,' I reply, although spending the evening alone with my philandering husband is the last thing I want. I open the freezer and rummage to find something for dinner. 'Actually, Vita, I wanted to ask you something.'

Vita lifts Kwami from the bassinet. 'Yes?'

'Did Ike have a friend over the other day?'

She glances at me with a puzzled expression. 'No. Why?'

'It doesn't matter.' Unearthing a frozen steak, I set it on a plate to thaw.

'All right, well, I'll leave you to it.' Vita shifts Kwami onto her hip and takes Ike's hand. 'Say goodnight to Mummy, Ike.'

Ike hides his picture behind his back. 'Night night, Mummy.'

'Night night, Ike.' I kiss the top of his head. 'Sleep tight.'

After they've gone, I tackle the evening meal. Beginning with the potatoes, I peel and slice them thinly before layering them in an oven dish with garlic and cream. After throwing a salad together, I open a bottle of *Cabernet Sauvignon* and, while the Dauphinoise potatoes are baking, pop upstairs to tidy my hair.

I appraise my appearance in the dressing table mirror, thinking how perfect Jenna always looks. On impulse, I tug off my T-shirt and jeans and wriggle into a little black dress. I add gloss to my lips and squirt *Chanel Coco Mademoiselle* onto my wrists and neck. It's Mark's favourite.

Mark pauses in the doorway. He raises an eyebrow, noting the table set for two. 'Something smells good. Did I forget an anniversary?'

I prod the searing steak with a fork. 'No. Vita offered to have the boys so you and I could have dinner together.'

'Well, you look nice.' He sits down at the table and pours wine into our glasses.

'Thank you.' I smile and set his plate in front of him. 'Sirloin steak, medium rare.'

'Looks great.' Mark lifts his wine goblet and chinks it against mine. 'Welcome back, darling.'

I place the overproof dish close to Mark and pass him the serving spoon.

'My favourite.' He dishes up a generous portion of potatoes and helps himself to salad. He cuts into the steak and pops a piece in his mouth.

'Good?' I ask.

He grins. 'Just the way I like it.'

Hope you choke on it, I think. But starting a row won't help me achieve what I want. 'Actually, I'm glad to have this opportunity.' My pulse quickens as I slice into a mozzarella burger. 'I want to talk to you again about me being involved with the business.'

He reloads his fork, pausing for a moment before bringing the food to his mouth. 'I thought we agreed it was too soon?'

'We didn't agree anything…' I stop myself to avoid a confrontation. I put down my knife and fork. 'I need to be doing something, Mark. My brain's stagnating.'

'It's not a good time.' He chews and swallows. 'We have a conference in a fortnight and Jenna's done all the prep. It will take too much effort to bring you up to speed. Perhaps in a month or two.'

Heat rises in my face. 'But I need something now.'

'Okay, okay. I'll have a word with Jenna.' He shovels more food into his mouth.

'Oh, of course. Jenna.' I push away my plate. 'It's my job. What's precious Jenna got to do with anything?' I get up. 'Just what the hell's going on between you two?'

CHAPTER THIRTY-FOUR

Saturday's post consists mostly of junk mail, so Monday morning finds me loitering in the hallway where I'm waylaid by Vita.

'Hanna.' She grabs my arm. 'Ike needs more skin cream. Can you phone the GP and ask him to leave out a prescription?'

'Yes.'

Outside, tyres crunch on the gravel drive. Heavy feet mount the steps. I need to get there first.

'Make sure they do it this morning,' continues Vita.

The letter box opens and the postman's stubby fingers push a wad of letters through the flap to land with a thud on the doormat.

At that moment, Jenna strolls out of the kitchen. Vita's still clutching my arm while I try to break free. Jenna's at the door, stooping to pick up the mail.

'I'll collect it on the way back from preschool,' I say, and finally Vita releases me.

Jenna's sorting through the bundle of letters.

I step forward. 'Anything for me?'

'Yep.' She holds out an official looking letter.
I snatch it. 'Thanks.'

On the bed, my heart races as I tear open the envelope. The table of figures mean nothing, but my eyes home in on the short paragraph beneath:

The alleged mother is not excluded as the biological mother of the tested child. Based on testing results obtained from analyses of the DNA loci listed, the probability of maternity is 99.9998%. This probability of maternity is calculated by comparing to an untested, unrelated, random individual...

So, Kwami is my child. I'm not even surprised. But what about my daughter? I recall so vividly her beautiful face, starfish hands and heart-shaped birthmark. Can she really have been just a dream?

That's it. In a moment of clarity, I decide to stop taking the meds. I should consult Tom, but I don't want him talking me out of it. If it's medication causing the hallucinations, the sooner I get them out of my system the better. I don't have time to wean myself off. Cold turkey is the way to go. Kwami's my child and I've neglected him for far too long.

CHAPTER THIRTY-FIVE

'I've been thinking, I can take the morning shift for the boys.'

Vita glances up from the changing mat. 'Are you sure?'

'Yes. I'm loads better since starting the new medication.' I don't tell her I've ditched it. I'm not suffering side effects. 'Anyway, I've always been an early bird.'

Vita hauls herself up from the floor, cradling her knees where she's been kneeling on them. 'Oh dear.' She always seems so competent, but I should stop taking her for granted.

Steadying herself, she bends again to lift Kwami. 'Well, it would certainly help if you got the boys up and dressed in the mornings.' She lays Kwami in the bassinet. 'But I'm more than happy to continue doing the nursery run.'

'Great. I'll hand the boys over to you after breakfast.' For a moment, I feel proud of my progress. After all, Tom said to pace myself and I don't want to overdo it. But as Vita disposes of the dirty nappy in the bin and moves wearily across to the sink to wash her hands, I'm consumed with guilt. She's been doing the lion's share of childcare duties while all I've contributed is a bit of light housework. I must do more. 'In fact, why don't I have the boys this morning? Ike doesn't have preschool today.'

'If you're feeling up to it.'

'I am. I'll take them for a walk.' Lifting Kwami back out of the bassinet, I dress him in a knitted jacket before settling him in the pram.

Meanwhile, Vita helps Ike on with his wellies and rain suit. Smiling, she opens the French doors. 'Have a nice walk with Mummy.'

I manoeuvre the cumbersome pram off the patio. The lawn and gravel driveway are easy, but the woods another matter. I struggle over troughs and rough earth, cursing Vita for insisting an old-fashioned Silver Cross would be better than a big-wheeled buggy.

Ike runs in and out of the trees, splashing his red wellies through the puddles.

'Don't go too far,' I call, battling to keep the pram on the track. As I reach the top of an incline, I pull on the pram brake and peek under the covers. The fresh air has worked its magic and Kwami's asleep. I smile. I'm determined to build a closer bond with him and Ike.

Ike crashes through fallen leaves and broken twigs like he has a friend chasing him. First, he runs one way, then giggles as if someone has tagged him before turning and running back through the trees. I smile. Perhaps we do have something in common? The child's clearly as potty as me.

Spotting a hollow oak tree, I call out to him. 'Look, Ike. You could climb right inside this tree. It's like a little den.'

'We don't want to.'

'Okay.' Then realising what he said, 'Who's we?'

'Me and Chi.' He reaches as if to grasp an invisible hand before running off through the trees again.

'Wait.' I release the brake and wheel the pram along the ridge behind him. This imaginary friend thing is getting out of hand.

As we leave the woods, we bump into Sorrel.

'I knocked for you,' she says, 'but your mother-in-law told me you were out with the boys.'

'I thought it was time to make an effort, but I think my brain may be turning to mush.'

Sorrel changes direction and joins me. 'Everything all right?'

'It would be if I didn't have to deal with this monstrosity.' I gesture to the pram.

She grins.

'If Vita hadn't gone ahead and bought the damn thing, I might have convinced Mark a buggy would be more useful.' I give Sorrel a sideways look. 'So, have you told your parents yet?'

She frowns. 'Don't start…'

'Okay, okay, but I'm not going to let it drop.' I change the subject, lowering my voice although Ike's some way ahead. 'You know you said Ike had a friend with him the other day?'

'Yeah?'

'Vita says he didn't have a play date.'

Sorrel shrugs. 'I saw what I saw.'

'I know. I believe you. I think he was playing with her again just now. I didn't see anyone, but he said he was playing with Chi.'

Sorrel nods. 'Probably one of the others.'

'Others?'

'The special others only a few people can see. The world is full of humans and others.'

'But Ike hasn't got special powers.'

'Children don't need them. They're open to things that adults close their minds to. Unless, like me, the door gets left open.'

'If it was one of these others, is that a bad thing for Ike?'

Sorrel shakes her head. 'No, I didn't get bad vibes from the little girl.'

'What did she look like?'

'Ike's age, yellow coat, curly hair… don't worry, she's definitely one of the good ones.'

'Good ones?'

'Guardian angels.'

———

'Heed little owlet…'

I'm jolted awake by the same haunting melody as before, but different words. Climbing out of bed, I slip into my robe, pad to the bedroom door and ease it open.

'Tu-whit, tu-whoo.' Louder now and coming from upstairs.

I creep along the landing towards the stairs leading to the second floor. The contractors have been renovating up there and the stairwell's roped off, so no one can accidentally wander up and fall through rotten floorboards. I unclip the rope and make my way up.

'Think you're so wise.' The sound is coming from a room at the back where workmen were repointing the mullion. I stoop under a ladder propped against the wall and squeeze past buckets and cans of paint. The bedroom, a replica of my own, is deserted. As I cross the floor and step into the turret room, the tune ceases, like someone flicked a switch. There's nothing much in the tiny space – a few tools, brushes and a

roller, and the window's been left open, presumably to clear paint fumes. I move across and take hold of the sash window, intending to slide it closed, then gasp. On the ledge, a metre or so from the window, sits a small, solitary figure.

'If only you knew…'

I cover my mouth. Ike's staring across the lawns towards the Darius site. How the hell did he manage to climb out of the window? I daren't call out for fear of alarming him.

Shedding my robe, I slide the window wide and step one leg over the low sill. Once I have my footing, I climb through, taking a moment to adjust my balance.

Miraculously, Ike hasn't heard me. He's swinging his legs while gazing down at something on the ground.

Holding my arms out like a trapeze artist and hardly daring to breathe, I inch along the ledge towards him.

Ike shuffles and I freeze. I need him to move away from the edge. I speak softly and deliberately. 'Hello, Ike. What are you doing out here?'

'Watching Gainde.'

I gulp. 'Gainde, huh. Bet he's ready for supper. Would you like to come and help me feed him?'

'Yes please, Mummy.' Ike twists around, his eyes bright.

Too fast. He wobbles and I stifle a scream. 'Careful,' I say, in as calm a voice as I can muster. 'What shall we give Gainde for tea?'

Perhaps Ike's pleased that I'm finally acknowledging his invisible friend, because he scoots back from the edge, takes my extended hand and stands up. Moving in tandem, we make our way back to the window. Once there, he clambers through with ease. I follow, slam the window closed and exhale, my heart pounding.

Ike stares up at me, wide eyed and trusting. I want to yell, tell him how stupid he is, but I don't. Instead, I pull him into a hug.

He wriggles. 'Stop it, Mummy. You're hurting me.'

'Sorry.' I release him and fasten the window securely. Later I'll vent my wrath on whichever stupid builder left it open. 'Come on. Let's go and feed Gainde.'

CHAPTER THIRTY-SIX

Ike stirs Coco Pops around the bowl, seemingly unperturbed by the events of last night. I haven't told Mark. Since our argument, we've given each other a wide berth and I don't want to rock the boat.

Kwami's on my lap so, when the doorbell rings, it's Mark who jumps up to answer it. 'That will be Temi.'

'Temi?' I say.

'Yes, back from the seminar in Leeds.' Mark hurries to the hallway.

I follow with Kwami in my arms.

Mark opens the door. 'Hello again, old friend.' He slaps Temi on the back.

Temi greets Mark warmly before glancing in my direction. 'Hanna. How are you?'

'Fine.'

He gestures towards Kwami. 'And the baby?'

'Good.'

There's an awkward moment before Mark addresses me. 'I'll debrief Temi in the office. Could you stick the kettle on?'

Back in the kitchen, I rest Kwami on my shoulder as I

flick the switch on the kettle and spoon coffee into a cafetiere.

'Look at my milk, Mummy.' Ike giggles. 'It's brown.'

Kwami fidgets and the coffee grounds spill. 'For heaven's sake, Ike. If you're not going to eat that, you may as well go and find Nana.' I open the French doors leading to her apartment.

Ike sticks out his bottom lip as he slides down from the table and totters out of the kitchen in search of Vita.

Moments later, Jenna appears. 'Any biscuits?'

I step away from the worktop. 'In the cupboard. So, Temi's back?'

'Yes.' Jenna locates a packet of chocolate digestives and sets them out on a plate. 'And it sounds like he's brought good news. Mark's happy.'

If there is something going on between her and Mark, she's got some front.

'It's all looking very positive for the conference.' She pours boiling water into the cafetiere. 'Could be the first of many.'

'Things are turning around, then.'

'All down to Temi.' Jenna pushes down the plunger. 'If we get a successful conference under our belt, it will provide good reviews for our web portfolio.'

She heads back to the office and I set Kwami down on the changing mat. I'm wondering if I exaggerated things between Jenna and Mark? I undo Kwami's babygro. Jenna's been out with her mates several times in the past few days. Perhaps it was the meds making me paranoid? I remove the wet nappy and wipe Kwami's bottom. I don't know how I feel about Temi coming back. I'd assumed we'd be cutting ties, but if he's made new contacts, Mark will be desperate to keep him here. I fasten the clean nappy. Something about Temi's presence unsettles me. He knows so much about us, and I don't know whether to trust him. He doesn't rate me highly, that's for sure. Still, perhaps it's no bad thing if he underestimates me...

Jenna returns. 'Forgot the sugar.'

I lift Kwami from the mat and get up. 'So, this mini conference...'

'Not so mini now. Could be quite prestigious. Temi's stoked up interest from VIPs and delegates all over the UK and Nigeria. Mark's really chuffed.'

'Large numbers, then?'

'Not too many to handle. Why?' She grins. 'Fancy dipping your toe back in the water? I'm sure I could delegate you a few tasks if that doesn't sound patronising?'

'No, I'd need to ease back in gradually.' I smile as I pat Kwami's bottom. 'Actually, I'd like that.'

Mark raises the matter that evening. 'Jenna says you were asking about the conference?'

I load the last of the plates into the dishwasher. 'Just showing an interest.'

'Well, I'd rather you stayed out of it.' He puts his empty mug on the draining board. 'I told you, Jenna's done all the prep. It's not fair for you to interfere now.'

'I didn't ask to, Jenna suggested it. Why don't you ever take my side?'

'It's not a question of sides...'

'Forget it, I don't need this.' I place his mug in dishwasher and slam the door closed.

'No, you don't.'

I spin round. 'What's that supposed to mean?'

'Well, let's face it, you're not exactly firing on all cylinders, are you? Why not concentrate on being a mother before thinking about returning to work?'

'I am being a mother and it was always the plan that I'd pick my job up again once the baby could be left with Vita.'

'Yes, but that was before…'

'Before what? Before I went crazy, you mean?' I march towards the door. This time it'll be me who storms out. 'Sometimes I think you don't care about me at all.'

It's not until I'm outside that I realise I'm still wearing slippers. Pulling my cardigan around me, I take long, calming breaths.

CHAPTER THIRTY-SEVEN

'Didn't you hear the doorbell?' Jenna says as she strolls into the kitchen. 'It's Tom.'

I look up from my book. 'No, sorry.'

Tom's brushing raindrops from his jacket shoulders as he follows her in. 'I'm a bit early.'

'That's all right,' I say, 'but you're soaked. Take off that coat and Jenna will make you a hot drink.'

Jenna lifts three mugs down from the dresser. 'We've not seen you in a while, Tom.'

'No.' Tom takes off his glasses and cleans them with a piece of kitchen roll.

Mr Biggles is curled on my lap. I tickle him around the ears, noticing how Tom remains near Jenna rather than joining me at the table.

'I've been working pretty much non-stop at the hospital,' he continues. 'They had a staffing gap and I was asked to help out.'

Jenna spoons coffee into mugs. 'Same as me, then.'

Tom replaces his glasses. 'Sorry, what?'

She grins. 'Covering a staffing gap.'

'She means my maternity leave,' I interject.

'Yes, once Hanna's back to her efficient self' – Jenna pours hot water – 'I'll have to find another job.'

Tom looks crestfallen. 'Don't you like it here?'

Jenna gestures towards the window and the gardens beyond. 'Who wouldn't want to work here?'

'But you don't live locally?'

'No.' She passes him a coffee. 'I was in Brighton before.'

'Probably find it all a bit tame up here, then?'

'I don't mind.' She sets a mug down in front of me.

'Thanks,' I say.

'Well,' Tom fiddles with the zip of his Filofax, 'if you ever want to do anything, you know, go for a pizza or something…'

Jenna laughs. 'Are you asking me out on a date, Tom McCarthy?'

Tom's cheeks flush. 'No, yes, maybe. Suppose I was?'

'I'd tell you, sorry, but I don't think so.' Jenna picks up her mug and strides out of the room.

'Damn.' Tom thuds the kitchen island with his fist.

'Don't mind me.' I ease the cat from my lap and stand up.

Tom spins around like he's just remembered I'm there. 'Sorry Hanna.'

'Come on, you. Bring your drink.' I lead the way into the snug.

When we're settled, Tom asks how I am.

I shrug. 'I'm okay.' I don't tell him about the incident on the roof.

He raises an eyebrow. 'I sense there's something you're not telling me.'

I frown. 'Mark and I argued again about work.'

'What exactly did he say?'

'He repeated that it's too soon, but it's not. I need something other than the boys.'

'Describe how the conversation went.'

I do my best to recount our exchange.

Tom nods. 'It sounds, from what you've said, as if things became emotionally charged almost immediately.'

'I guess so. I suppose I was pretty defensive.'

'Next time, try using I-statements.'

'I-statements?'

'Yes. Rather than, "You didn't" or "You don't care", try saying something like, "I don't feel supported when you make decisions without consulting me. In future, I hope we can discuss it and come to a decision together".'

I snort. 'That doesn't sound like me at all.'

Tom shrugs. 'There will always be difficulties when discussing work. It was assumed you'd give up your job for a while when you had children, and then Vita stepped in, leaving you feeling worthless as a mother. You need to talk to Mark again. Make sure he understands where you're coming from.'

'I'll try.'

He sips his drink. 'Did you do anything about the DNA test?'

'Yes, I did.'

'And?'

'Kwami's definitely mine.'

Tom nods slowly. 'And does it make a difference?'

'Actually, I think it does. I feel more settled now I know for sure.'

'That's good.'

'I took the boys out for a walk again.'

'Great. How about Vita? Have you managed to establish new boundaries?'

'We've agreed I'll take the morning shift with the boys.'

'Good. Creating autonomy for yourself should reduce conflict.'

After I've shown Tom out, I go back to the kitchen, where I find Jenna making a cheese sandwich. She waves a knife in the air. 'Want one?'

'Yes please.'

She butters another round of bread and slices more cheese.

'No sandwich for Mark, then?' I ask, filling two glasses at the tap.

'He and Temi have gone out.' She transfers the sandwiches onto plates and carries them over to the refectory table.

I bring the water and join her. 'And Vita?'

'She's taken Kwami with her to fetch Ike from preschool. How did your session with Tom go?'

'All right.' I glance at her. 'You do know he fancies you?'

She laughs. 'I know, right?'

'Are you going to go out with him?'

'It wouldn't be fair. He's not my type.' She sips her drink. 'I felt quite sorry for him, actually. Stammering his way through that.'

'Perhaps you should have said yes?'

She raises an eyebrow. 'I told you, he's not my type.'

My heart beats faster. So, who is her type? Mark?

Jenna studies me, an amused expression on her face. 'Did you hear what I said?'

I feel sick. Is this the moment she tells me she's screwing

Mark? She's so brazen. I lift my head. I'm ready. 'Yes, I heard you.'

She laughs. 'I don't think you did.' She waits a beat. 'MEN aren't my type, Hanna. Surely you knew that?'

I stare at her, feeling my cheeks burn. Of course, it's obvious.

'Honestly, Hanna. How long have we known each other?' She snorts with laughter. 'Your face. It's all right, I'm not gonna make a pass at you. You're not my type either.'

'Yes, I'm looking forward to it…'

As I step into the office, Mark cuts the Zoom session short. 'Yes, got to go. Speak soon.'

'Who was that?' I ask.

'Deòiridh Skinner. One of the delegates for the conference.'

I don't quite catch the name. 'Jury Skinner?'

'Deòiridh' – he spells it out. 'Celtic, I think. She's well known in her field.'

'Which is?'

He doesn't answer.

'Look.' I perch on the edge of his desk. 'I'm not trying to take anything away from Jenna. At least, not until I feel up to it. But I really need something to keep my brain active and I think it would be good for me to have a few tasks to do. Helping Jenna will stop my mind from dwelling on other things.'

Mark leans back in his swivel chair. 'What other things?'

'I don't know. My head gets so messed up sometimes. Looking after the kids isn't enough. It's not that I'm not busy, but it's the wrong sort of busy. I need something other than the kids.'

He stares at me.

'I think it's the only way I'll start to feel normal again.'

He sighs. 'All right, you win. To be fair, Jenna's quite keen to have you involved. But let her take the lead, okay?'

I smile and kiss him on the cheek.

CHAPTER THIRTY-EIGHT

Vita's already in the kitchen fixing Ike's breakfast when I come downstairs.

'You're up early.' I take a cereal bowl from the cupboard and help myself to granola.

'Mark tells me you're assisting Jenna with the conference?' she says.

Jenna marches into the room. 'Yes, and it's going to be bloody marvellous. I'm delegating a whole load of things for her to do.'

'So, I guessed you'd want me to take charge of Ike and Kwami again,' continues Vita.

'Yes, please.' I reply. 'If that's all right? It will only be for a couple of weeks.'

She turns her attention to Ike. 'It's not like Nana has anything else *she'd* rather be doing.' She ruffles his hair.

Jenna and I exchange a glance. Vita never misses an opportunity.

'Actually, I've already started a list,' says Jenna. 'Press announcements, advertisements, speaker bio's, equipment inventory…'

'Thank you.' I grin. 'Sounds right up my street.'

'I know. Event planning always was your forte.'

'I'll need access to a computer.'

'You can use the Acer. It's just been upgraded. Could you start with background histories for the speakers? I'll email you the delegate list.'

I pour almond milk over my cereal and eat standing up. I don't care how much humble pie I have to consume to get Vita to mind the kids. It's great to feel valued again.

Before getting started, I pop across and knock for Sorrel to tell her about my newly negotiated responsibilities.

'So, you'll be busy over the coming weeks,' she says.

'Just for the next fortnight until the conference. I still hope to manage a few walks, but I might need to adjust my daily routine.'

Sorrel nods. 'It's good. I mean, if it's what you want, then it's good. But don't overdo it. You need to keep a balance.'

'I know.' I pause in the doorway. 'Have you told your parents yet?'

'They're coming up next weekend. I'll tell them then.'

I hurry back to the house and, not wanting to crowd Mark and Jenna, commandeer the snug as my personal workspace. An hour later, I've pushed the couch aside, set up the laptop and opened Jenna's email. There are over forty people on the delegate list, with half a dozen highlighted as requiring speaker bios. I recognise one of the names immediately and message Jenna.

Who exactly is this Deòiridh Skinner?

Not sure, but she's a Keynote Speaker, so
she must be important. A doctor. Worked in
Africa I think…

I soon discover Deòiridh Skinner has published journal articles and books in the field of anthropology. Until about five years ago, she was a regular on the conference circuit, then she disappeared from the public eye. Perhaps that's how Mark managed to procure her?

I draft her bio.

Deòiridh Skinner. After completing a Master's at Cambridge in 1975, Deòiridh moved to California to undertake a Doctorate in Anthropology at Berkeley University. She has since travelled the world researching cultures and voodoo practices, and developing the specialism for which she is renowned.

Jenna enters the snug with her hands behind her back. 'I've a present for you.'

'What is it?' I take the proffered parcel and rip it open to find a new mobile phone. 'Ooh, thank you.'

'Don't thank me, thank your husband,' says Jenna.

I grin, knowing Jenna put Mark up to it.

'Stick it on charge,' she says, 'and I'll show you how to link up to the Acer. Oh, and could you draft me some copy for advertisements and press announcements? You're so much better with words than me.'

'Sure, but you'll have to do the technical stuff. I've never created Facebook Ads.'

'I might put something on LinkedIn too.' She smiles. 'We're gonna make a great team.'

CHAPTER THIRTY-NINE

Vita shows Tom into the snug. 'Look who I found lurking in the hallway.'

He smiles enthusiastically. 'Ready for our session?'

'Oh blast. Sorry Tom, I meant to text you.' I gesture my ladened work desk. 'I've got loads to do.'

He raises an eyebrow. 'Not even time for a quick catch up?'

Reluctantly I close my laptop. 'Okay.'

Tom takes the only armchair not covered in paperwork, while I move a pile of ledgers and sit opposite.

'Well,' he says. 'I see things have changed.'

I grin. 'I get so much satisfaction when I'm being useful.' I don't admit my new responsibilities are beginning to consume me.

'And you don't get that sense of satisfaction from looking after the children?'

I squirm. 'It's bad, isn't it?' I cover my face with my hands. 'I'm a terrible mother.'

'No, you're not,' Tom says. 'Your brain just needs more

stimulus. That doesn't make you a bad mother.' He studies me closely. 'How are you sleeping?'

'Better. I'm tired, but it's a good tired.' I don't tell him my head buzzes all night with checklists and spreadsheets.

He nods towards the door. 'Vita let me in. She seems in her element.'

I laugh. 'Yes, we're both happy.'

From outside the room comes the sound of hammering.

Tom glances up. 'Sounds as if it's all go?'

'The electrician's finishing off the lighting, and the builders are making good in the other downstairs rooms.'

'This conference must be a huge financial investment.'

I grimace. 'It is. Mark had to get a business loan. Hopefully the money coming in from the delegates will cover costs. And, if we get more conference bookings, Mark thinks we'll be able to make a start on Darius block. That way we can offer onsite accommodation for future events.'

Jenna sticks her head around the door. 'Sorry to interrupt. Hanna, did you have any luck with the portable loo quotes?'

I wince at Tom. 'Sorry.' I move back to the desk, open the laptop and pull up a webpage. 'This company is local, and they do posh loos for gigs and weddings. The only thing is, their luxury loos start at five hundred pounds a unit.'

'Ouch,' says Jenna.

Tom gets up. 'I'll leave you to it. But Hanna, don't overdo it, okay?'

'I won't.' I continue to address Jenna. 'So, what shall we do about the loo?'

'I might ask Steve the Caterer if he can recommend anyone cheaper.'

'Will the caterers need access to the kitchen?'

'No, they roll up with their own vehicle. It's completely

self-contained. They'll erect a marquee on the lawn between Caleb and the Darius site.'

I turn to say goodbye to Tom, but he's gone. 'What if the weather's bad?' I ask Jenna. 'A marquee might be draughty.'

'We can use the communal area in Caleb for delegates to sit and eat. It will only be the hardy smokers who venture out to tent city. Oh, and I must remember to tell Temi he's sleeping in the main house for the duration. We'll need all the Caleb rooms for breakout groups.'

At lunchtime, I take a short break and go to check on the boys. Vita has everything in hand and has even found time to prepare me a salad. 'You look tired,' she observes. 'Don't go overdoing it.'

'I'm fine,' I say, shovelling food into my mouth, anxious to get back to work.

By teatime, I'm ready to report on progress. I message Jenna.

> I've finished research on the background speakers and drafted bios for the delegate packs. I'll email them across and you can send them out for approval.

Great, thanks.

I'm still working when she comes to find me at six o'clock.

'I've set up a spreadsheet and allocated a number to each of the breakout rooms.' I tell her, showing her the laptop screen. 'Do you know yet what equipment we need?'

'As a minimum, tables and chairs, plus whiteboard and pens, but several rooms will require a computer and projector in addition. We also need microphones for the main Conference Hall and video equipment to record lectures, so they can be viewed afterwards online. And some participants will be joining via Zoom.'

'So, do I need to look at hiring video equipment? Or computers with webcams?'

'We'll need specialist conference webcams with 360-degree capability.' Jenna taps her chin thoughtfully. 'You know, I might see if I can get someone to come and video the lectures? It will cost more, but they'll edit them for us. Let me see what I can find out.'

CHAPTER FORTY

On the day of the conference, I rise early, shower, and do my hair and makeup before going downstairs.

Vita and Ike are already in the kitchen. Ike's making syrup trails in his porridge while Vita packs a picnic.

'Morning,' I say. 'Need any help?'

'I think I'm good.' Vita tucks a couple of bottles of Fruit Shoot into the insulated bag, along with an icepack.

I glance out of the window. 'You've a nice day for it.'

'Yes, and it says on the website they have a nature trail. That should keep Ike occupied. Now, where did I put my sunglasses?'

'Here,' I say, spotting them on the kitchen island.

'Thank you.' She slides the glasses into a pocket on the side of the bag.

'Want me to help you load?'

'Yes please. If you've time.'

I lift Kwami from his bassinet and secure him in the car seat before carrying it out to the Citroën. Vita stows picnic and nappy bags in the boot, while I strap Ike into his booster seat.

Checking the baby car seat is secure in the front passenger seat, I open the back door to say goodbye to Ike. 'Have a lovely time, and mind you do what Nana says.'

Ike bounces up and down. 'We're going on a bear hunt,' he sings.

I close the door, raising my eyebrows at Vita. 'Good luck.'

She gives me a brief wave before checking the rear-view mirror and reversing the car out of its parking space. I'm sure she'd prefer to be visiting Flatford Mill to admire Constable's countryside rather than hurtling around the grounds on a themed nature trail.

Heading back indoors, I make a final check of the table in the hallway. I set everything out last night – register, name badges and delegate packs, but it doesn't hurt to be sure.

My role is welcoming the guests. Most will be bused in from Colchester, fifteen miles south. Others will drive from Airbnbs located in the small villages around us. Hopefully they'll follow the directions emailed out and park sensibly in the area behind Aaron and Bartholomew blocks. We weren't able to afford parking wardens.

My tummy flutters as I spot a small group of delegates approaching the open front door. Taking a deep breath, I step forward, greeting them with a friendly smile and my rehearsed patter. 'Hello. Welcome to *The Sanctuary*. Please sign the register and find your badge. Here's your delegate pack. Would you like a complimentary pen?'

Despite the sunshine, many wear coats. Jenna and I anticipated this, and I swap outer layers for raffle tickets to enable speedier retrieval from the hired hanging rails at the end of the day.

'Hello, my dear.'

I spin round at the sound of his voice. 'Hello, Stefan.'

Mark's godfather hugs me. After extracting myself as quickly as politeness allows, I step back. 'It's nice to see you again.' I take his coat, gesturing towards the Conference Hall doors. 'Won't you take a seat? We can catch up later.'

There's a buzz in the air as the delegates anticipate the arrival of the Keynote Speaker. Mark hasn't yet returned from collecting Deòiridh Skinner from Bury St Edmunds.

Finally, the Range Rover pulls up on the driveway. I stand in the hallway, trying to quell my butterflies. I don't know why I'm so apprehensive. Footsteps crunch on the gravel before Mark breezes in with Deòiridh and suddenly everything makes sense. The glamorous woman in a designer camel coat and clutching my husband's arm, is the alluring woman we met in Lagos.

Despite a train journey and a twenty-mile drive in the car, she looks relaxed and fabulous. As they enter the Conference Hall, the delegates rise and applaud. Temi winks at me as he closes the double doors.

Feeling redundant, I hover in the hallway in case of late arrivals. The catering company are providing morning and afternoon refreshments, as well as lunch for eighty, so there's little for me to do, and Mark made it clear I was not to attend the lectures.

As I pace up and down, something bugs me. Something doesn't make sense. Grabbing one of the surplus delegate packs, I flick through to the Speaker Bios page. As I scan through the typed words, I feel sick. I researched Deòiridh myself, but there's no way that elegant and beautiful woman graduated in 1975. That would put her in her sixties. I'll never hear the last of it from Mark if I've made a mistake.

An hour later, I hear robust applause, together with appreciative whistles. When the doors open, Deòiridh's first to emerge. She's shed her coat and is stunning in an emerald-green shift dress and gold pendant necklace. Delegates swarm around, keen to engage her in conversation, but Mark, ever the gentleman, protectively takes her arm and guides her through the front door towards Caleb block.

Jenna, in tailored black trousers and smart boxy jacket, follows close behind, escorting the rest of the delegates along to the breakout sessions.

The hallway's empty when Temi appears at my side. 'All right?'

'Yes, thanks. Did it go well?'

'Very well. Deòiridh's keynote speech was marvellous.'

I notice he pronounces Deòiridh's name correctly.

He studies me carefully. 'You didn't come in?'

'No, Mark wanted me available in case anyone needed anything.' Noticing a stray delegate loitering in the hallway, I attempt to prove my worth by making a beeline for her. 'Can I help you?'

'Er, yes…' She blushes. 'I was looking for the Ladies?'

'There are portable loos outside but,' – I point to the powder room under the stairs – 'you can use the facilities in here as long as you don't shout about it.'

'Thank you.' She smiles gratefully.

Temi pats my arm. 'I'll leave you to it. I'd better head over to Caleb.'

I step into the Conference Hall. Only the technical crew remain, frantically rewinding cables and gathering up video equipment. Ignoring me, they hurry past on their way to capture discussions in breakout groups. The room is in disarray. Moving along the rows, I gather up dropped papers and straighten chairs in readiness for the afternoon's plenary.

At lunchtime, I head across to Caleb. On the way I pass smokers huddled together under the marquee. Despite the April sunshine, they look a little chilly. Most of the delegates are in Caleb's communal area, noisily chatting as they tuck into *Steve's Bowl Food – vegetarian and vegan options available.*

Spotting Jenna, I hurry towards her. 'Everything going okay?'

Her eyes sparkle. 'It's all going great. We had a small hiccup with one of the projectors, but a nice guy from Kings sorted it. We've had so many positive comments.'

'Anything more I can do?'

'Oh!' She grabs my arm. 'The feedback sheets! I left them in the office. Could you hand them out as they file into the Conference Hall for the Retrospective? Then, be a dear, and collect them up again afterwards?'

'Sure.'

Someone clears their throat into a microphone. I turn to see Mark in the centre of the throng. 'The afternoon session is about to begin. If you'd like to make your way back to your respective breakout rooms…'

The communal area clears. With nothing else to do, I make myself useful helping Steve and his team gather up dirty crockery.

Steve winks. 'I could offer you a job.'

I check my watch – ten past two. Twenty minutes until the delegates move back to the Conference Hall. Heading for the office, I locate the feedback sheets on Jenna's desk. By the time the delegates arrive for the plenary, I'm there to greet them at the Conference Hall doors.

An hour later, I'm collecting the forms back in. The delegates are animated as I smile politely, exchanging raffle ticket stubs for coats.

When the hallway's virtually clear, Mark places a hand on his godfather's shoulder. 'Stefan. I believe we've earned a drink. Come this way. You too, Isaac.' He ushers the two men into the kitchen.

Temi follows, accompanied by Deòiridh, while Jenna brings up the rear.

Spotting a handful of hangers-on, I approach. 'Are you waiting for taxis?' Having established they are, I wait with them, making small talk until the cabs arrive.

I wave them off from the front steps and close the door. My feet are killing me and I'd like nothing better than to disappear into the snug and remove my shoes. I'm about to do just that when raucous laughter floats out from the kitchen. As I move past the doorway, I glance in to see Mark opening bottles of champagne. Corks fly and wine fizzes and sprays across the kitchen island. What a mess. I step into the room as Jenna passes around overfilled glasses.

'Cheers,' shouts Mark.

His favoured visitors join in with gusto. 'Cheers.'

I grab a cloth from the sink to mop up the spilled champagne.

'Hey,' calls Mark. 'I think Steve left some bits for the afterparty. They should be in the fridge.'

Obligingly, I open the fridge door, quickly locating cling-filmed plates of cold cuts and cheeses. Assuming the role of waitress, I carry them to the table.

Mark's cheeks are already ruddy. 'Couldn't have gone better,' he declares. He's sitting beside Deòiridh, an arm draped casually around her shoulder.

As the drinks flow, the party becomes rowdier. Mark opens more champagne and raids the fridge for bottles of beer. Isaac offers round a box of cigars.

I perch on a stool beside the kitchen island, sipping half a glass of bubbly and trying not to fret about spillage from careless drinkers. I wince as cigar ash drops onto my lovely refectory table.

Jenna shoots me an occasional sympathetic look but I'm mortified when she attempts to draw me into the conversation. From my bar stool, I have a clear view of my husband. I watch his fingers travel sensually up Deòiridh's spine. When they reach the nape of her neck, his thumb gently caresses her naked skin. My cheeks blaze with heat. Sliding from the stool, I creep out of the room. No-one will miss me.

CHAPTER FORTY-ONE

I gaze around the room – the littered table with dirty glasses and crusted plates, empty wine and beer bottles cluttering the kitchen. 'So, it went well?'

'It went great.' Mark slots four slices of bread into the toaster. 'Everyone was complimentary about the venue and the speakers.'

'That's good.'

'Oh, Stefan and Isaac stayed over. They kipped in the snug.'

My pulse quickens. 'Did Deòiridh stay?'

'Yep.' The golden toast pops up and he spreads it with butter.

'Where did she sleep?'

Before answering he pours hot water into the cafetiere. 'She took my room, and I bunked in with Temi.'

'Hmm.' Should I challenge Mark about his behaviour last night? But he was drunk and, after my own craziness of late, perhaps I should cut him some slack.

'Actually.' He sets the cafetiere and a plate of toast on a

tray. 'Deòiridh's got a break in her diary, so I've persuaded her to stay on for a few days.'

'Why?'

'I want to pick her brains.'

'What about?'

'All manner of things.' He picks up the laden tray. 'I'm taking her and Temi out for dinner this evening.'

'Do you want me to come?'

'No, you'll be bored. We shan't be late back.' He strolls along the corridor making for his office. Is Deòiridh in there?

After he's gone, I wander into the snug. As I enter, a sour smell assails my nostrils – booze, body odour and cigarettes. I draw back the curtains and open the window. My space has been violated.

Heading over to Caleb block, I find Temi and Jenna stacking chairs and tables. 'Can I help?' I ask.

'The hire company are supposed to pick everything up at eleven.' Jenna runs fingers through her spiky hair. 'Would you mind going through the rooms and checking the equipment against this?' She holds out a copy of the inventory spreadsheet.

'Sure.' Taking the list from her, I move from room to room, checking off equipment. Mostly the list tallies, but a MacBook is missing and I wonder if Mark has it in his office? Also, I can't locate the video equipment. Perhaps the guy filming took it away to do the editing? I'll have to check with Jenna.

When I exit the building, she and Temi are busy dealing with the equipment collection. I'll email her later. I make a note of the missing items on the spreadsheet and head back over to the kitchen.

Vita and Ike are engaged with some sort of craft project

because the table's covered with coloured paper, crayons, glue and stickers.

'I'll have the boys for a while,' I say. 'You must be shattered.'

Vita rubs her eyes. 'I could certainly do with a break.' She hauls herself up from the chair with a sigh, before heading out to her apartment.

Kwami's babbling happily in the bouncer, his fingers sticky with squashed banana. I grab a wet wipe and clean him up.

'Are you going to help me make a dinosaur, Mummy?' asks Ike.

I shake my head. 'I'm not very good at dinosaurs.' I fold a piece of coloured paper and slide it in front of him. 'Why don't you make a nice card for Nana?'

Mark, Deòiridh and Temi are lingering over breakfast when I enter the kitchen next morning. Having woken with a headache again, I head for the cupboard in search of paracetamol, take two tablets and wash them down with water.

Turning my attention to the cluttered worktop, I load the dishwasher while throwing surreptitious glances in Deòiridh's direction. It was two a.m. when she and Mark rolled in. I know because I was giving Kwami a bottle at the time. For someone gallivanting until the early hours, she looks remarkably fresh. There's no way she's over sixty.

'Come on.' Mark gets up and heads for the door. 'I want to show you that data.'

Deòiridh tucks her hair behind her ear, giggling as she ducks under Mark's arm. I catch their intimate smile. Bitch.

Temi stays behind.

'Did you have a nice meal last night?' I ask.

'Me? No, I was in Hadleigh, meeting up with an old school friend. I only got back half an hour ago. I wish I had eaten.' He rubs his belly. 'Too much beer on an empty stomach is not to be recommended.'

So, he didn't dine with Mark and Deòiridh. My heart is heavy as I make myself a cuppa and join Temi at the table. 'Are you avoiding me?'

He laughs. 'Well, you made it pretty clear last time I was here that you didn't exactly want me around.'

'I know.' I sip my drink. 'I'm sorry. I wasn't myself.'

He studies me. 'You seem better now. Jenna told me you were invaluable in the lead up to the conference.'

'Yes.' I sigh.

'What's the matter, Hanna?'

'I suppose I'm feeling a bit of a spare part now the conference is over.'

He reaches out and pats my hand. 'If I know Mark, he'll already be planning the next one. I'm sure your skills will be required again very soon.'

CHAPTER FORTY-TWO

Mark wanders into the kitchen. 'Anything to eat?'

I sway Kwami in my arms. 'You should have joined us for lunch. I called you three times. We waited until almost two before sitting down.'

He frowns. 'Deòiridh and I were in the middle of something.'

I glare at him. 'On a Sunday?'

'Sorry.' He lifts a tea towel from the dish on the worktop and frowns at the remains of an apple crumble.

'It's not me you need to apologise to.' I move Kwami onto my shoulder. 'Your mother cooked roast lamb with all the trimmings, and Ike was so disappointed.'

'I'll make it right. Mum didn't leave a plate for me?'

'It's in the fridge. You'll need to microwave it.'

He opens the fridge and prods the cling-filmed meal with gravy congealed on the plate. 'Perhaps I'll have a sandwich.' He grabs a couple of slices of bread and cheese.

'No Deòiridh?' I ask.

'She's gone to bed.' He butters the bread and slices the cheddar. 'She suffers with migraines.'

She's not the only one. 'Poor thing. Must be all those long meetings.'

Mark looks up sharply.

I smile sweetly.

'Any piccalilli?'

'Should be in the fridge.' Kwami shifts his head side to side and I rub his back. 'So, how much longer is she staying?'

'Who?' He spreads a thick layer of pickle on the cheese. 'Deòiridh?'

'Yes.'

'For as long as I can persuade her.' He cuts his sandwich diagonally in two. 'She brings a whole new perspective to what I'm trying to achieve.'

'So I see.'

He flicks me a puzzled look. 'You're paranoid.'

'Where's she going to sleep? You can't keep doubling up with Temi.'

'I won't need to. Temi's off at the end of the week. Deòiridh can have his room in Caleb and I'll move back into the main house.' He takes a bite of his sandwich.

Kwami's fallen asleep so I lay him gently in the bassinet. 'Temi's leaving?'

'Yep, he's found his own place.' He picks up his plate, leaving the worktop covered in crumbs. 'Believe me, Hanna, there's nothing going on between me and Deòiridh. Perhaps you need another session with Tom?'

———

Next morning I'm alone in the kitchen when Jenna pops in. 'Hi,' she says. 'Nice weekend?'

'Not especially. Mark and Deòiridh have been thick as thieves.'

'Tell me about it.' She fills her water bottle at the sink. 'They've barely stopped scheming since she arrived.' She glances at me. 'Oops, have I said the wrong thing? You're not worried about her, are you?'

'Just wondering what they have to discuss all the time.'

'She's very experienced with the conference circuit and has loads of useful contacts. I'm sure you have nothing to worry about.' Jenna heads back to the office.

After she's gone, I don jacket and boots and head outside where I find Sorrel on a bench at the edge of the lawn.

She waves as I approach. 'Hello stranger. You walking?'

'Just a short one while Kwami's at nursery.' We set off together around the side of the house and through the kitchen gardens. 'Did you speak to your parents at the weekend?'

She grimaces. 'I did.'

'How did it go?'

'Better than expected. They're still "processing." Dad said nothing, I think he was in shock. Mum took it better than I thought she would.'

'It's good that they know.'

'Yeah. They're going to make an appointment with your husband to discuss things.'

'Well done.' I squeeze her arm. 'Sorry I haven't been around. It's been so manic.'

'S'okay. How was the conference?'

'A big success. I loved having the chance to do something worthwhile.'

'But?'

I sigh. 'It's just…'

'Just what?'

'Oh, I don't know. A bit of an anti-climax now it's over.' And not so easy to keep my eye on Mark and Deòiridh when I'm not involved with the business…

We admire the trees in the orchard, thick with blossom.

Sorrel smiles. 'I always think blossom looks like snow.'

'It does a bit.' I stifle a yawn.

'Am I boring you?'

'No, sorry, I'm just tired.'

'I'm not surprised. All that work and a young baby. Shall we head back?'

We retrace our steps in silence.

'What's up?' Sorrel asks.

'Nothing.'

'Yes, there is. Has it got anything to do with the attractive red head?'

I scowl. 'What do you know?'

'Uh-oh, touched a nerve.' I don't respond, but Sorrel continues. 'I get a strange feeling about her.'

'What sort of feeling?'

'Something about her aura. I think she could be dangerous to you and Ike.'

'Me and Ike?'

'Yes. Watch your back.'

As we head towards the house, I reflect on Sorrel's words. According to her parents, the odd things she sees and hears are all in her mind, perhaps even made up to get attention, but I'm not so sure. There's something about Deòiridh, and I don't think it's jealousy or the attention Mark shows her. I hadn't considered her to be an actual threat.

When I open the front door, raised voices travel from the kitchen.

'I told you. I don't trust her.'

That's Vita. I thought we were past this. Does she still not trust me with the boys? I slip off my boots and take a deep breath before stepping into the room.

'She…' Vita cuts off abruptly.

I glance from her to Mark. 'Everything all right?'

'Everything's fine with me.' Mark breezes past on his way to the office.

My heart beats fast as I address Vita. 'Sorry, did I interrupt something?'

'No.' She tugs a handkerchief from her sleeve. 'Everything's fine.'

'Are you crying?'

She blows her nose. 'It's just hay fever.'

But Vita doesn't suffer from hay fever and, if she's got a problem with me, it's unlike her not to tell me to my face. 'Fancy a cuppa?' I flick the switch on the kettle and lift two mugs down from the dresser.

'No.' She glances at the clock. 'I've got to pick up Kwami.' Taking the Citroën keys from the hook, she heads off.

I make myself a tea and I'm about to sit down when Temi wanders in.

He sniffs the air. 'Do I smell coffee?'

'No, but I'll make you one.'

'Thanks.'

We sit together at the table. 'Everything all right?' he asks.

I sigh. 'I'm not sure. I think I just walked in on Vita having a go about me.'

Temi places a hand on my arm. 'That is probably unlikely.'

My eyes fill with tears. 'Vita's always had it in for me.'

'Sorry, I didn't mean to…'

'You don't know anything about it,' I snap.

CHAPTER FORTY-THREE

'What time did you go to bed last night?' I ask.

'Oh, early hours.' Mark has his head in his MacBook. 'Deòiridh and I were going over the feedback sheets from the conference. Hope we didn't disturb you?'

I unload the dishwasher, stacking plates noisily as I put them away in the cupboard.

Mark slams the laptop closed before tucking it under his arm and heading for the door. 'Jenna says you're updating the equipment inventory for the hire company. Is it finished? I don't want to get an extra bill for going over the return date.'

I put the cutlery away. 'There were a couple of things missing. I emailed Jenna about it.'

Mark stands at the door with one hand on the door jamb. 'Missing? Jenna didn't mention anything.'

'Yes, video camera, tripod and a projector. I assume the photographer has them.'

'Oh hell.' Mark steps back into the room. 'If I lose the deposit that really will be the final straw.'

Good job I didn't mention the missing MacBook. 'I'm sure they'll turn up. I'll speak to Jenna.'

'Turn up? You'll be lucky.' He wipes a hand across his face. 'Bloody Jenna. Why hasn't she told me? This is all I need.'

So, Jenna's out of favour now. I wonder how she feels being usurped by someone else. I flick the switch on the kettle. 'Do you want a coffee?'

'Yes please.' He flops down on a kitchen stool.

'It's probably not the best time to mention this,' I say as I make our drinks, 'but can I ask you about Vita?'

'What about her?'

I sit down beside him. 'When I came in yesterday, I caught you both arguing. Was it about me?'

'Not everything's about you, Hanna.'

'Sorry I…' To my chagrin, I burst into tears.

Mark stares in astonishment. 'What's the matter with you?'

'I don't know, I'm just tired.'

He places a hand on my shoulder. 'I told you it was too soon to come back to work. You've overdone it.'

'No, it's not that.' Hot tears flow down my cheeks. 'I loved working with Jenna on the conference and I don't mind being tired. It's just… sometimes I feel so worthless.'

'You need to rest.' He cups my face in his hand. 'You look exhausted. Are you sleeping?'

I close my eyes. 'Not really.'

'You need a night off. Mum and I will mind the boys tonight and I'll sort you out with something to help you sleep.'

I head up to bed early and find a bottle of Zolpidem on my bedside table. *Take one 10mg tablet with a drink of water one hour before bed.* Mark and Vita have the boys so I do as the label says and I'm out like a light.

I wake at eleven p.m. and, feeling thirsty, head down to the kitchen. While filling a glass with water, I'm alerted to raised voices coming from the snug.

'I've told you. There's nothing to worry about, Mother.'

'Why won't you listen? You know nothing about that woman.'

That woman? So, they're not arguing about me. I creep to the doorway to listen.

'And you do?' says Mark.

'Yes.' Vita's tone is derisive. 'Believe me, I do.'

'You don't know what you're talking about. Many colleagues hold her in the highest esteem.'

Are they talking about Deòiridh?

'I don't doubt that,' says Vita.

Mark sighs. 'I can't understand why you're getting so worked up.'

'Because I've seen that look before. Heard those exact same arguments.'

'What are you talking about?'

'Your father, Mark. It's just the sort of bullshit your father would come out with.'

'Oh, here we go…'

'Yes, here we go. He always went on the attack when threatened.'

'Christ, you're as bad as Hanna. She suspects me of having an affair with every female in the vicinity.'

Is that really what he thinks?

Silence, then Vita's voice again. 'It's like Nduka's back…'

'Really, Mother, have you heard yourself?'

Vita continues in a calm, firm voice. 'I know what I'm talking about Mark, and I have evidence to prove it.'

'Evidence? What evidence?'

'Evidence that your father abandoned his family for fame and prestige. You're in danger of following in his footsteps.'

'Don't be ridiculous.'

'It's not me who's ridiculous. Don't test me.'

'For heaven's sake…'

Mark's footsteps cross the room and I jump back, fearful he's coming into the kitchen. Luckily, he strides off along the corridor and the office door slams.

I find Vita on the couch, dabbing her eyes with a hanky.

'Hello,' I say. 'I didn't realise you were still up?'

She glances at me. 'Did you manage to sleep?'

'Yes. I came down for some water.' I wave my glass. 'Is your hay fever playing up again? Why don't I make you a drink? What about a hot chocolate?'

'No, I'll get indigestion.'

'Look, why don't you get yourself off to bed? I can see to Kwami if he wakes.'

'Well, if you're sure?' She gets up, smooths her skirt and tucks the handkerchief into her cardigan pocket. 'I think I might be coming down with something. Perhaps I'll have a Lemsip.'

I jolt awake. What was that? Rubbing my eyes, I check the time. Nearly two. Kwami will wake soon for a feed. Pushing off the duvet, I get up and use the ensuite.

Back in the bedroom, I pull on my dressing gown and pad along the landing. I hover outside the boys' door for a moment, listening, but all's quiet. Easing the door open, I creep in. Kwami's sound asleep, so I tuck his blanket around him and turn to Ike who's sleeping too, his limbs flung wide. I adjust his quilt and quietly leave the room. Glancing along the landing, I notice the guest room door is ajar, but there's no light on. So Deòiridh's still up. Is she with Mark? So much for minding the boys…

Heading downstairs, I tiptoe along the corridor and try the office door, but it's locked.

My throat is parched again, so I wander through to the kitchen. As I run the cold tap, something outside catches my eye. A light, bobbing around on the lawn. Is it a torch? I lean across the sink and peer out of the window, but I can't see anything. Did I imagine it?

Lifting the keys from the hook, I unlock the French doors, slip on my gardening clogs and step out onto the patio. The night is starless, the moon obscured by dark clouds scudding across the sky. There are no lights in Vita's apartment. I turn around to face the chapel, but there are no lights on in there either.

An owl hoots and leaves rustle in the treetops. A chill runs across the back of my neck and, despite my dressing gown, I shiver.

I go back inside and lock the door. After filling my glass, I lean against the sink, staring out into the darkness. The sky clears and the moon reappears, its soft hue reflected on the grass. But that wasn't the light I'd seen. Outside, I'd had the strongest sense that I wasn't alone.

Back in my bedroom, I lay down and close my eyes. Where is Mark?

CHAPTER FORTY-FOUR

'Come on, Ike.' Vita picks up his Spider-man rucksack. 'We'll be late.'

Ike slides down from his chair and follows her out to the hallway.

Mark gets up too. 'I've work to do,' he mumbles, heading to the office.

I remain in the chair by the range. I can't stop thinking about last night. Was Mark with Deòiridh? What were they up to?

Temi pokes his head around the door, spots me and hesitates.

'It's all right,' I say. 'I won't bite.'

'Are you sure?' Grinning he rubs his arm. 'Think I'm still bearing scars from last time.'

'I know. Sorry. I've been having terrible moods swings. I hadn't been sleeping, but I'm better now. Coffee?'

He takes a seat. 'Yes please.'

I make our drinks and carry them over to the table.

'Thanks. You said you're feeling better now?'

'Yes, Mark's given me some sleeping pills.'

Temi frowns. 'I'm not sure pills are always the best answer.'

'It's just until I get back into a routine.'

Kwami begins to wail, and I pick him up. 'Temi' – I jiggle the baby in my arms – 'can I ask you something?'

He smiles. 'Of course.'

'Remember when we were in Lagos, that old woman at Nduka's funeral?'

'Ada. Yes, I remember.'

'She said we needed to have two funerals, and you told me if we didn't, Nduka might come back and haunt us.'

He laughs. 'It is just a Nigerian superstition.'

I take a bottle of milk from the fridge. 'So, you don't think it's true?'

'Hanna, what's the matter?'

'Oh, nothing.' I pop the bottle in the microwave. 'You're probably right. It's the sleeping pills.'

He waits, his eyes deep and soulful. I'm going to miss having him around. 'I hear you're moving out?' The microwave pings and I take out the bottle.

'Yes, in a day or two. A friend has lent me his apartment in London.' He smiles. 'I just have to keep his houseplants alive while he's away in the States.' He sips his drink. 'It will free up my room for Deòiridh.'

I check the milk is the right temperature before sitting down to feed Kwami. 'How much do you know about her?'

'Why do you ask?'

'It's just… her and Mark seem inseparable.'

Temi scratches his chin. 'She is very charismatic.'

'Mmm.' I attempt a laugh, but my voice cracks. 'Not sure that's what I wanted to hear.'

'Are you worried? About the two of them?'

'Not specifically, but their closeness winds Vita up. I've never known her be so angry with Mark.'

'Hmm.'

'Oh, ignore me. I'm just being silly.'

I'm gazing down at Kwami when I feel Temi's hand on my shoulder. 'In my experience, it is wise to trust one's instincts.'

Following Temi's note of caution I avoid taking any more pills. Even so, I sleep soundly until woken by Kwami crying. I check my alarm clock – six-fifteen a.m. He's slept through. Clambering out of bed, I hurry along the landing and into the boys' room. How does Ike sleep through this racket? When I pick up Kwami, he begins rooting at my chest. 'Nothing there, I'm afraid,' I say, my milk having dried up weeks back. 'Let's find you a bottle.'

I carry him downstairs, noting the empty kitchen. 'Where's Nana? She's usually up by now.'

Mr Biggles winds himself round my ankles, mewing.

'I guess you haven't had breakfast either.' I tip a few biscuits into his bowl.

Kwami begins to fret, so I stick a sterilised bottle in the bottle maker and press the button.

Jenna appears in the doorway. 'Someone's hungry.'

'Sorry, did he disturb you? He slept through though, so I can't complain.' The machine bleeps and I attempt to scoop formula into the bottle while Kwami wriggles in my arms.

'Here, I'll take him.' Jenna jiggles him on her lap while I prepare his feed. He stops crying and regards her with interest so, rather than risk upsetting him again, I hand her the filled bottle.

'Hey, what did your last slave die of?'

'Do you mind? I should check on Vita.'

Before Jenna can argue, I pad across the patio to Vita's apartment and knock on the door. 'Hello? Vita?' I put my ear to the door. There's movement inside. After a few moments, Vita opens the door, her face deathly pale.

'Are you all right? It's not like you to…' I glance past her and gasp. The apartment's been ransacked. Books pulled from bookcases and drawers emptied onto the floor. Even in her tiny kitchenette, cupboard doors are flung open, and rice and granola litter the work top. 'What in the world…'

Vita stares into space.

I take her arm. 'Come on.' I lead her across the patio and into the kitchen.

Jenna glances up. 'What's happened?'

I shake my head, helping Vita to the chair beside the range.

Jenna passes Kwami to me. 'I'll fetch Mark.'

Moments later, Mark races in. 'Are you all right, Mother?'

'She's had a bit of a shock.' I set Kwami down in his bassinet. 'Someone's broken into the apartment.'

'Shit.' Mark lifts a poker from beside the range and hurries out of the door.

While he's gone, I switch on the kettle. 'It's okay, Vita. Mark will sort everything out.'

She doesn't respond and I notice she's clutching a broken mug. Gently I ease it from her grasp, replacing it with a cup of strong, sweet tea.

'It's a bloody mess over there,' Mark says on his return. Lifting the phone from the wall, he dials 999. 'Hello? Police? There's been a break-in.' He gives our address. 'No, it's my mother's apartment…'

I squeeze Vita's shoulder.

'No, the perpetrator is no longer on the premises.'

'What did they say?' I ask, as he puts down the phone.

'They're sending someone to take a statement.'

'That's it?'

Mark shrugs. 'I don't think anything of value is missing.'

'I don't understand. Why would someone break into Vita's apartment, rather than the main house?'

CHAPTER FORTY-FIVE

Is that a baby crying? I sit up groggily and rub my eyes, listening. Of course, it's Kwami. I haul myself out of bed. He's slept through again, but I'm still shattered. After the break-in, Vita hadn't been up to looking after the boys, so yesterday was manic. A wave of nausea washes over me and I steady myself leaning against the dressing table until it passes. Staggering along the landing, I head into the boys' bedroom, pick up the crying baby from his cot and carry him back to my room. Kwami's nappy is heavily soiled, so I lay him on the bed and strip off his clothes. I wipe his bottom and fasten a clean disposable, leaving him on the bed while I dump his wet clothes in the ensuite.

As I wash my hands, I glance in the mirror. My mouth is dry, and I run my tongue around my lips, shocked as I realise I haven't yet spoken a word. I didn't blow Kwami a raspberry or pull a funny face. I didn't even hug him. Like an automaton, I simply attended to his needs. The poor kid is starved of affection.

I hurry through to the turret nursery and pull open a drawer to find him some clean clothes. Spotting something yellow underneath the other clothing, I tug it out. A babygro with a line of little elephants each holding the tail of the one in front. It's cute. I sink down on the floor and hug it to my chest. I miss my daughter so much…

'What is wrong with you?'

I glance up. Mark's in the doorway holding Kwami. I blink. 'What?'

'Kwami was screaming his head off. I found him on the bed, naked apart from a nappy. Why would you leave him like that? He might have rolled off.'

'I came to get a clean babygro,' I murmur, turning the sleepsuit over in my hands.

Mark pushes me aside, bashing my head on the side of the cot, and grabs a white babygro from the drawer before marching back into the bedroom.

Dazed, I stay slumped on the floor, rubbing my head and listening to Mark chattering to Kwami in the next room. 'There you go, mate. Soon have you sorted. That's better, isn't it?'

'How are you?' asks Tom a few days later.

'I'm not sure.'

Tom slides his glasses up the bridge of his nose. 'Tell me.'

I sink down on the couch. 'I seem to be experiencing short-term memory loss.'

'Can you give me an example?'

'You know when you walk purposefully into a room and can't remember what you came in for?'

Tom nods.

'Well, it's kind of like that. I was changing Kwami's

nappy, I went to fetch a fresh babygro and completely forgot what I was doing. Mark found the baby lying on the bed, abandoned.'

'So, you were distracted?'

'Perhaps. But also, I keep forgetting things.'

'Like what?'

I cringe. 'I forgot to pick up Ike.'

'Tell me what happened?'

'I was in the kitchen when Mark rushed in and grabbed the car keys. He said preschool had called because no-one had collected Ike.'

'And you were supposed to fetch him?'

I shake my head. 'I remember Vita mentioning something about getting her eyes tested, but I don't remember her saying she couldn't pick up Ike.'

'So, it was more of a misunderstanding?'

'I don't know. It's as if my brain's slowed right down. What do you think's going on with me?'

'How are things between you and Mark?'

I squirm. 'Not great.'

'Can you elaborate?'

'It's my fault.' I give a half-hearted smile. 'I'm feeling jealous, but it's completely irrational.'

Tom steeples his fingers. 'Why do you consider your feelings to be irrational?'

I shrug.

Tom leans back. 'Hanna, have you made any changes to your medication?'

My cheeks burn. Should I tell him?

'If you were thinking of adjusting your medication,' Tom continues, 'you'd need to do it slowly. You can't just drop it without experiencing negative side effects.'

CHAPTER FORTY-SIX

I'm feeding Mr Biggles when a cry travels from the hallway. I rush out there and start up the stairs. Then I freeze. Ike's on the top step holding Kwami. How on earth did he lift the baby out of his cot?

Taking a deep breath, I say calmly, 'Stay there, Ike.'

'Baby cry,' he says.

I continue creeping up. If Ike drops the baby, can I catch him? 'It's okay, Ike,' I soothe. 'It's okay.'

Ike's face crumples. I'm ten steps away when he leans forward, teetering on the edge. I need him to step back, to sit down, but I'm afraid anything I say might result in him losing his grip.

Five steps to go… 'Good boy, Ike.'

Two steps from the top, I reach forward and snatch Kwami from Ike's grasp. Bounding up the remaining steps, I grab Ike with my free hand and drag him away from the stairs. 'What did you think you were doing?' I yell. Shifting the baby to my left hip, I shake Ike's arm. 'You might have dropped him.'

Ike stares at me, wide eyed. Too late, I realise how rough

I'm being, when he turns and sprints along the landing to his
bedroom.

———

'I'll mind the boys this afternoon,' I tell Vita.

'Are you sure?'

'Yes. I need to spend time with Ike. He's still wary with
me after yesterday.'

Vita shakes her head. 'I can't understand how he managed
to reach into the cot, let alone carry his brother.'

'I know. Let's hope some fresh air will cheer him up.'

'Well, I do have letters to write…' Vita never really got
into emails and I envy her use of snail mail. I'd love to write
and receive letters. But who would I write to? During the
period Mark and I were trying for a baby, I became supersen-
sitive whenever one of our friends got pregnant and this
resulted in me distancing myself. What would I even say after
all this time?

Kwami fills his nappy just as we're about to leave for our
walk. I strip him down, redressing him in fresh clothes and a
padded all-in-one.

Ike regards me with suspicion. When I try to get him into
his quilted gilet and boots he begins to snivel. 'I want Nana.'

'You can't have Nana. She's writing letters. You've
got me.'

Once outside, it doesn't get any easier as the pram
wheels skid on the uneven ground. I battle on while Ike lags
behind. 'Come on, Ike,' I call for the tenth time in as many
minutes.

He scowls, looking down at his feet and taking dolly
steps.

'Look at the pretty flowers.' I point at an umbrella-like

cluster of white froth along the hedgerow. 'That's called cow parsley.'

Ike continues to avoid eye contact.

'We might see a squirrel,' I say. 'Let's look for a squirrel.'

Ike glances about, not up in the trees, but over his shoulder. No wonder he's walking so slowly.

'What is it?' I pull on the pram brake and go back to where he's standing.

There's a scuffling sound in the bushes. Are we being followed? Grabbing Ike's hand, I hurry back to the pram and release the brake. I push fast, still hanging onto Ike. The pram slips and slides while Ike stumbles and falters, and I yank his arm to stop him from falling over.

'Want Nana,' he wails.

'Well, she's not here.' I march along, dragging him beside me.

Suddenly the pram veers off the path and slips free of my hands, heading for a slope. I let go of Ike and charge after it, managing to grab it just before it crashes into a large oak tree.

My heart's beating fast. 'That was close.' I turn to Ike, but he's disappeared. 'Damn.' Hauling the pram back onto the path, I pull on the brake. Kwami cries. 'Shh.' I jiggle the pram handle. 'Ike?' I call. 'Ike?'

I run a few metres one way, then the other, scanning bushes either side. He can't have gone far, I only let go of his hand for a moment. Running back to the pram, I release the brake and retrace our steps. He's probably heading for home and his precious Nana.

After a few minutes, I catch a glimpse of Ike's blue gilet through the trees. I pull the brake on again and run towards him. 'Ike,' I shout.

He's standing in a clearing, staring at nothing.

I grab his arm. 'Don't ever do that again.'

He has the strangest look on his face and the hint of a smile.

'Ike, what are you looking at?'

'Gainde,' he says.

My pulse quickens. I stare in the direction he's looking but there's nothing there.

'Gainde,' I repeat, deciding to play along. 'How do you do, Gainde.' I pretend to shake hands.

'Gainde don't shake hands.'

'Sorry. Well, come on, Gainde. You come with me and Ike, and I'll make you both a hot chocolate when we get home.'

'Gainde don't like hot chocolate.'

'Whatever.' I grab Ike's hand and drag him back to the path.

He pulls and tugs, digging his heels into the wet leaves. It's surprising how strong he can be when determined. 'No,' he cries. 'Gainde…'

'There is no Gainde.'

'Gainde,' Ike repeats, sobbing.

I bend down and put my arms around him. 'Look,' I say. 'No Gainde. There is no Gainde.'

Ike tries to pull away.

I scoop him up and carry him, kicking and screaming, to the path where I hoist him onto the pram. Releasing the brake, I push one-handed back towards the house. With my other hand I hold Ike while he thrashes, kicks and goes rigid. He sobs and Kwami wails as if they're in competition, but I march on, determined to get home. As we near the house, the boys reach a crescendo and Norris, sweeping leaves on the edge of the lawn, looks over in alarm.

'What?' I shout rudely.

I'm manhandling the pram onto the patio as Mark opens the French doors. 'What the devil's happened?'

'This kid is impossible.' I lift Ike down from the pram and pass him to Mark. 'Here, you have him.'

Mark takes him and Ike lays a hot, tear-stained face on his father's chest, his sobs now punctuated by shudders.

Mark pats his back. 'He's terrified. What the hell have you done?'

Vita opens the door to her apartment. 'Whatever's going on?'

I stare at their condemning faces. 'Here.' I gesture to the pram. 'You can have this one too. I'm done.' Still in wellington boots, I march through the kitchen and into the snug. My hands shake as I pour myself a brandy. I knock it back and pour another, trying to steady my breathing.

CHAPTER FORTY-SEVEN

When I reach the lawn, Sorrel's on the bench. She has a notepad on her lap as she sketches the east elevation.

'That's really good.' I point at the gargoyles. 'You've really captured their gruesome little faces.'

'Thanks.' She slides the pencil into her pocket and tucks the pad under her arm. 'We walking?'

'S'pose you heard about yesterday,' I ask, as we take the path through the trees.

'Couldn't really miss it.' She giggles. 'I think the whole of Suffolk heard you coming across the lawn with two screaming brats.'

I grimace. 'Not my proudest moment. Ike won't have anything to do with me. He backs away whenever I come near him.'

'What happened?'

I sigh. 'I met Gainde.'

'You saw him?'

'No. That's just the point. I couldn't see anything, but Ike was convinced he was there.'

'What about the little girl?'

I turn to face her. 'You think there's actually another one?'

'I sense her. Some sort of protector.'

'Protector from what?"

She shrugs. 'I'm not sure.'

'Oh, well.' I scoff. 'That's okay then.'

She glances at me. 'You should be pleased someone's watching over Ike.'

We walk on in silence.

'Sorry,' I say, after a few moments.

'S'okay.'

'How come you know all this stuff?'

She laughs.

'What?'

'You asked me how I know. You didn't question that I know.'

'Bang, bang, bang.' Ike bashes upturned saucepans with a wooden spoon while Kwami, watching from his bouncer, shrieks with excitement. I rub my brow. My head's splitting and I wish I could lay down, but Vita's gone to Stowmarket to meet a friend and won't be home for hours.

'I know,' I say to Ike. 'Let's go upstairs and play.'

I lift Kwami from his bouncer and Ike follows me upstairs. In their bedroom, I set Kwami down on the playmat, where he kicks happily under his baby gym. Ike plonks himself down on the mat, his expression sullen.

'Let's build a castle.' I pull the lid off the plastic tub of Duplo and soon Ike's engrossed.

Kwami becomes fretful, so I transfer him to the cot. In moments he's asleep. I glance at Ike, cross-legged on the mat.

Perhaps if I rest my eyes, just for a few minutes. I lie down on Ike's bed…

I wake with a start. The boys! But Ike's busy colouring and Kwami's still asleep. I check my watch: four-thirty. I need to feed them soon. Stumbling into the ensuite, I splash water on my face.

'I'm just going down to start your tea,' I whisper to Ike as I step back into the bedroom. 'I'll come and get you in a few minutes.'

He nods, completely absorbed with his crayoning.

I dash downstairs. In the kitchen, I'm greeted by Mr Biggles who rubs against my ankles, protesting noisily. 'All right, all right.' I tip cat biscuits into his bowl, place a tray of fish fingers in the oven and pop a bowl of baked beans in the microwave.

It's only minutes before I'm racing back upstairs to fetch the boys, but before I reach their bedroom door, I hear crying. I hurry in and over to Kwami's cot. 'Okay little guy…' But the cot's empty. Then I hear water running.

I hurry into the ensuite and gasp. 'No, no, no.' The bath taps are on and the plug in. Kwami's lying in the bottom of the tub in a babygro and nappy, while water laps around his ears.

I reach in and snatch him up. His cries grow frantic as I carry him into the bedroom. 'It's okay, it's okay,' I soothe, laying him on the bed and stripping off his wet clothes. I pick him up and wrap him in a bath towel. Ike's still on the mat doing a jigsaw puzzle.

'Did you put Kwami in the bath?'

Ike looks up, blinking. 'No, Mummy.'

'You must have done.'

He cowers, shuffling backwards on his bottom.

'Don't you ever do that again,' I yell.

'What's going on?' I look up and Mark's in the doorway. 'Why are you shouting at Ike?' He strides into the room and picks up the quivering child. 'Can't you see he's scared?'

'He put Kwami in the bath,' I say. 'He might have drowned.'

'What are you talking about?'

'I popped down to get tea started and Ike must have…'

'You left the boys upstairs on their own?' Mark shakes his head. 'What's the matter with you?'

Could I have been in such a fugue that I put Kwami in the bath?

From downstairs comes the piercing beep of the smoke alarm. Mark glares at me before running downstairs with Ike in his arms.

I'm shaking as I dress Kwami.

In the kitchen, Ike's tucking into baked beans on toast. On the worktop, a tray of charcoaled fish fingers lays beside the dismantled alarm. Wordlessly, I take a bottle from the fridge and pop it in the microwave to heat.

'I'm beginning to wonder if it's wise to leave you alone with the boys,' says Mark.

I spin around. 'What do you mean?'

'Let's see' – he counts off incidents on his fingers – 'you forget to pick up Ike, you abandon Kwami on the bed. Twice now, you've accused Ike of trying to injure his brother. Can't you see he's petrified of you? Carry on like this and someone will report us to social services. Do you want to lose custody of the boys?'

'No, of course not.' Kwami wails as I jiggle him ineffectively. 'I…'

'You'd better sort yourself out, Hanna.'

The water pours from the faucet as I perch on the edge of the bath. I reach over and add a generous glob of my favourite relaxation bath oil.

There's so much space between Mark and I. Sure, our marriage has had its moments, but nothing like this. We no longer seem to have anything in common. I don't know how we're going to find our way back.

I waggle my hand in the water creating lavender bubbles. I'm not sure I even recognise the man I married. Those first few years were so happy. Mark studied hard, worked all hours and there was no money, but we had each other and that was enough. Candlelit picnics on the rug; cheap plonk and fish and chips eaten from the paper; walking home in the rain because we couldn't afford a cab and rubbing each other's hair dry with a towel in front of the sitting room fire… Mark was so loving and incredibly charming – a bit of a flirt if I'm honest – but it was him and me against the world. We were a team, united, unbreakable.

Am I being paranoid? First, I thought there was something going on between Mark and Jenna, now I'm convinced he's having an affair with Deòiridh. I've never been a jealous wife. What's wrong with me? I sigh. It's hardly surprising my husband's seeking love elsewhere. I haven't been exactly attentive. The way he looked at me earlier… it made me afraid. Does he even love me? For goodness' sake, I almost drowned my child. Perhaps I came off the meds too quickly, but how could I be so distracted that I put Kwami in the bath fully clothed?

I turn off the water and slip out of my bathrobe before easing myself down under the water. With my fingers I make patterns in trails of bath oil. Shapes float in and out of my subconscious, like cloud rabbits in *Watership Down*. As I doodle absentmindedly, a face appears. Gently I play with the edges. Not quite right... there, that's it. I stare into the beautiful face of my baby girl... and then she's gone, dispersed into the water. How long will she continue to haunt me?

CHAPTER FORTY-EIGHT

'Can I leave Kwami with you this morning?' I ask Vita. 'I need to patch things up with Ike.'

She purses her lips. 'If you think it's a good idea…'

Ike doesn't look up as he stirs the remains of his breakfast cereal.

'We'll find a big fish, shall we, Ike?' I coax.

I can tell he's torn. He loves the fish. Reluctantly, he slides down from his chair, and doesn't protest as I help him into his gilet and boots.

We set off through the trees, passing a beautiful sea of red and white campion, but I've learnt that flowers don't impress Ike. Reaching the Japanese Garden, we kneel on the grass beside the bridge and gaze into the little pool.

'Where is the fish?' he asks.

'We have to be quiet and patient,' I whisper.

I glance up, hopeful a ray of sunlight might penetrate through a gap in the trees, but no such luck. I shiver. It's such a gloomy place, not even peaceful with the incessant buzz of insects. Something brushes my shoulder. I shuffle forward on my knees to avoid giant leaves of alien vegetation bowing down menacingly. According to Norris, the plant is called Brazilian Rhubarb. Any fish that has survived in these murky waters has likely grown to the size of Nessy.

There's movement under the water. A flash of something orange. 'Look!' I point.

'Is it a fish?' cries Ike.

The fish surfaces with a small splash before diving once more into the still, dark water.

'He's gone,' I say. 'Come on.'

Hauling ourselves up, we stroll on through the woods. A twig cracks and I turn but there's no one there. 'Sorrel?' I call, and then, 'Norris?' but there's no reply.

As we arrive at the clearing, I gasp. The right hand of St Eduardo, usually raised to bestow a blessing, has broken off at the wrist and lays on the ground. Last time I'd put the damage down to wild animals, but this looks more like the hand of God.

From high in the trees, a crow caws before descending with a precision rivalling that of a cruise missile. I duck, but he's so close that the air shifts and Ike buries his face against my legs. The bird lands on top of St Eduardo's statue and ruffles his iridescent feathers.

'It's just Mr Crow,' I say, feigning bravery I don't feel. 'Hello, Mr Crow.'

Ike peers up and the crow nods its thick, grey beak.

'Come on. Let's go home.' My heart races as we hurry back through the trees and I don't slow down even when a bramble scratches my cheek.

As we reach the stile, we find Norris repairing the top rail. He glances up, startled by our sudden appearance. 'All right, Mrs Konteh?'

'One of the statues,' I stammer. 'It's been damaged.'

'Struck by lightning, I shouldn't wonder,' he says. 'It'll

'ave been the storm last night. I'll take a look when I've finished up 'ere.'

'Will he be able to fix it, Mummy?' Ike asks, as we make our way along the path.

'I hope so.' But I can't help thinking that Mark won't want to spend money restoring an old statue. He'd rather spend it on a more contemporary feature or a sculpture to impress his corporate visitors.

I'm still turning over Norris's words as I swing open the gate. I didn't hear a storm last night. I must have slept through it. But how did lightning find its way through those tall firs?

We're almost home when I spot an ambulance outside Bartholomew block. Grabbing Ike's hand, I quicken my pace.

'No, Mummy…' Ike complains as I drag him along.

I skid to a halt beside Sorrel's open door just as Jenna steps outside. 'What's happening?' I demand.

'It's Sorrel,' Jenna answers. 'She's had a miscarriage.'

I stare open-mouthed as two paramedics carry Sorrel past on a stretcher. 'I should go with her.'

'No.' Jenna takes my arm. 'You've got Ike, and anyway, Cathy's going.' She gestures towards our part-time care assistant who's climbing into the back of ambulance. 'Sorrel's parents will meet them at the hospital.'

The ambulance drives away, and Jenna and I take Ike back to the house.

'I'll drop Ike over with Vita,' Jenna says once we reach the kitchen.

'Thanks. That will be really helpful.'

'Okay. Won't be a mo.'

I flop down in the chair by the range.

Minutes later Jenna returns. 'Cup of tea, I think.' She switches on the kettle.

'When did it happen?' I ask in a shaky voice.

'Cathy found her this morning when she was doing her rounds. It must have begun in the early hours.'

'I should have called for her,' I murmur.

'It wouldn't have made any difference. It's just one of those things.' She shakes her head. 'We didn't even know she was pregnant.'

I attempt to stand, but my legs wobble. 'I should go to the hospital.'

Jenna places a hand on my shoulder. 'I told you. Sorrel's parents have been informed. They'll take it from here.'

CHAPTER FORTY-NINE

I don't spot Sorrel right away. She's in the last bed looking pale and small. 'Hi,' I say, pulling up a chair.

She opens her eyes. 'Hi,' she answers in a husky voice.

I squeeze her hand. 'Your mum and dad have been with you?'

She nods, biting her bottom lip. 'I lost the baby.'

'I know.'

Her eyes fill with tears. 'They weren't even able to tell me whether it was a boy or a girl.'

'I'm sorry. It's so unfair.' She must have been almost sixteen weeks. How do they class that as a miscarriage?

'I think it was a boy.' She turns her face to the wall. 'Silly me. I thought it was Ike or Kwami she was after. Not my little one.'

'Who's she?'

'That Deòiridh woman.' She glances back. 'I told you she was dangerous. I read it in her aura. She collects children's souls.'

'Hush, try to rest,' I soothe.

Her eyes flash with anger. 'You don't believe me. I knew

the others wouldn't, but I hoped you knew me well enough by now to know that I'm not lying.'

'I do know.'

'But you think I'm crazy.' She sighs. 'You'll see. You'll all see.'

I get up. 'I should let you rest.' I swallow, having trouble forming the words. 'I'm so sorry, Sorrel, but I'm afraid it's just one of those terrible things that happen sometimes. It's not anyone's fault.'

She reaches out and grabs my wrist. 'Promise me something?'

'What?'

'You won't do anything silly.'

'What do you mean?'

'It doesn't matter.' She blinks. 'I wouldn't have been allowed to keep the baby, but I wanted the best for him, you know?'

'I know. You'll always be his mum.'

'Do you think there's a heaven?'

I hold her hand again. 'I don't know.'

'Neither do I, but it would be good if there was, because then I'd know I'll see him again.'

I kiss her forehead.

The next afternoon, Jenna finds me in the snug. I can tell from her expression that something's wrong.

'What is it?' I ask.

She sinks into the armchair. 'Sorrel attempted to take her own life.'

'Oh no,' I cry. 'Is she okay?'

'Her parents visited yesterday afternoon and had her

moved to a private room. Apparently, she was uncommunicative, but the hospital staff had warned them to expect that. They stayed an hour before going back to their bed and breakfast. At five-thirty this morning they were called and told she'd tried to commit suicide.'

'No, no, no.'

'Apparently, she went into the bathroom after lights out, laid down in a warm bath and slit her wrists. She did a pretty good job, apparently. If it hadn't been for the nurse checking in on her, it would have been too late.'

'I should have realised.' I wring my hands. 'She said some odd things when I was with her yesterday.'

'You couldn't possibly have known what she was planning. No one knew.'

'What will happen now? Will she come back here?'

'No. She's to be moved to a secure unit for her own protection.' Jenna gets up and steps towards the door. 'It's so sad, isn't it?' She shakes her head. 'The hospital cleaner spotted a message written in steam on the bathroom mirror. One word. *Sorry.*'

CHAPTER FIFTY

What happened to my little girl? Was she adopted by some rich and loving family desperate to have children? At least that would mean she's okay. Perhaps one day she'll track me down, come to find me…

A voice cuts through my thoughts. 'Hanna?'

I glance up at Tom sitting opposite.

'You were miles away. What were you thinking about?'

I don't reply. It's been two weeks since Sorrel's suicide attempt. For days I've been on edge, liable to fall either way.

'Mark tells me you've not been doing so good.' Tom steeples his fingers. 'Is this to do with what happened to Sorrel?'

'She knew something bad was going to happen. She warned me to take care.'

Tom leans forward. 'Take care?'

'She was wrong. It wasn't my child in danger, it was hers.'

'It's very sad that Sorrel lost her baby.'

'Perhaps I'm envious,' I murmur. 'If my baby was dead, I'd want to join her. Not that I'm religious.'

'You're envious?'

I glare at him. 'I envy her bravery. Here am I, dreaming of ways to check out and yet it's Sorrel who has the balls to go ahead and try it.'

Tom's eyes are searching. 'You feel suicidal?'

I laugh. 'It's okay, Tom. Although I'm sure everyone would be better off without me, I promised Sorrel not to do anything stupid.' I gaze out of the window. 'She knew what she was asking. Perhaps I did too? I should have said something to the hospital staff. I might have stopped it happening.'

Tom touches my arm. 'It's not your fault, Hanna. If someone's determined to take their own life, it's very hard to prevent that from happening.'

'But supposing she'd died? What a waste. She's just beginning her life, whereas the best of mine is over.'

'What do you mean by that?'

'I'll never have another child, not after the complications when Kwami was born.' I sigh. 'I have two sons and neither is really mine.'

'You don't accept the results of the DNA test?'

'Oh yes, biologically Kwami's mine. But it doesn't feel like it. Every morning I glance into my bathroom mirror and see a strange woman staring back. She goes through the motions, talks to people, interacts, but she's not me.' I laugh. 'It's ironic, really. Sorrel said someone took the soul of her baby. Perhaps she's taken my soul, too?'

CHAPTER FIFTY-ONE

Mark glances up as I wander into the kitchen. 'Nice to see you up and dressed. How are you feeling?'

'A bit better actually.' I flick the switch on the kettle. In desperation I'd resorted to Zolpidem again. 'It's amazing what a couple of decent nights' sleep will do.'

'I'll do that. Come and sit down.' He busies himself making tea. 'So, the sleeping pills are helping? Deòiridh said they were good.'

I didn't know the pills were her recommendation. Still, I mustn't complain. Since moving into the Caleb block apartment, she's kept herself to herself. 'Thanks.' I take the mug and cradle it in my hands. 'I thought I might come back to work today. Jenna's asked me to write some website copy about our plans for Darius.'

'Well, don't go overdoing it.' Mark closes his MacBook. 'It's not worth making yourself ill again.' He heads along to the office.

I sip my tea while scrolling through emails on my mobile, trying to locate the template Jenna sent me for the website.

When the phone rings, I jump. I don't recognise the caller ID. 'Hello?'

'Hanna? It's me, Sorrel.'

'Sorrel. How are you? I'm so sorry about everything that happened.'

'Thanks. I know you understand.'

'Are you still in the secure unit? I didn't think you were allowed to make calls.'

'No, I'm home.' She sniggers. 'Although I may as well be in a secure unit. Mum's driving me mad.'

'She's just worried about you.'

'Listen. I have to tell you something and I don't have much time. I've been doing some research. Well, when I say I've been researching, actually Will has.'

'Will? So, he's back?'

'He never went away. Anyway, you need to listen, Hanna. You and your kids are in danger.'

'Look Sorrel, I know you're trying to help but I've not been well myself. I had a bit of a relapse after what happened to you. My mind playing tricks on me again…'

'That's just it. You're not imagining things.'

My heart beats faster. 'What do you mean?'

'Will's been looking into this Deòiridh woman. There's loads of stuff about her online. It's all pretty weird. She's older than she looks, and she's been mixed up in some bad shit. Will said to ask if you remember the torso found in the Thames?'

'Vaguely. Wasn't it a little boy? Some sort of ritual killing?'

'Exactly. And they never caught the people responsible. During the investigation, Deòiridh was one of several experts consulted.'

'With her background and knowledge, that's hardly surprising.'

'Will believes there was a cover up. It looks very dodgy. I swear she put a hex on me to make me lose my baby.'

'A hex?'

'A spell. I think she's a witch.'

Sorrel's clearly become more disturbed since the miscarriage. 'Sorrel, I know you're trying to help, but you can't jump to conclusions. And the torso in the Thames? Deòiridh is just the sort of person they'd consult on a case like that.'

'No, there's more. She's been involved in stuff in the States as well. Seriously, Hanna. You need to watch your back.'

'Well, I've hardly seen her lately. She commutes to London most days and, even when she doesn't, she keeps her distance.' I sigh. 'Look, email me links to the stuff Will's found and I promise to look at them.'

'Okay, but Hanna?'

'What?'

'Trust no one, and definitely not your husband. Yes Mum… sorry Hanna, I've got to go.' She hangs up.

I stare at the phone in my hand. Perhaps Mark was right? Sorrel sounds crazy. The phone pings with an email – links to articles on the torso in the Thames. I shudder as I read how the headless and limbless body of the little boy (the police named him Adam) was discovered. Even now, seventeen years later, they've not been able to prove who did it. Another news article suggests it might have been ritual killing linked to voodoo. Tiny pellets of clay containing particles of gold were found in Adam's belly - a black magic potion…

'Hanna?'

Mark's calling. I close the webpage. The research will wait until I'm alone.

CHAPTER FIFTY-TWO

'No sign of Vita this morning?' I ask, stirring a pan of porridge on the range.

Mark shrugs. 'She must have slept in.'

A few weeks ago, Mark would have been the first to comment on Vita's absence. The ever-devoted son, he'd have headed over with a cuppa to rouse her. Not that it happened often. Unless nursing a cold, she'd be in the kitchen supervising, even when not on grandchildren duty. But since the break-in, she's seemed more vulnerable. Older somehow.

'How was she last night?' I ask.

'Her usual self.' Mark doesn't seem at all bothered as he carries on reading the newspaper. I'd heard them arguing again yesterday. Perhaps he's not looking forward to facing her this morning?

I lift the pan from the hob and set it aside. 'The porridge is ready, but it's hot. Can you watch the boys?' I pour a mug of tea, add a splash of milk – just the way Vita likes it – and carry it across the patio. 'Vita,' I call as I knock on her door. 'I've brought you a cuppa.'

I get no response, so I set the hot mug down on the

doorstep and knock again, calling louder. 'Vita? Are you okay? I wondered if you'd overslept?' Still no reply. I shiver, recalling the break-in a few weeks before. Surely the burglars haven't returned…

Retrieving the spare key from under a flowerpot, I unlock the door, pick up the mug and head inside. There's no sign of Vita downstairs, so I go straight up to her bedroom and knock again, but this time I don't wait.

Pushing open the door, I find the room in darkness, the drapes still drawn. When I place the mug on her bedside table, Vita doesn't stir. She must be feeling rough. I open the curtains and turn back to the bed. 'Are you all right, Vita?'

Her eyes are wide like she's in shock and a tiny sound comes from her throat. A small stream of spittle dribbles down her chin. She doesn't move.

'Vita!' I run to the door. 'Mark,' I scream. 'It's your mum. Come quick.' Hurrying back to the bed, I take her hand. 'Don't worry, you'll be okay.'

Moments later, Mark appears at the bedroom door. 'What's the matter?'

'Sit with your mum,' I tell him. 'I'm calling an ambulance.' I rush back to the kitchen, grab the phone and dial 999. 'Ambulance please…'

I give our address, but the female responder wants more detail. 'Is she breathing?'

'Yes, but she can't move or talk. I think it's a stroke.'

'Ambulance is on the way,' says the woman.

I gaze about the kitchen. Kwami, in his bouncy chair, is gurgling happily while Ike, unable to wait for porridge, chases cereal around a bowl. Vita wouldn't approve of Coco Pops, I think.

We're shown into the family waiting room while the doctors examine Vita. Mark sits on one of the plastic chairs, scrolling through his phone. I remember how worried he was when his father had a heart attack. Now his mother's had a massive stroke and he seems to be taking it in his stride. I don't get it.

Unable to settle, I pace up and down. Vita and I were never close, but over the past few weeks we'd got on better. Now this. I feel guilty. If only I'd checked earlier; if only it had happened last night when Mark was with her. But "if onlys" don't change anything.

The door finally opens and a doctor joins us. 'It is a stroke, and a bad one. A stroke on the left or the right side of the brain affects half your body,' he explains. 'But one like this, in the middle, affects absolutely everything.'

'How long do you think she was lying there?' I ask.

He shakes his head. 'It's hard to tell. If we'd caught it earlier, we might have been able to do more. As it is, we just have to wait. If she survives the next twenty-four hours, there's hope.'

CHAPTER FIFTY-THREE

Ike holds his stomach. 'My tummy hurts.'

'You're probably just hungry.' The act of packing his Spider-man bag frequently brings on this little ploy. Nevertheless, I glance at him. He does look a little pale…

He promptly throws up all over his clothes.

'Oh dear, it's all right.' I carry him upstairs, sponge him off, and change his T-shirt and trackie bottoms. Back downstairs, I settle him on the chair by the range.

'Is he all right?' asks Mark.

'Yes, but I'll have to cancel my visit to your mother.' Despite the odds, Vita had survived the stroke, but, when her faculties failed to return and the doctors explained she needed twenty-four-hour care, Mark made alternative arrangements.

I flick the switch on the kettle. 'He's too poorly for preschool and I can't take him with me.' I'd decided not to take Ike to visit Nana. Perhaps it was cruel, but I didn't want him seeing her the way she was. I don't think she'd want that either.

Placing a spoonful of sugar in a jug, I dissolve it with a

little boiling water before topping up with cold. My mum used to make this for me when I was poorly.

Mark continues munching toast.

'You could go?' I suggest. He hasn't been to see his mother once since she transferred to the nursing home. It's always me bringing her flowers and magazines she'll never read. What a living hell. For a fit and vivacious person like Vita to end up in a state like this seems desperately unfair.

He shakes his head. 'I'm expecting a call. I can look after Ike though, if you take Kwami with you?'

'Okay,' I agree, not wanting to let Vita down. I pop a straw in the sugared water and place it on a small table beside Ike. 'Just small sips.' I tuck a throw around him and kiss him on his forehead. 'Daddy's going to look after you.' I make a final check of Kwami's travel bag before setting him in the baby seat. 'You sure you'll be all right?' I ask Mark.

He humphs with exasperation. 'I'm not totally useless.'

As I unlock the Citroën, I hear Ike's voice calling 'Mummy'. He always used to cry for Nana when he was unwell. It breaks my heart to leave him so poorly. I fix the baby seat into the passenger side and climb into the driver's seat. As I start the ignition, I hesitate. Don't be silly. I give myself a little shake. Ike will be fine with Mark.

———

Vita's asleep when we arrive, so I take a seat beside her and occupy Kwami with a story from one of his baby books.

Finally, she stirs.

'Hello,' I say. 'It's me, Hanna. I've brought Kwami with me today.'

She can't speak and yet there's something about her eyes. Is she frightened about what's happened to her? 'It's okay.' I reassure. 'You're going to be okay.' She makes no reaction. I pop Kwami down on a blanket and settle to the small tasks I do each time I visit – brushing her hair, massaging her hands and straightening her pillows. I'm not sure it helps, but it makes me feel better to be doing something.

'Would you like me to read to you?' I pick up a novel from her bedside table and frown. Barbara Cartland. Not Vita's usual cup of tea. It must be from the hospital library. Still, better than nothing.

As I open the book and begin to read, Vita's eyes grow wide.

'Sorry,' I say. 'Shall I stop?'

She doesn't respond.

I close the book. 'What is it? Are you in pain?' I put down the book and press the call bell.

A care nurse pokes her head around the door. 'Everything all right?'

'I'm not sure. I think my mother-in-law was trying to communicate something.'

The nurse checks Vita's vitals before giving me an apologetic look. 'She's fine, but perhaps you should let her rest?'

After she's gone, I study Vita's face. She stares ahead, as if looking right through me. 'What is it, Vita? What are you trying to tell me?'

After a few moments, I get up to leave. 'Next time I'll bring something else to read.' I pick up Kwami. 'Bye Nana.' I wave his hand. 'See you soon.'

I arrive home to find an ambulance on the driveway. I slam my foot on the brake. Mark runs down the steps as I leap from the car. 'What's happened now?' I yell.

He tucks something inside his coat and fastens the zip. 'It's Ike.'

I feel blood drain from my face. 'I knew he was ill. I shouldn't have left him.'

Mark shakes his head. 'No, it's not that. He's had an accident.'

As we move towards the ambulance, the paramedic raises a hand. 'Sorry, folks. Only room for one.'

Mark and I exchange a glance. 'You go,' I say, running back to the Citroën. 'I'll find someone to mind Kwami.'

I leave Kwami with one of the care assistants and follow Mark to the hospital. We sit in the same waiting room with its uncomfortable chairs and obligatory box of tissues.

Mark rubs his face. 'He was feeling better and said he was hungry, but I was on a call, so I told him to wait. Somehow, he managed to open a door on the range. When I saw what he was doing I yelled, but the door slammed closed on his fingers.'

'No!' I cover my mouth.

'You should have heard him scream.' Mark drops his head into his hands.

'He'll be all right.' I lay my hand on his arm.

'His finger was on the floor.' Mark's voice trembles. 'I didn't know what to do.'

I stifle the urge to vomit.

'I picked it up, wrapped it in ice and…'

The door opens and a doctor steps into the room. 'Mr and Mrs Konteh?'

I grip Mark's hand.

'I'm afraid your son has lost his little finger and the tip of his ring finger. The burns, however, are superficial.'

'You're not able to sew the finger back on?' asks Mark.

The doctor shakes his head. 'It was badly damaged, but we find children of this age usually adapt well.'

'Oh no.' Tears roll down my cheeks. I reach forward and grab a tissue.

Mark squeezes my hand. 'What happens now?' he asks.

'We'll take him to theatre and tidy things up. You can see him before he goes down.'

'And recovery?' asks Mark.

'He'll need to stay in for a few days but, all being well, he'll be home within a week. You'll need to bring him back to have the dressings changed.' He opens the door. 'Sister?'

A matronly woman appears in the doorway. 'Yes, Doctor Kemp?'

'Take the Kontehs to see their son.'

CHAPTER FIFTY-FOUR

'Please can I have another pancake, Daddy?'

'Sure, buddy.' Mark and I exchange a smile. Ike's thriving on the attention, but we don't mind. As long as he's okay.

'There you go, mate, and another for Mummy too.' Mark slides a second pancake onto each of our plates.

'Oh, go on then.' I squirt maple syrup onto Ike's breakfast and slice it up.

Ike spears a piece of sticky pancake with his fork. It's amazing how quickly he's recovering. Mark winks at me as he joins us at the table. As he smothers his own pancake with syrup and tucks in, there's a warm glow in my belly. The accident has united us - we're the closest we've been since Kwami was born. We're finally turning a corner. For the first time I can actually see us as a proper family.

'I've been thinking...' Mark pops the last piece of pancake in his mouth and swallows. 'I could get one of the care assistants to give you a hand if you like. Cathy maybe?'

I feel my lips purse. 'I can manage.'

He pats my hand. 'I know you can, but it's a big house

and with Mum not around… I thought Cathy could do two days a week.'

I glance across at Kwami in his bouncer. 'Perhaps you're right.'

―――――

Cathy takes no time at all to establish a routine and, a couple of days later, I get the chance to go across to Vita's apartment to find her a more suitable book. She's an avid reader and her bookcase is arranged by genre and author. I inspect the shelves – mostly autobiographies, plus a few historical novels and the odd crime thriller. Quite an eclectic taste.

Wondering what she might have been reading before the stroke, I crouch down to check the small side table beside her armchair. I find a book with a leather spine and flip it open. A diary. I snap it shut. I can't read Vita's diary. Glancing back at her bookcase, I note the diary's brown leather spine matches a row of books on the top shelf. I lift one down. Yes, all diaries.

I knew Vita had documented her travels over the years. She even mentioned once she might use her journals to write a memoir. The diary in my hand is from 1980, the year Mark was born. If Vita had planned to publish her work, surely it wouldn't hurt to dip into this volume? Feeling a shiver of apprehension, I flip open the pages.

I'm so lucky. I can't believe I deserve such happiness. I was not prepared for the love I'd feel for my son. I'd do anything, anything for him. Motherhood may signal the end of my career, but I can live with that. Mark is the most wonderful gift…

Vita had delighted in becoming a mother, even though it meant the end of her career. I experience a pang of guilt. She was a far better mother than me. I close the diary and slide the book back on the shelf before selecting another – 1984. Settling myself in Vita's armchair, I read.

> *Nduka works so hard. He's a good man and I should be grateful, but I wish he'd pay me and Mark just a little attention. The boy needs a father and I need a husband. It's five years since he came to my bed. Does he even find me desirable?*

My cheeks burn. I shouldn't be reading this, but I'm unable to stop. It sounds as if Nduka, like Mark, was a workaholic. The gap between him and Vita was clearly widening.

> *Tonight, I dressed prettily but Nduka didn't notice. Oh, the shame! I can't write the words – and yet I must. Tonight, I tried to seduce my husband, but he shunned me. I'm such a failure. He doesn't love me anymore. Did he only perform his conjugal duties to gain a son?*

When did Nduka leave? I'd always wondered what made him abandon Vita and Mark. I skim forward a few pages.

> *We don't deserve this. Nduka is my
> husband and Mark's father. We deserve better.*

Her words reflect bitterness, as her affection and love for Nduka shifts into something else. Is this what it will be like for me and Mark? Is this where we're heading? We've had eight years together. Perhaps that's the limit for love between a couple. Perhaps I should be grateful for what we've had…

'Hanna.' Mark's calling me from the kitchen. Tucking the diary under my jumper, I run back to the house.

———

Once dinner's over and Ike's in bed, I settle down in the snug with the diary.

> *I have my suspicions that Nduka is having
> an affair. It isn't the first time. He returned
> to Nigeria before me and quickly developed a
> circle of admirers. By the time he sent for
> Mark and I, he was established and well
> respected…*

I flip over a few pages.

> *I find it so difficult to fit in. The other
> wives have already formed cliques. I'm always
> on the outside looking in. Nduka assures me
> he's not up to his old tricks. When I first
> met DS…*

My heart races. DS? She can't mean Deòiridh Skinner? I continue reading.

...I was not worried. True, she's beguiling and spell-bindingly beautiful, but I believed her to be out of Nduka's league. He's so much older. But then how old is she? I'm not sure anyone really knows.

Deòiridh couldn't have been Nduka's mistress. This happened years ago. And yet, Vita comments on DS's age…

They spend so much time together, but if I act the jealous wife, things will not end well. Instead, I attempt to become her friend. But I quickly realise DS needs no friends. She's intelligent, influential and completely self-sufficient. DS needs neither man nor woman…

A tear plops onto the page and I realise I'm crying. Will Mark repeat the sins of his father?

CHAPTER FIFTY-FIVE

Mark staggers into the kitchen, panting.

'Good run?' I ask.

'Six kilometres,' he croaks, checking his Fitbit. 'Getting better.' He fills a glass with water and downs it in one.

'Well done.' This fitness fad is a new thing, but I can already see results. As I admire his toned biceps, I spot what looks like cling film on his upper arm. 'What's that?'

Mark grins. 'Tattoo. I've always wanted one.'

I feel a flutter of unease. 'That was a big decision.'

'Well, I got to thinking' – he brings his elbow across his chest, stretching his triceps – 'I'll be forty soon and…'

'Shouldn't we have discussed it first?' I interrupt.

He drops his arms. 'I don't tell you what you can and can't do.'

'Well, you do actually…' I mutter.

Mark opens the fridge and takes out oat milk, blueberries and spinach to make a smoothie.

'Let's have a look then,' I say, attempting to keep the mood jovial. I peer through the film covering. 'Some sort of weird eye, isn't it? Looks like an Egyptian hieroglyph.'

He adds the ingredients to the liquidiser. 'Kind of.'

'But what does it mean?'

He fits the lid and hits the start button.

I raise my voice to be heard above the noise. 'What made you do it?'

'Do what thou wilt…' Mark yells back.

———

I sit in the clearing, staring at the Mowgli statue. It always reminds me of Ike, raised by Mark and I as our own.

Although Mowgli's curled up, he's not asleep and he's wearing a wary expression. Who wouldn't be with a wolf to mind you, but I notice he's not actually looking at the wolf. He's frightened by something else.

I get up and move closer, bending so my face is level with his. Nothing there. Just a lone pink marsh orchid hidden in the long grass. Perhaps he's scared of the woods. I glance around at the benevolent but now damaged figure of Father Eduardo. I knew Mark wouldn't prioritise the repair. Surely it would make more sense to have Mowgli facing the monk, gratefully acknowledging his benefactor, but it's as if the child hasn't noticed Father Eduardo. I take a few backward steps away from Mowgli and glance back. From this angle, the terror on the child's face is palpable.

Ouch. I bend to rub my ankle. I really should look where I'm going. But what caused me to stumble? Some sort of paving stone with a jagged edge. Reaching down, I tug away the ivy. A plinth and, carved into the limestone, words. *Father Eduardo. Born 15th April 1808. Died 12 October 1875.*

———

As soon as I get back to the house, I rush into the snug and scan the top shelf of the cabinet. Where are the gardening journals and architectural books? They've been replaced by a selection of oversized china vases.

I hurry through to the office. 'Mark, what happened to the old books in the glass cabinet?'

'What?' His brows knit together. 'How should I know?'

I feel like I've been slapped.

Jenna glances up. She gestures towards the door and mouths, 'Give me a minute.' A few moments later she follows me into the kitchen. 'Sorry, it's my fault.'

'What is?'

'When you had that fall you mentioned Norris might like the old gardening books. Remember you said something about him massacring the garden? Anyway, I told him about them and he asked if he could borrow them.'

'You had no right.'

Jenna's cheeks colour. 'I'm sorry. I thought you intended them for him? He's only borrowed them. I'll get them back.'

I sigh. 'Okay.'

'I'm glad you're getting back into research.' She smiles. 'It's good for you.'

———

Next morning, Jenna arrives lugging a big canvas bag. 'Here you go.' She hefts the bag onto the kitchen island. 'Safely returned.'

'Thanks.' I unzip the bag and peek inside.

'Fancy coming to lunch with the board of trustees tomorrow?'

I hesitate. 'Is it okay with Mark?'

'Sure. He asked me to invite you.'

'Will Deòiridh be there?'

'No, she's in Paris. Didn't Mark tell you?'

I'd been worried my renewed closeness with Mark was waning, but perhaps he was just busy yesterday and is now trying to make amends. Kwami babbles in his bouncy chair and I smile. 'That would be great. I just have to figure out what to wear.'

'Did Mark give you an update on Sorrel Jordan?'

'No?'

'It seems her miscarriage brought things to a head. Apparently, she and her mum are getting on much better. Her GP's got her on a new drugs trial for the epilepsy and she's going to start a Foundation Course at Art College in the fall.'

'Oh, I'm really pleased.' I wonder if Will's still on the scene. Sorrel might not have shared all her secrets…

Jenna heads back to the office, leaving me unpacking the books. Some are instructional – when to prune, how to identify plants, Latin names, etc. Norris probably enjoyed looking through them.

I soon locate the one I want, a maintenance log, the front part filled with records of work undertaken – chimneys swept, stairs replaced, work completed in the chapel. The last quarter of the book consists of architectural designs for different sections of the garden.

Kwami emits a high-pitched squeal.

'Okay, I won't be long,' I murmur, thumbing through the pages. An original plan for the Italian Garden… sketches of the folly… an itemised list of the statues… Here it is, the layout for the tableau in the woods. I examine the design closely. Why did they move Father Eduardo's statue? And why does Mowgli look so scared of him?

CHAPTER FIFTY-SIX

The AIWASS trustees are not due to arrive until ten a.m. so I have plenty of time to drop the boys at nursery and preschool. When I return, two corporate vehicles are parked on the drive and Jenna's in the kitchen making coffee.

'The bigwigs are here then?' I whisper, as if they might overhear me.

'Did you see those cars?' Jenna whistles. 'Mercedes SUVs… someone's making some serious dosh.'

'Where are they now?'

'Mark's schmoozing them with a grand tour. They're coming back for refreshments before we leave.'

The front door opens and Mark calls from the hallway. 'Jenna?'

She winks at me before picking up the tray and heading for the office.

I hurry upstairs to get changed. I've decided on a blue shirtdress that I haven't worn since before my pregnancy, and I'm delighted to find it fits. After checking my hair and refreshing my lip gloss, I make my way downstairs and hover in the hallway.

Eventually the office door opens. Stefan and the other trustees amble out, lingering in the corridor to admire the artwork.

'Splendid portraits,' one of the gentlemen remarks.

'Isn't that Crowley?' says another.

'Yes,' Mark answers, 'and this one here is my father, Nduka Konteh.' Spotting me, Mark gestures in my direction. 'And, for those of you who haven't met her, this is my wife, Hanna.'

One of the VIPs extends his hand. 'Wilson Barnes. Pleased to meet you.'

Is it my imagination or does he lick his lips?

Mark steps between me and the visitors. 'We'd better get going. The table's booked for half past.'

We're ushered out to the vehicles and Isaac opens the rear door of a Mercedes. 'In you get, ladies.'

Jenna and I exchange a glance before clambering aboard.

'You ladies all right back there?' he asks as we pull away from the house.

'Yes, thank you,' I reply.

He catches my eye in the driver's mirror and winks. Jenna rolls her eyes.

When we arrive at *The Pig and Whistle*, I'm surprised to see Temi. He comes over to greet us and shakes hands with the visitors before planting a kiss on my cheek. 'Long time, no see.'

'I didn't know you were joining us,' I say.

'Mark's entertaining the big guns today,' Temi whispers. 'I'm here for moral support. Catch up later?'

At the table, I'm introduced to the remaining trustees. Alun Stephens smiles politely, while Sebastian Goff barely acknowledges my presence.

Stefan pats the chair next to him. 'Come and sit here, my dear.'

Not wanting to offend, I squeeze through and take the seat between him and Wilson Barnes, who seems fixated on my post-pregnancy cleavage.

'Alwyn will be sorry not to have met you.' Wilson's eyes glint. 'He always appreciates a pretty face.'

'He couldn't make it?' I inquiry politely.

'Prior engagement, I understand. More wine?' Stefan tops my glass to the rim.

The waiter grovels attentively as we work our way through starters and mains, and I lose count of how many bottles of wine are consumed. I hope the police won't be out patrolling for drink-drivers.

During dessert, Isaac produces cigars and I struggle with the smog for a while before pushing aside my cheesecake. 'Would you please excuse me?'

The men shuffle their chairs to let me out. After a quick stop in the Ladies, I head through the side door and into the pub garden in search of fresh air when I spot Temi outside on a bench.

He smiles. 'You escaped too.'

I wave a hand in front of my face. 'Too muggy in there.'

He shuffles along the seat to make room. 'How are you?'

'Better.' I sit down. 'Actually, things have been good lately.'

'I'm glad to hear it.'

From inside comes a loud guffaw, followed by a chorus of booming laughter. I gesture towards the pub door. 'They seem to be enjoying themselves.'

'Undoubtedly.' Temi raises an eyebrow. 'And all on you and your husband.'

I wince, hoping the investment will be worthwhile. 'What does AIWASS even mean?'

Temi shrugs. 'I don't know that it stands for anything much. You've possibly noticed the word spells out the initials of their Christian names?'

'Oh, I see.' I laugh, counting the men off on my fingers. 'Alun, Isaac, Wilson, Alwyn, Sebastian and Stefan.'

Temi nods.

'At least no Deòiridh today.'

He shoots me a look. 'She had to go to Paris. A last-minute thing, but she'll be back in a few days.'

So, if she'd been available, I wouldn't have been invited? I swallow down a sob. 'I've been reading some of her work.'

'She's very knowledgeable.'

'I found a report on the mutilation of albino children in Tanzania.'

A muscle flexes in Temi's cheek.

'Is that why we managed to adopt Ike? Because of his vitiligo? Did you pull strings?'

'I'm not sure I should…'

'Mark said Ike was in danger, but I never understood why. Reading that report…' I shudder.

'African witch doctors consider albinos to be special. Their body parts are believed to bring wealth and good luck.'

My hand flies to my mouth. 'No!'

'Every year, albino kids are picked off the streets. Later, dismembered bodies are found, missing limbs, hair and teeth. Even genitals hacked off with machetes.'

'Please, stop!'

'I have personally been involved in the transportation of two children to Philadelphia for treatment to horrific injuries,' he continues. 'One was fitted with prosthetic limbs. What is even more shocking is some of the parents collaborate, believing their children to be cursed.'

I cover my ears with my hands.

'Don't ask me to apologise for pulling strings.' Temi gets up, his eyes sparking with anger. 'I will continue to use fair means or foul to help such unfortunate children.' He turns and strides back into the pub.

My cheeks feel flushed, so I give it a couple of minutes before following him inside. I hang back as he says farewell to the guests.

Mark returns from the bar, having settled the bill. I dread to think what it cost. He claps his godfather on the back. 'I have a fine bottle of Cognac back at *The Sanctuary*. Can I tempt you?'

'That's very good of you, Mark,' Stefan replies, 'but if it's all the same, I think we'll hit the road.'

The visitors divide themselves between the two SUVs and we wave them off, before Jenna and I climb into Mark's Range Rover to head for home.

On the journey, I replay Temi's words in my head. I've never seen him so angry.

Back at *The Sanctuary*, Jenna excuses herself. 'Think I need a little siesta after all that wine.'

'Good idea.' I turn to Mark. 'I'll just go and check on the boys.'

He places an arm tenderly around my shoulders. 'They're fine. Cathy can manage. Come and relax.' Taking my hand, he leads me into the snug. 'Baileys?'

'Oh, go on then.' I sink into the couch while he pours the drinks.

He hands me a glass before setting his brandy down on the side table and focusing his attention on an old-fashioned record player, his latest acquisition.

'I thought you were holding out for one with a *His Master's Voice* horn,' I tease.

'I'm still on the lookout, but this does the job for now.'

I grin. He's so chuffed with his eBay win.

Mark extracts the vinyl from the *Hunky Dory* album sleeve, blows on it and sets it on the turntable. Moments later, Bowie blasts out from the speakers. '*Ch-ch-changes…*'

'Oh, I love this one.' I tuck my legs up under me, tapping my hand on the arm of the couch.

Mark picks up his glass and sits beside me. I snuggle up against him, sipping my drink. This feels so nice.

As Bowie launches into *Life on Mars*, I pull away, reaching for the book on the side table. 'What's this?'

'It's one of my father's.'

'I didn't think you kept any of his books?'

'I didn't. Deòiridh gave it to me. She borrowed it some time ago and obviously couldn't return it, so gave it to me.'

I sit up straighter and examine the cover. 'What is it?'

Mark takes it from me. '*The Book of the Law* by Aleister Crowley.'

'Isn't he one of the portraits in the red corridor?

'Yes. It's interesting actually and might be right up your street. Crowley writes about a belief system called Thelema. It's over a hundred years old, but very far reaching…'

'I'm surprised you're interested in an ancient belief system.'

Mark hesitates a moment, and I fear I've said the wrong thing, but he smiles indulgently. 'Crowley was very popular in the sixties.' he explains. 'His philosophy advocated pursuit of an individual's will. Many musicians credit him with the development of their art. John Lennon as well as David Bowie. And Jimmy Page, the guitarist from *Led Zeppelin,* was so taken with his views that he bought Crowley's old house in Scotland.'

'Is that where *The Beatles'* transcendental influences came from? I always thought that was George?'

'No, I think that's something different. Although Crowley did believe in reincarnation.' Mark laughs. 'Deòiridh thinks Kwami might be a reincarnation of Dad.'

I shiver. We never did have a second funeral for Nduka. Could his spirit be in torment? Could Kwami be... no, don't go there.

Mark reaches down to the stack of albums beside his chair and retrieves *Sgt Pepper*. 'Look at this.'

I slide closer.

'Now...' He studies the album sleeve. 'There he is. Back row, next to Mae West.'

'Crowley or your dad?' I jest, wanting to hang on to this funny, good-humoured Mark.

'Crowley, silly.'

I stare intently. 'The bald guy?'

'Yes.' Mark strokes the album cover affectionately. 'Who'd have thought my father was a fan.'

Fan of *The Beatles* or Crowley?

CHAPTER FIFTY-SEVEN

I unload my shopping bag onto the kitchen island. 'I thought I'd make something nice for tonight,' I say, stowing prawns and seabass in the fridge.

Mark glances up from the newspaper. 'I won't be here, will I?'

'Oh? Where are you then?'

'I told you. I'm picking up Deòiridh from the airport.'

'I don't think you did. I didn't even know she was coming back.'

He folds his paper. 'Of course she's coming back. All her stuff is here. Her flight lands at six. Don't worry about supper. We'll stop off for something on the way home.' He lays the newspaper on the table and strolls out of the room.

I drop into a chair and put my head in my hands. Bugger, bugger, bugger. Just when I thought Mark and I were on track, that bloody woman comes back into our lives.

Mr Biggles rubs himself against my ankles. I lift him onto my lap. His purr is comforting but it's not enough. Have Mark and Deòiridh been in touch the whole time she's been away?

Mark's in the kitchen unpacking a box.

'What's that?' I ask as he pulls out a chunk of polystyrene.

'New coffee machine.' He lifts a black Tassimo from the box and plugs it in at the wall.

'You'll do Jenna out of a job.' I chuckle.

He plays around pushing the buttons. 'Bloody thing…'

'Here, let me.' I remove a piece of packaging wedged under the lid. 'You probably need to run it through a couple of times with water first.'

'Christ's sake.' He slams his fist down on the counter.

I flinch. He's been short tempered since Deòiridh returned.

'Sorry.' He steps back.

I lift out the water holder and fill it under the tap. 'Where's Jenna, anyway?' When he doesn't reply, I turn to face him. 'Has something happened?'

'Jenna's gone.'

'Gone?' My hand shakes as I insert the plastic disk, click down the lid and press the start button. 'Gone where?'

He shrugs. 'I had to let her go.'

'Jenna?' I repeat.

Mark's attempting to open a packet of coffee pods. 'Turns out she wasn't as honest as we thought.'

'What do you mean?'

He takes a knife from the drawer. 'The missing equipment. Video camera, screen, MacBook.'

I feel sick. 'Jenna wouldn't do that.'

'I called her out on it.' He stabs angrily at the plastic wrapping. 'She's lucky I didn't involve the police.'

'Are you sure it's not a mistake?'

His nostrils flare. 'Quite sure. I don't know why you're so bothered. I didn't think there was much love lost between the two of you lately.' He drops the knife and tugs at the packet so hard that it rips and coffee pods spill. 'Damn it!'

'Why don't you let me sort this?'

Mark turns on his heels, immediately tripping over Mr Biggles. 'Bloody cat.' He strides down the corridor to his office.

I slam my hands down on the worktop. Damn. I bet Deòiridh had something to do with this.

CHAPTER FIFTY-EIGHT

A telephone call comes through on the hands-free. I hit the button. 'Hello?'

'Hanna? It's Temi.'

'Oh.' We haven't spoken since he got bolshy at the pub. 'Hi.'

'How are you?'

'Up and down.'

'Can you talk?'

'Yes, although I'm not sure how stable the line will be as I'm on my way to visit Vita.'

'You're in the car?'

'Yes.'

'Let's hope the signal holds. How's Vita doing?'

'No change. Did you know Jenna had left?'

'No, I didn't. That's a bit sudden.'

'Yes, and it seems not completely amicable. Where are you, anyway?'

'Attending a seminar in North Wales. Guess who I bumped into over dinner last night?'

'No idea.'

'Alwyn Williams.'

'Alwyn… oh, the trustee who didn't show for the lunch?'

'Yes. We had a few drinks and he confided in me. There's been a bit of a falling out with the other members of the board.'

'What about?'

'Some sort of ceremony Deòiridh's organising. Hold on, I wrote it down…' There's a rustle of paper. '*The Hermetic Brethren of Molech*. Apparently, the trustees are members of a secret society. Deòiridh invited them to a private function last week at *Tredeger House*.'

'Where's that?'

'South Wales. Three of the trustees live close by. It's run by the *National Trust* but used to be owned by the Morgan family. Have you heard of Evan Morgan, the Black Monk?'

'No?'

'He was a contemporary of Crowley.' Temi sighs. 'I think Deòiridh's a bit of a magpie, gathering ideas from this and that belief system and adapting them to fit her own personal truths. She wrote… to…' The line stammers before dropping out.

'Damn,' – I bang the steering wheel – 'I've lost you. Hello?'

'Hello?'

'Sorry, I went under some trees. You were saying?'

'Yes, Deòiridh wrote to the trustees threatening that if they didn't perform certain acts, they'd be thrown off the board.'

'How come she has a say about who's on the board?'

'I've no idea. Anyway, they all turned up. Alwyn said after dinner things got weird when Deòiridh commanded them to go home and make an animal sacrifice.'

'What?'

'Alwyn thought it was a joke, until she contacted him direct saying she wanted proof of death. And it couldn't be some random wild animal. He was supposed to sacrifice a creature he loved. His pet dog, for Christ's sake.'

'That's crazy.'

'Alwyn said that's not what he signed up for. He refused to do it.'

'Good for him.'

'Yes. He told her to go ahead and throw him off the board, but he's really cut up about it. I'd better get back. I'm due in the lecture theatre in ten minutes, but I wanted to let you know.'

'Thanks Temi.'

'And Hanna? If Deòiridh's back at *The Sanctuary*, be careful.'

Vita's asleep when Kwami and I arrive, so I set Kwami down and tidy Vita's bedside table. A note is propped against the water jug and the envelope bears my name. I tear it open.

Dear Hanna

I didn't want to leave without speaking with you, but Mark insisted I go immediately.

I want you to know that whatever they're saying, it's not true. I hope you know I'd never repay you by stealing from you.

I suspect it was Deòiridh who stitched me up. She's never liked me and wanted me out of the way.

I had no choice but to go. Mark said he'd call the police if I didn't leave the premises and Deòiridh said she'd make sure I never work again.

Hanna, please, take care of yourself. I'm not sure what the two of them are cooking up, but I fear it's nothing good.

Stay safe, you and the boys.

Your friend,

Jenna x

CHAPTER FIFTY-NINE

'See you later,' calls Mark.

I run into the hallway, just as he and Deòiridh are heading out through the front door. 'Where are you two off to?'

Mark answers with his hand on the door jamb. 'Lunch with prospective clients in Ipswich.' He sighs. 'I did tell you.'

'Oh, did you? Will you be back in time for Ike's bedtime story?'

He waves dismissively. 'Sure.'

As soon as they've gone, I hurry along to Mark's office and locate his MacBook. A quick scan of the search history reveals he's been perusing translated transcripts from a series of video interviews carried out by Deòiridh in Uganda.

In the first, she interviews the local schoolteacher:

DS – Tell me what made you aware of this practice?

Teacher – A child found in the next village, his head and private parts missing.

DS – That's when it became closer to home?

Teacher – Yes, but it was when one of our own children was found bleeding in the bushes, castrated but still alive, that we started our crusade against child sacrifice.

Child sacrifice? I scroll through an investigative report for *Anthropology Magazine.* It includes an interview with a former witch doctor, reputed to have murdered many children:

I was left alone with the child. I brought a sharp knife, like a guillotine, down on his neck.

I shudder.

Statistics follow, detailing the number of children who have disappeared. Also, a transcript of an interview with the Minister of Ethics and Integrity. In it, he admits to believing in spirits, but disapproves of his ministers consulting with them. Clearly the Ugandan government is trying to respond, but not fast enough. Officially there have been two dozen ritual killings in the past year, but further comments by an aid worker suggest the number is much higher, with not all cases followed up. There are extracts from the reports:

A three-year-old boy's body found horribly mutilated – organs, liver, pancreas and heart missing, his left hand hacked off; a four-year-old in a pool of blood with his penis cut off; an eighteen-month-old girl with her throat slit. Villagers blame the witch doctors. Parents take their children everywhere with them. General panic is rife, and no one has been convicted over recent cases.

Appalled, I click on another link - an interview with a survivor who escaped:

Men grabbed me and carried me to a shrine in the woods. The witch doctor (a woman) shouted at the men, and they laid me down on the ground and ripped off my clothes. The witch doctor got very angry. She hit me with a stick. Then they let me go and I ran.

The police report suggested the boy was lucky he didn't meet the witch doctor's standards. He'd been circumcised so, in her eyes, was blemished. Many villagers were now having their sons circumcised and their daughters' ears pierced, to offer them some protection.

I gag. It's barbaric that this sort of thing happens in the world today and, according to these reports, ritual killings are on the increase.

After drying my eyes, I continue reading:

Some people believe that if the bodies of children are buried under new buildings, their company will be become powerful and wealthy. The sacrifice of children is also used as part of the initiation for new witch doctors... blood spilled from a child and squirted into the face of the initiate allows the spirit to enter and gives them power.

The report ends with a graphic account of a visit to a witch doctor, who explains how clients bring him human body parts – heart, liver, blood of a child – as food for the spirits. He acts as go-between, taking the clients into the woods, where they deposit the human remains.

I click back on the search history and find another paper written by Deòiridh. This one about the Inca's cultural ritual of Capacocha:

It is considered an honour to be selected as a sacrifice to the gods. The ceremony is more humane than African prac-tice. Children need to be healthy, strong, beautiful and of high status. For the ceremony, the child is dressed in fine clothes and adorned with jewels, before being given an intoxicating drink. Some are killed by strangulation, some by a blow to the head, others are buried alive...

I stop reading and close the MacBook. How can Deòiridh write about this stuff?

By six p.m. Mark and Deòiridh are still not back, so I bath the boys and let Ike play for a while. He flicks through his books and yawns.

'Time for bed, little man,' I say.

'But Daddy said he'd read to me,' he wails, clambering into bed.

'Daddy's working, but I'll read to you.'

I tuck him in and begin to read, but he's asleep before I get to the third page.

'Let's see if you can be as good as your brother,' I say to Kwami as I sit in the armchair to give him his bedtime bottle. After I've burped him, I lay him down in his cot. He sucks noisily on his dummy. Vita never approved of a comforter, but it's the only way I can get him to settle. I sigh. One day, perhaps I'll have the patience to rock him to sleep in my arms. I switch off the central light and turn on their night-time stars. If Ike wakes to darkness, he yells.

I tiptoe across the room. '*Soar away raven…*' comes from outside. Fearful the singing might disturb the boys, I softly close their door behind me.

'Spirit and ghoul…' Padding lightly along the landing, I glance upstairs to the second floor and shudder. I haven't ventured up there since finding Ike on the roof.

The song calls me on. '*Eerie the portent…*' Unclipping the rope, I place a foot on the bottom step and ascend. Halfway up, moonlight streams in through the window. I gaze out. Not moonlight but a strange orb, suspended a few inches from the glass. *'Chills to your soul…'*

I rub the pane. What the hell is it? Some sort of drone? Is it watching me? I duck behind the curtain and lean against the wall, my heart racing. Get a grip. I take a few deep breaths and when I peer out again, it's gone. It must have been a reflection. I close the drapes and head downstairs.

I'm almost at my bedroom door when the tune starts again. *'Poor little songbird...'* I hurry into my room and retrieve my mobile phone from the charger before climbing the stairs again.

'Smothered in bed...' What sort of creepy lullaby is this? Hardly daring to breathe, I alight on the landing. I've come so far; I must go on. *'Even a bird song...'* I tiptoe along, listening at each door. The builders have made the roof water-tight and the structure sound, but floorboards are missing and I'm grateful for my phone torch.

The last room is the one that's a duplicate of my own. I push open the door and shine the torch. It's in a fearful state, musty with strips of mouldy wallpaper hanging from damp walls. *'Can't wake the dead.'* As I cross the floor and step into the linked turret room, the singing stops. I pause as if playing musical statues.

The tiny space is empty. Even the workmen's tools have gone. Over by the window, smudged footprints bear witness to Ike's episode on the roof. I stand still, engulfed in sadness, for the room's replica, the pretty space below, should have been my daughter's nursery. But then, as the wave of sorrow washes over me, it cleanses, leaving behind a residue of peace and calm.

CHAPTER SIXTY

'And into downward-facing dog.' The yoga teacher demonstrates on all fours.

Placing my palms on the mat, I push up into my hips.

'Spread those fingers and toes.'

Before being fired, Jenna had gushed with enthusiasm about the yoga instructor she'd managed to secure. 'He's a real Buddhist monk, you'll love him.'

'Oh, I don't know.' I'd groaned. 'Walking is more my thing.'

'Walking's fine when the weather's good, but what about on cold, wintery days? Yoga sessions in the chapel couldn't be more convenient. You need to relax, and we could do with an insider's take on the quality of his teaching.'

The first half hour is fine although, from the individual attention the yoga instructor pays me, I find it hard to believe this athletic thirty-something is really a monk. Nevertheless, concentrating on getting my body to stretch and adapt into the yoga postures requires focus. I shoot surreptitious glances at the bunch of sprightly sixty-somethings making up the rest of the class. Their bodies are so much more flexible than my own. Heaven knows what I'll be like when I'm their age.

'Now, into the cross-legged position – *padmasana* – for the breathing exercises. Breathe in – one, two, three, four, and hold the breath in… then breathe out – one, two, three, four. That's good. Now, in your own time…'

I try to concentrate on counting, but my mind wanders. Since Deòiridh returned, Mark's closed himself off and, with Sorrel, Jenna and Temi all gone, I feel very alone.

'Now *savasana*, or corpse pose. Let your feet flop out and your hands open towards the ceiling. Close your eyes…'

The stillness and quiet is an invitation for bad thoughts to crowd back in, and I sense my old anxieties returning. How long before they become full paranoia once more? Counting breaths was better than this. I open my eyes. My mat's situated in an alcove near the stained-glass windows. Trying not to move my head and attract the instructor's attention, I let my eyes rove and count gargoyles on the ceiling. *One, two, three…* I stare at their grotesque faces. Who would position these ugly faces along the cornice of such a beautiful room? Perhaps we could have them boxed in? No, Mark would never agree. What on earth are they doing indoors, anyway? Aren't they supposed to be on the outside of houses to ward off evil spirits? *Eleven, twelve, thirteen.* That can't be right. I count again. Thirteen. I turn my head towards the other side of the room and count the faces grinning down. Thirteen.

Sitting up, I twist around to check the back wall, but a giant fresco takes up the whole space. No gargoyles. I turn back to the front where, in olden days, the altar resided. Just a plain piece of coving.

Realising the yoga instructor has his eyes on me, I mouth, 'Sorry,' and get up. Loosely rolling my yoga mat, I dump it down beside him as I leave the chapel. Twenty-six gargoyles. That's not right.

Hurrying into the snug, I drag a chair across to the bookcase and grab the book I'd been looking at a few days before. I flick through the hand-written log showing work planned for the gardens in 1852, along with details of maintenance work that had taken place in the monastery. The monks were nothing if not meticulous record keepers. I quickly find what I'm looking for.

For maintenance work in the chapel. Repair work to the altar rail and small repairs as necessary to thirty gargoyles. Mr F Sinclair.

So where are the other four gargoyles?

I head back to the chapel and pace up and down outside. Although the class has ended, the students seem in no hurry to leave, wandering out at a leisurely pace and bestowing enlightened greetings on everyone. The instructor is last, acknowledging me with a curt, 'Namaste'.

Pushing open the door, I stand in the middle of the floor. Turning slowly, I check what I already know to be true. Thirteen gargoyles positioned either side of the chapel, all evenly placed and matching each other. None on the back wall and none on the front. I realise the front wall is a new addition and move closer to give it a tap. Hollow, a panel wall blocking off a section of the chapel. I head back through the door and out into the corridor.

Idiot, I think, staring at the toilet block. When the monastery became a hotel, they must have used a section of the chapel to create the powder room.

I step inside. Three cubicles, plus a double vanity unit, all to the left of the doorway. That leaves a small section of the old chapel, perhaps two meters square, unaccounted for. Why have I never noticed the discrepancy? I tap the right-hand wall and find it to be hollow too.

Returning to the corridor, I ignore the disapproving faces looking down from ornate frames and examine the wooden panelling behind them. The dark polished sections, almost black with age, run vertically and I slide my fingertips across the joins. Perfectly flush. Stepping back, I stare at the paintings once more. Since Vita's stroke, no one has supervised the cleaners and their work has become tardy. I move closer, peering at finger marks disturbing dust on the frame of the Crowley portrait. Standing on tiptoe, I reach behind the painting and discover a keyhole.

In the evening, I leave Mark and Deòiridh in the snug sharing a bottle of malt whiskey, but instead of going up to bed, I hide in the powder room. I lock the door of the cubicle and perch on the toilet seat with my feet resting on a pipe.

An hour passes with nothing happening, and I'm cold and stiff. Just as I'm about to give up and go to bed, the snug door opens. Light footsteps outside. The sound of a key in a lock…

After five minutes I come out. The secret door is closed. I need the key.

CHAPTER SIXTY-ONE

'Back soon,' calls Cathy as she sets off on the nursery run.

'Okay.' I give it another fifteen minutes before creeping upstairs to Mark's bedroom. I know the coast will be clear, as he and Deòiridh went straight to his office after breakfast. I open up the cufflinks box, but there's no sign of a key. Nothing in the dresser or drawers either. Frustrated, I gaze about the room. His new cashmere jumper lays crumpled on the armchair and I pick it up to fold it. As my knuckles brush the soft wool, a musky fragrance tickles my nostrils. Patchouli – perfume favoured by sixties hippies. No prizes for guessing where that's come from. I place the neatly folded jumper down, my attention drawn to the moleskin trousers he wore yesterday. Nervously, I rifle through the pockets and extract a single key. I slide it into my jeans pocket, grab a pair of Mark's shoes and dash down to the kitchen.

Cathy's back, loading the dishwasher.

'I'm going out for a while,' I tell her, grabbing the car keys from the hook. 'I've chores to do in town. I can collect Kwami from nursery, but I won't be back in time for Ike. Could you pick him up from preschool at lunchtime?'

'Sure,' she answers. 'No problem.'

———————

In Hadleigh, I park in the market square and head straight for the shoe repairers where I hand over Mark's loafers. 'Soles and heels, please.'

'Thirty minutes?' says the cobbler.

'Thanks. Oh, and a copy of this.' I hand him the key.

I make my way to Crabtrees and purchase a latte. Sipping my drink, I watch the clock. Suppose Mark notices the key's missing?

Thirty-five minutes later, I'm back in the cobblers and handing over a twenty-pound note. 'Thank you.'

After collecting Kwami, I head home. I drive erratically, focused on getting the key back. Guiltily, I glance at the baby in the car seat. I don't usually speed with the kids.

As I turn into our gate, I catch sight of something yellow. Slamming my foot on the brakes, I unbuckle my seatbelt and climb out of the Citroën. I swear it was a child, but Ike doesn't have a yellow mac. Moving over to the bushes, I part the branches, peeping in and poking around. Nothing there – no sign of anyone.

I get back into the car, release the handbrake and continue up the drive. I'm almost at the house when I notice Ike's bicycle on the gravel. I brake sharply. The car skids. There's a horrible crunching sound. I step out of the car to find the balance bike wedged under the front bumper.

'Oh no!' cries Cathy. She and Ike are sitting on the front steps.

'The bike shouldn't have been out here,' I snap. 'Ike's not allowed to ride on the drive.'

Cathy's face pales. 'I didn't know.'

I turn back to the car and lift Kwami from his car seat. Shifting him onto my hip, I grab my handbag from the footwell. As I head for the front door, Cathy bends down to Ike. 'Go inside and wash your hands, there's a good boy. I'll only be a moment.'

Ike runs into the house.

I glance at Cathy, expecting an apology.

She blinks, wiping a tear from her eye. 'You don't know how lucky you were. Five seconds earlier and it might have been Ike under your wheels.' Pulling a tissue from her sleeve, she blows her nose. 'I'd better go and do Ike's lunch.' She heads inside, leaving me on the steps glancing back down the drive. Whatever or whoever was in the bushes may have just saved Ike's life.

———

I join Cathy and Ike in the kitchen, feeling relieved now that I've returned the key. 'I see that Mark's car's gone,' I say to Cathy. 'Did he say when he'd be back?'

She still looks shaken after Ike's near miss. 'Not until late, I think. He said they wouldn't be back for a meal.'

'I can look after the boys this afternoon, if you like,' I suggest, while taking a baby bottle from the fridge. 'Why don't you get off a little earlier?' I pop the bottle in the microwave.

'Don't you want me to make your dinner?'

'I'll probably just have a jacket potato with Ike.'

She gives a small smile. 'Well, if you're sure.'

With the boys in bed, I grab a torch and make my way into the corridor. Sliding the Crowley portrait to one side, I put the key in the lock. It's stiff, but after a couple of attempts it turns. Cautiously, I pull the door open and step inside, immediately stumbling on the uneven floor. I switch on the torch. The beam illuminates a trap door. I tug at the handle, but it won't budge. Shining the torch around the perimeter, I discover it's bolted. I grip the torch between my teeth and wriggle the rusty bolt until it finally slides free. I swing open the hatch and shine light down into the darkness revealing a ladder.

Securing the hatch to a hook on the wall, I cautiously lower myself down the hole. The rungs seem endless, but eventually my feet touch firm ground. Stepping off the ladder, I shine the torch. What is this place? A basement with stone floor and walls. Is it some sort of catacomb or crypt? I shiver. It's cool rather than damp, and much larger than the chapel above, with numerous pillars dividing the space into smaller areas.

Ahead, the crypt opens into a central chamber. To one side stands a large stone table. I move closer and run my fingers across the surface. The edge is engraved with some sort of hieroglyphic design. Beside the table are two metal buckets. I shine torchlight into them. Nothing, although the bottom of one is coated with a dark brown residue. I sniff a metallic smell. Blood?

Reeling back in shock, I bump into a camera set upon a tripod. It must be the videoing equipment hired for the conference. So, Jenna didn't steal it after all, but what's it doing down here? I right the tripod and step into another circular space with chalk markings on the floor – two triangles, one above the other with symbols at each tip. Animals perhaps, but none I can distinguish.

On the far wall is a curtained nook. I'm drawn to it as if bewitched. I approach cautiously, lift the curtain, and scream. A grotesque horned beast stares back, nostrils flaring and eyes of darkest red.

Staggering away from the mask, I race to the steps, hastily climb the ladder and slam the trap door. Stepping back through the secret door, I lock it and replace the painting.

Breathe. My heart rate slowly returns to normal. Outside, Mark's car sweeps into the courtyard. I dash upstairs, pull off my jeans and trainers and hurl myself under the quilt.

CHAPTER SIXTY-TWO

'Fancy spag bog for lunch?' I ask Mark, taking a packet of mince from the freezer.

He glances up from the newspaper. 'I won't be here.'

'Why? Where are you going?'

'Deòiridh and I have a business lunch.'

Again? I want to say, but I keep quiet.

Once Mark and Deòiridh have gone, I grab the master keys and head across to Caleb block. Cathy has the boys, so I don't need to worry about them. Casting cautious glances over my shoulder, I unlock Deòiridh's door and let myself in.

Unlike Mark's room, her apartment's immaculate and, apart from the complimentary bowl of fresh fruit on the table, you wouldn't know anyone was staying here. Not wanting to waste time, I hurry through to her bedroom. The bed has been made and her makeup neatly arranged on the dressing table.

On the bedside table are three books – *Dark Bayou: An Account of the Infamous Louisiana Homicides* and *Do What Thou Wilt: The Life of Aleister Crowley.* Do what thou wilt. Mark used those words when I challenged him about his tattoo. The third is a leather-bound Bible. The cover is water-damaged, and the speckled frontispiece reveals it to be a King James, dated 1875. It falls open at *The Book of Leviticus* where I find a piece of yellowed paper listing references. I run my fingers across the pages to locate the first: Lev 18:21 *'And thou shalt not let any of thy seed pass through the fire to Molech…'*

Molech? Wasn't that the name Temi mentioned? The Brethren of Molech?

Setting the Bible down, I turn my attention to the cupboard below where I discover a bundle of news clippings. I lift them out. The top ones relate to the story of the torso in the Thames. I thumb through. Odd words are circled in red pen – *Calabar bean* – also known as Doomsday, causing paralysis. Ground seeds from the *Datura plant* – a sedative.

Rifling further, I come across a photocopy. It's an extract from a book, a letter written by Crowley in 1945. An underlined section jumps out. *'It is absolutely essential to begin a magical diary, and keep it up daily… Begin with an account of your life, going back before your birth…'*

What? How can you keep a diary about the time before you were born? It must have intrigued Deòiridh though, as she's highlighted it. I wish I could find her magic diary. A bit further on she's asterisked, *'this will start you on a discovery of who you are, and eventually lead you to your recovering the memory of previous incarnations.'*

Previous incarnations? Is that what this is about? Past lives?

I flip the paper over. On the back has been sketched what looks like a family tree. The subject is Aleister Crowley. Deòiridh seems obsessed by him. The tree shows his parents, Edward Crowley and Emily Bertha Bishop. Also, his grandparents and great grandparents. Underneath someone has scribbled, *'Edward Crowley b. 12th October 1875, d. 1st*

December 1947. Father Eduardo b. 15th April 1808, d. 12th October 1875.' Father Eduardo? Does Deòiridh believe Crowley to be a reincarnation of the wicked old monk?

I shove everything back where I found it and move across to the wardrobe. As I open the door, I'm greeted by an earthy waft of familiar perfume. I suppose it's better than moth balls. In the bottom I find two more books, their titles impossible to translate.

Opening one, I flick through to a section of illustrations and gasp. The images are graphic. Black and white engravings, photographs and diagrams depicting horrific scenes of mutilation. The subjects look like something you might find in an abattoir - not animals but people, with limbs and joints labelled like cuts of meat. I gag.

Hurriedly, I replace the book and pick up the other. This one focuses on female genital mutilation. Terrible diagrams of women and photographs of pubescent children.

What sort of woman reads stuff like this? It must be illegal to have copies of such things. Are they the tools of her trade?

When I arrive in the kitchen, Cathy and Ike are having an early lunch while Kwami babbles in his bouncer.

Cathy glances up. 'Beans on toast? There's plenty.'

'No, I'm all right thanks.' I hunt through the cupboard to find the paracetamol.

'Headache again?' She winces. 'Why don't you have a lie down?'

I pour a glass of water and swallow two pills. 'I might just take a nap in the snug.'

The door opens and I sit up with a start.

Mark wanders into the room. 'There you are. Cathy mentioned you weren't feeling too good. Are you okay?'

I rub my temples. 'Bad head. I've taken paracetamol, but they haven't touched it.'

'Mark?' Deòiridh calls from the hallway.

'In here.' He perches on the edge of the couch.

She pokes her head around the door. 'Oh, hello Hanna.'

'Hanna has a headache.' Mark strokes my hair away from my forehead.

She frowns. 'Poor you. I know what that's like.'

'Have you got anything stronger than paracetamol?' he asks her.

'Of course.'

'How did lunch go?' I ask when she's gone.

'Fine. We made some good contacts.'

'Did you go back to *The Pig and Whistle*?'

'No, a new place. A golf hotel near Dedham Vale.'

Deòiridh returns. 'Here, take a couple of these. They'll soon sort you out.' She holds out a packet of pills and a glass of water.

They're blister packaged, but still I hesitate. 'Is it okay to mix these with my other pills?'

'They'll be fine,' says Mark. 'Deòiridh takes them all the time for migraines. Go upstairs and have a proper lie down. I'll get Cathy to stay on and mind the kids.'

CHAPTER SIXTY-THREE

My head feels like a lead weight. Disorientated, I haul myself to a sitting position. Those pills really knocked me out. How long have I been asleep? I check my mobile – three-fifteen a.m. Why hasn't Kwami woken up?

Swinging my legs out of bed, I stagger across to the ensuite and splash water onto my face before tiptoeing along the landing to the boys' room. Ike and Kwami are both sound asleep.

My throat's parched, so I head downstairs for a drink of water. After filling a glass from the faucet, I wander back into the hallway, tugging at the neck of my T-shirt. I'm so hot. I ease open the front door, trying to avoid the familiar creak. A fresh breeze wafts in around my knees. Ah, that's better. I blink, rubbing my eyes. There are three SUVs parked on the driveway. What the hell's going on?

I close the door softly and tiptoe towards Mark's office but, as I pass Crowley's portrait, I pause. The frame's crooked and the secret door slightly ajar. Surely they're not all down there?

I go inside. The trap door is closed but not bolted. I lift it open and secure the rope on the hook. A rhythmic echoey sound floats up from below.

Carefully, I ease myself through the hatch and down the ladder. When I step off the bottom rung, I creep silently forward and conceal myself behind a pillar.

I peek out. Robed figures sit in a circle, chanting in a strange language I don't recognise. Two of them shake wooden sticks with bells. The chanting builds as one of the figures stands and moves to the centre. Throwing back her hood, she reveals her auburn hair. Deòiridh.

She raises her arms. 'Welcome Brethren.' The chanting fades. 'Tonight,' she continues, 'we gather to initiate our newest member to the role of Adeptus Minor.' She beckons and one of the seated figures gets up. Head bowed, he stands before her.

Deòiridh places her hands on his shoulders. 'From this moment brother, you will be known by the name Azizi.'

The others whoop and applaud before rising to their feet to surround Deòiridh and the newly christened Azizi.

He pulls down his hood and I gasp. Mark.

Then everything goes black.

When I open my eyes, I'm lying on the couch in the snug with Mark leaning over me. I push him away. 'No.'

'Shh,' he says. 'Don't get so worked up.'

I struggle to sit upright. 'I've every right to be worked up. What was going on down there?'

He looks puzzled. 'Down where? You need to stay calm, Hanna. You're working yourself into a state.'

I spot movement across the room and Deòiridh steps from the shadows. She hands something to Mark.

'Here, have a nip of this.' He holds a hip flask to my lips.

'No.' I brush it away. 'Where are the children?'

'The children? Upstairs in bed, of course. It's you we're worried about. You've been sleep walking.'

I shove him hard. 'I have not been sleepwalking.' Glancing down, I realise I'm only wearing a T-shirt and knickers. My cheeks burn as I push past him to stagger across the room and out to the hallway. 'How do you explain this then?' I demand, tugging open the front door.

Mark and Deòiridh exchange a glance.

I turn and stare out into the night. Mark's Range Rover is the only vehicle on the driveway. My legs buckle and everything swims.

CHAPTER SIXTY-FOUR

Sunlight streams in through the window. I sit up, rubbing my eyes. What happened? Images flood back – robed men chanting in the basement, some sort of initiation ceremony, Deòiridh and Mark… was it a dream?

My mobile phone vibrates on the bedside table. I reach out and pick it up. 'Hello?'

'Hanna,' says Temi. 'I was worried when I didn't hear back from you. How is everything?'

'Not good.' I rub my forehead. 'I'm not sure I can tell what's real and what's not.' I swallow a sob. 'I don't know what's happening to me.'

'It's time you got out of there.'

'But why?'

'I can't explain, not over the phone, but you and the children need to leave tonight. Pack a bag. I'm coming to meet you.'

'Surely it can't be…'

'Listen. I'm afraid of what might happen. I'll meet you at the pub we went to that time for dinner. You remember?'

'*The Pig and Whistle*, yes, but I…'

'Hanna, it's important. There's a train from Cardiff just after four. I can be in Colchester by eight and I'll get a taxi to the pub. Meet me there. Bring the boys. And Hanna? Tell no one.'

'Okay.'

'I'll see you soon.'

I hang up and haul myself out of bed. Yesterday's clothes are heaped on a chair. I pull on jeans and a T-shirt, and creep along the landing to the boys' room. It's empty. Cathy must be minding them. Lifting a small wheelie case from the top of the wardrobe, I unzip it and set it down on Ike's bed, before opening drawers and piling in some of his clothes and favourite soft toys. Turning to Kwami's chest of drawers, I do the same – babygros, vests, jumpers, nappy wipes, a pack of disposable nappies. I'll have to buy more on the way. But on the way to where? I haven't a clue. I only know I must get the boys to safety.

I zip up the case and pad across to the door. The coast is clear, so I scoot back to my bedroom and stow it in my wardrobe.

Grabbing a rucksack, I fill it with a few of my own clothes and toiletries. What else? Passport. I stuff it into the side pocket of my bag, along with my driving licence, credit cards and the little cash I have. I don't have passports for the boys, but no matter.

I hide the rucksack with the wheelie case, close the wardrobe doors and head downstairs.

Mark glances over as I come into the room. 'Hi. How are you feeling?'

'Not great.' I join Cathy and Ike at the table.

'Show Mummy your dinosaur,' says Cathy.

Shyly, Ike turns the paper so I can admire his masterpiece.

'That's brilliant.' I force a smile. 'We need to put it up on the fridge.'

'Cathy' – Mark gives her one of his charming smiles – 'would you mind taking the boys upstairs?'

'Sure.' She lifts Kwami from his bouncer chair and takes Ike's hand. 'Come on, Ike. Shall we go and find your library books?'

Mark takes a seat opposite me. 'We need to talk about last night.'

I stare at him. 'It wasn't a dream.'

'You had a bit of an episode,' he continues.

'Did I?' My tone is non-committal.

'I've spoken to Tom. He's busy, but he can fit you in for a session tomorrow.'

I shrug.

'Hanna, did you hear what I said?'

'Yes,' I snap. 'You want me to see Tom again.'

'If you don't, we'll need to look at alternatives. Things can't go on like this.'

———

Mark's in his office for the rest of the day and Cathy has the boys, so I hide in the snug. At lunchtime, she brings me a sandwich and I eat half of it before closing my eyes again. My head's splitting.

Around six o'clock, Deòiridh's voice floats in from the hallway. Half an hour later Mark's Range Rover drives away. They've gone out to dinner. They're probably discussing me. What a problem I am and how to get rid of me.

At seven, Cathy pokes her head around the door. 'The

boys are tucked up in bed. Sound asleep, bless them. I'll be off now if that's okay?'

I lift my head from the cushion. 'Yes, of course. Thanks Cathy. I don't know what I'd have done without you today. I'm feeling pretty wretched.'

She frowns. 'You sure you'll be all right? Suppose they wake?'

'I'll be fine. Thanks Cathy.'

I hear the front door slam and give it another ten minutes before hurrying upstairs. Pulling a jumper over my T-shirt, I slip on my jacket and retrieve the bag and suitcase from the wardrobe. After a final scan of the room, I slide the rucksack on my back and wheel the case out onto the landing, making for the boys' room.

'Come on, Ike.' I shake his shoulder.

He sits up, rubbing his eyes. 'Read story?'

'Mummy will read later. Look, I'll put some books in your bag. Can you get up now? We're going on an adventure.'

Ike nods sleepily and clambers out of bed.

'There's a good boy.' I help him into his gilet and slide his Spider-Man bag onto his shoulders. 'You can bring Blue Bear.' I tuck the bear under his arm.

Kwami squirms as I lift him from the cot. 'You're nice and cosy in your sleepsuit, aren't you?' I place him on my hip and move onto the landing.

Ike yawns.

'Come on, Ike.' Picking up the wheelie case, I coax him slowly down the stairs. Once outside, I secure the children safely in their car seats and load rucksacks and case into the boot.

With a last glance at the house, I climb into the driver's seat, buckle my seat belt and start the ignition. Steadily, I steer the Citroën out through the iron gates and along narrow lanes towards *The Pig and Whistle*. I'll be early, but it doesn't matter.

I haven't gone far when I catch sight of a vehicle coming up fast behind me. 'You can't get by here.' I mutter, my eyes flicking from the rear-view mirror to the road ahead and back again.

The vehicle flashes its headlights. It's an SUV, and is almost touching the Citroën's bumper. I stare in the mirror, but their lights are dazzling; too bright for me to work out who's driving. Whoever it is, they're in a hurry. I'll have to let them pass. Perhaps there's somewhere further on where I can pull over?

I press my foot down on the accelerator, but the SUV keeps pace. Then BANG - they rear-end the car. My body jolts forward. What on earth…

There's a moment of silence before Ike whimpers.

CRASH - my rear bumper again. I have no option but to hit the throttle. We pass a couple of driveways, but I'm going too fast to pull over. My heart races. What are they playing at?

They're right on my tail when they hit us a third time. Ike cries out as I fight to stay in control. I tug the steering wheel sharp right, and then left as the road snakes. Around the bend, two cyclists meander lazily along the lane. I spot a farm entrance to my left and frantically spin the wheel, but it's too late. A tree looms up seconds before my forehead hits the windscreen. *A bird crashes into the glass… as if it already knew its fate.*

CHAPTER SIXTY-FIVE

As I regain consciousness, I realise I'm at home, lying on the couch in the snug once more.

'There she is.'

I turn my head. Mark's in the armchair opposite.

'What happened?' I stammer.

'You had a bit of an accident. Bloody cyclists riding two abreast, they should be prosecuted.'

'What?' My head's killing me. I reach a hand to my fore-head, feeling something sticky. I stare at my fingers. Blood. 'Do I need to go to hospital?'

'No, Deòiridh's taken a look at you. You're going to be fine,' Mark says. 'Citroën's a write off though.'

Deòiridh squats down in front of me. 'This will help.' She holds a glass to my lips.

I take a sip. The brandy burns as it slips down my throat, shocking me to wakefulness. 'The boys…' I try to sit up.

Deòiridh places a firm hand on my shoulder. 'The boys are fine.'

I glance from Deòiridh to Mark and back again. I had something urgent to do… why don't I remember? Whatever it was, it's gone, but I have a fierce need to see the boys. 'I have to check…' I struggle to get up.

Mark holds out a hand. 'Wait…'

'No,' says Deòiridh, 'let her go. She'll be reassured once she knows they're safe.'

I smile gratefully.

Mark takes my arm and guides me slowly across the room and upstairs. He pushes open the boys' bedroom door. 'See? Both soundo.'

I gaze at their tiny forms, snuggled up in their beds. They're fine. A wave of nausea washes over me and my knees buckle.

Mark supports me along to my room. 'Just rest.' He helps me to the bed. 'I'll check on you later.'

I sit up. The room's in darkness. My head throbs. Clambering off the bed, I stumble through to the bathroom where an inspection of my forehead reveals a small cut secured by three strips of surgical tape. There's glitter in my hair and I puzzle over it for a moment before working out it's tiny fragments of glass. The driver's mirror must have broken when I crashed. It's odd they put me to bed with a head injury. Basic first aid training dictates you don't let anyone sleep when they've bumped their head. Perhaps Mark's been checking in on me?

Everything's unusually quiet. I stifle a cough. My throat's dry and I could do with a soothing hot lemon. On the way downstairs, I look in on the boys. Kwami's in his cot, sucking contentedly on his thumb. Ike's bed is cluttered with soft toys, and it takes me a moment to realise that he's not in it.

Panic rises. I run out onto the landing, then back into the

boys' room where I check under Ike's bed. I even open the wardrobe, as if he would climb in there.

'What are you doing?' Deòiridh's in the doorway dressed in a long purple robe.

'Where's Ike?'

'Downstairs with Mark.' She crosses the room and closes the wardrobe before taking my arm. 'Let's get you to bed.'

She settles me back in my room. 'Here, drink this.' She offers me a glass. 'It will help.'

It tastes of lemon and ginger and, because I'm so thirsty, I obediently comply.

As she covers me with a quilt, her dressing gown gapes, revealing a glimpse of her chest. On her left breast is a tiny swastika, while her right breast bears another design, the same tattoo as Mark's.

'What's that?' I stammer.

'It's called the *Eye of Horus*. Now, get some rest.'

'Hello. How are you feeling?'

'I don't know, I…'

Mark moves closer and studies my face. 'You still look a little flushed.' He lifts something from the bedside table. 'Drink this.' Supporting my head, he holds a glass to my lips.

I sip cool, refreshing water. 'Thanks. I had the strangest dream… robed figures… in the woods…' I struggle to form words, but my tongue seems too big for my mouth.

'Shh.' Mark lowers my head onto the pillow. 'Just rest. You'll feel better soon.' Gently he strokes the good side of my forehead.

I close my eyes. 'That's nice…'

CHAPTER SIXTY-SIX

Mark has his head in his hands.

'Mark?' My voice is groggy and distant.

He glances up and takes my hand. 'How are you feeling?'

'I'm okay.' His eyes are puffy and swollen. Has he been crying? 'What's happened?'

'You had an accident. Don't you remember?'

My stomach lurches. 'The boys?'

He smiles. 'The boys are fine.'

'I remember being downstairs... Deòiridh was there... how long have I been up here?'

'A couple of days.' There's a catch in his voice.

'Mark, what is it? Is it... Vita?'

'No, Mum's about the same.' He takes a deep breath. 'While you were out of it, we received some bad news.'

I clutch his arm. 'What news?'

He attempts a smile. 'It's Temi. I know you and he didn't really get on, but...'

'Temi? What's happened?'

Mark covers his face with his hands again and his shoulders shake.

I sit up, wrapping my arms around him. 'Mark, you've got to tell me what's happened.'

He pulls away, rubbing his eyes with balled fists. 'No one realised he was suffering.'

'Suffering?'

'He hid it well, but he must have been depressed for a long time.'

'Temi wasn't depressed.'

'He was returning from Wales. Got as far as Liverpool Street before he…'

'He what?'

'Threw himself under a tube train.' Mark exhales. 'Temi's dead.'

Temi dead? How can Temi be dead? I rub my forehead. My brain's a fog. Why don't I remember anything? My throat's dry. I reach for the glass of orange squash on my bedside table and down it in one. I should check on the boys, but Mark said they were fine. I lay back on my pillow. I'm so tired… I close my eyes.

———

'Hanna?

'Mmm?' It's hard to open my eyes. When I finally manage it, Deòiridh smiles down at me.

'I've brought you a hot chocolate.'

'Thanks.'

After she's left, I glance at the drink on my bedside table. Slowly I haul myself to a sitting position and reach out, but I'm clumsy. The mug tips and milky drink spills across the bedside table.

Bugger. What a mess. I grab a handful of tissues, attempting to soak up the liquid dripping onto the carpet. Then I freeze. Voices are right outside my room.

'She's pretty out of it,' says Deòiridh.

'It's good she sleeps,' replies Mark.

'We need to keep her calm.'

'I know, I get it.' He sighs. 'If anything had happened to the boys…'

'It didn't.'

'I called Tom. He's not sure what more he can do.'

'So, what happens now?'

There's a pause before Mark answers. 'I've put a call in to *Mount Lodge*.'

'The mental health unit?'

'I have no choice.'

They're going to lock me up. It's not really a surprise. I've lost touch with reality. Why don't I remember?

I do remember one thing. Temi's dead. But there was something else… something to do with the accident. Where was I going? I rub my forehead. If only I could make sense of it all.

What was it Tom said? Postpartum psychosis? Back then I'd Googled the symptoms – religious delusions, hallucinations and nightmares so lucid you can't tell whether they're real or not. Paranoia, disturbing thoughts and panic attacks. If untreated, postpartum psychosis can lead to suicide or even infanticide. Is that why they're keeping the boys from me? Why was I in the car?

CHAPTER SIXTY-SEVEN

'You need to get up.'

'What…' I blink, my eyes assaulted by bright light.

Mark throws back the quilt. 'Tom's coming this morning.'

'Tom…' My eyelids softly close.

'No, you don't.' Mark grabs my shoulders and hauls me to a sitting position. My limbs feel as if they belong to a rag doll as he prods and pulls me until I'm wearing a T-shirt.

He chucks a pair of trackie bottoms on the bed. 'Put these on too.'

'Mark, I can't…'

'Yes, you can.'

I reach for the trackies and attempt to slip my legs into them, but I wobble and collapse back onto the bed.

Supporting me with one arm, he yanks up my trousers like I'm a toddler. Frowning, he says, 'You'd better brush your teeth. I'll be back shortly.'

I stagger through to the bathroom. As I glance into the mirror, a woman with dank, greasy hair and a pale haggard face stares back. She doesn't look like me. Have I lost weight? I pick up the toothpaste. It takes every ounce of my energy to squeeze a blob onto the brush.

'Ready?' calls Mark.

'Wait, I need a wee.' When I've finished, he comes in and takes my arm, leading me downstairs. I'm slow and frail like an old lady.

He settles me on the couch in the snug. 'I'll bring you a cuppa.' He tucks a throw around my legs. 'Tom will be here soon.'

———

'Hello Hanna.' Tom's voice is overly bright. I can tell he's trying not to appear shocked by the way I've deteriorated. 'How are you feeling?'

I lay my head back on the couch. 'Exhausted.'

He pulls up a chair and sits in front of me. 'Mark says you've not been well. I'm sorry to hear that. I thought we'd made progress.'

'We did, but then… the accident, and the news about Temi…'

'Yes, I heard about Temi. Quite a shock for everyone.'

Mark comes in with two mugs. He hands one to Tom and sets the other on a small side table.

I smile at him half-heartedly. 'Thanks.'

'I'll leave you to it,' he says.

Tom waits until Mark closes the door before continuing. 'Hanna, can you describe your symptoms?'

I rub my eyes. 'Tiredness mostly.'

'Mark says you've been having strange dreams?'

'I don't know whether they're dreams, hallucinations or reality. It's hard to tell.'

'What sort of dreams?'

'Religious gatherings in dark crypts, messages from birds, phantom dogs, ghostlike children…' I frown. 'Doesn't bode well, does it?'

'Well, those symptoms might suggest postpartum psychosis. In some cases, depression morphs into psychosis and it doesn't always happen right away. Any feelings of paranoia?'

I snort. 'Like believing my child's not mine, my husband's having an affair and everyone's out to get me? That kind of thing?'

Tom folds his arms. 'You know, Hanna, it might be time for us to seek specialist help. There's a unit not far away with a great reputation for dealing with these things.'

'So, you want to lock me up. I suppose it was only a matter of time.' I lean forward and grab his arm. 'Tom, can I ask you something?'

'Of course.' Pushing his glasses up the bridge of his nose, he waits expectantly.

'Did I try to hurt my children?'

After Tom's gone, Mark carries me back upstairs and settles me on the bed. 'Here, take these.' He holds out two pills. Meekly I swallow them, washed down with sips of water.

He closes the drapes. 'Try and get some rest.' Tucking me in like I'm a little girl, he kisses my forehead.

I roll over and close my eyes, but I can't stop thinking about the look on Tom's face. He didn't answer my question, but he was concerned. Could postpartum psychosis explain all the things that have gone on? Were the sightings of the little girl and the singing all hallucinations? My mind won't stop churning. It fits. And yet, if I'm suffering from psychosis, how come I'm capable of thinking this through logically and rationally? Wouldn't I be arguing it was all real?

I lift my head from the pillow. How long have I been asleep? Someone's crying. Is it Kwami? I pull on my dressing robe and head for the door, but it's locked.

I rattle the handle. 'Let me out.'

But no one comes.

I put my ear to the door. The crying's stopped, but I want to check the boys are all right. I bang on the door. 'Hey, let me out.'

Silence.

I stumble back to bed and curl into a ball. Why would they lock me in again? Do they really think me capable of harming the boys?

CHAPTER SIXTY-EIGHT

I'm woken by a hand over my mouth. 'Mmm…' I protest, thrashing about.

'Shh.'

Twisting my head, I stare up at Jenna.

She holds a finger to her lips before releasing me.

'What are you doing?' I hiss. Then I remember the locked door. 'How did you get in?'

She dangles a key in front of me. 'It was in the keyhole.'

I drop my head. 'They locked the door again. They think I'm a danger to the boys.'

'That's not it. They're up to something. It's you and the boys who are in danger.'

'How do you know?'

'Temi told me. We stayed in touch after that cow booted me out.' She grips my arm. 'You do know I didn't steal anything?'

'Of course, it was ridiculous, but why didn't you fight it? Clear your name?'

'Deòiridh's a powerful woman. She could have stopped me from working again.'

Everything comes flooding back and my eyes fill with tears. 'Is Temi really dead?'

'Yes.' Jenna pats my arm. 'I'm sorry, but there's no way he committed suicide. Someone wanted to shut him up. We'll talk about it later, but right now we've more urgent things to deal with. Can you get up?'

I swing my legs slowly to the floor.

'Shall I help you get dressed?'

'I'm okay.' Brushing her away, I pull on jeans.

Jenna eases open the bedroom door, while I grab my jacket and follow her. Softly, we tiptoe along the landing to the boys' room. Kwami's asleep in his cot, but Ike's bed is empty. 'Where's Ike?'

'They've taken him downstairs. Heaven knows what they're up to, but it won't be anything good.'

'I have to get him.'

'I'll come with you, but we need to be super quiet.'

'No, take Kwami to my car. I'll meet you there.'

'The Citroën's not there.'

Of course, the accident. 'Oh, shit.' I rub my brow. 'We'll have to take Mark's Range Rover. It's parked behind Bartholomew block.'

'We'll need a distraction.'

'Take Kwami downstairs and hide in the powder room. If I'm not back in fifteen minutes, smash the fire alarm and get outside.'

Leaving Jenna to sort out Kwami, I hurry downstairs to check the snug before going to the kitchen and grabbing Mark's car keys from the hook. Everywhere's deserted. I hesitate. Should I call the police? But after the last episode, they're not likely to believe me and, even if they do, they'll take an age to get here. No, I have to do this myself.

Tucking the keys in my jeans pocket, I tiptoe along the

corridor. The portrait of Crowley is displaced; they must be in the crypt. I rifle through my jacket pocket, exhaling with relief when my fingers close around the key I had cut.

No sign of Jenna yet, so I slide the key carefully into the lock and turn. I open the door and step inside. The hatch is closed. Although I'm weaker than I was, adrenaline helps me to lift it.

Chanting again. So, I wasn't dreaming. The initiation ceremony was real. I peer down into the darkness. Flickering lights. Candles? Soundlessly I ease myself down the ladder. When I reach the bottom, I creep to the nearest pillar and hide.

Holding my breath, I peer out. Six black-robed monks kneel along three sides of a chalk-drawn pentagram. Four of them are chanting, while the others beat a rhythm on small circular drums. In their midst is an altar bearing candles, along with two metal bowls with chains, like incense holders used in an Orthodox Church.

I gaze at the monks. Is Mark one of them? Who are the others? The trustees? Behind the altar stands a solitary figure, slight built and wearing a purple satin robe. It has to be Deòiridh.

The chanting and drumming subside, and the monks appear to enter a trance-like state. One rises to his feet. He wafts incense over the altar before extending a hand to Deòiridh. She moves forward and they stand side by side.

Assuming the role of Master of Ceremonies, the monk speaks. 'Behold. Your High Priestess, reincarnation of our servant, Aleister Crowley.'

'So be it,' reply the other robed men in unison.

'This very eve marks the turn of time,' he continues. 'Deòiridh, Adeptus Exemptus, has exceeded the 26,348 days

Aleister Crowley dwelt upon this earth. As your longest-serving servant and your High Priestess, she will…'

'Do what thou wilt shall be the whole law,' the others chorus.

He spreads his hands wide. 'From this moment henceforth, Deòiridh assumes the entity, Goddess of Aiwass. She and only she commands us on the true pathway to Molech.'

'Pure will is perfection in every way,' they chant.

Deòiridh faces the altar as the Master of Ceremonies approaches the wall. Lifting the horned mask from the niche, he fits it over her face. With a bow, he resumes his position on the pentagram.

She turns slowly, her hands aloft. Collectively we gasp, for the mask is transformed. Before us stands a living entity, its evil eyes glinting within deep eye sockets.

For a moment I cannot breathe.

'Bring forth the sacrifice,' the beast commands.

Sacrifice?

Two of the men move to a dark corner of the room, where they crouch down. What are they doing? I crane my neck… they're uncovering something. One of them scoops it up in his arms and carries it to the altar.

As he sets the bundle down, my heart skips a beat. Ike, naked but for his Spidey boxers. His body's floppy and it looks as if he's asleep. How did they get him down here without waking him? What are they going to do? Come on, Jenna, I need that diversion…

The men return to their places.

Deòiridh circles the altar, examining Ike. She lifts one limb, then another, before peering into his face and flicking his cheek with her fingers.

I flinch. Why doesn't he wake up? Then I realise his eyes are open. He's not asleep; he's been drugged.

She makes several circuits, each time setting down an artefact beside Ike's still body. First, a rosary made of wooden discs, then an amulet. Small stones follow, along with two skulls that look as if they come from birds. On her last rotation, she sets down a tiny item.

What is it? Gingerly, I take a step forward. Remarkably, they don't hear me. Something black, an inch long, the diameter of a pencil... I stifle a gasp. Ike's severed finger.

Deòiridh returns to a central position and the beast stares right at me.

I duck back. Did she see me? That's when I notice the tripod positioned halfway between the altar and the pillar I'm hiding behind. She's filming this. It's all for the camera.

She lifts a candle and holds it above Ike's head. A tiny drop of wax lands on his forehead.

I cover my mouth. No.

Ike's eyes go wide, but he doesn't cry out.

Deòiridh picks up a small bowl. She dips in a finger and anoints Ike with what appears to be oil. Her fingers draw shapes on his wrists and ankles. Setting down the bowl, she gazes up, mumbling words.

Is it a prayer? Whatever it is, it's not in English. Come on, Jenna. Smash that alarm.

Deòiridh stares down at Ike before taking something from the table and lifting it high. A flash of steel. A knife!

'No!' I scream. Racing from my hiding place, I dive into the midst of the circle.

The mouth of the Master of Ceremonies forms a small 'o' of surprise while the rest of the monks stumble back, startled by the intrusion.

I hurl myself forward, half mounting the altar, in my attempt to shield Ike's motionless body with my own. As I close my eyes, I hear someone scream. It takes a moment to realise it's me.

I open my eyes again. The Master of Ceremonies is approaching. As he nears, he lowers his hood. It's Mark.

He pulls my arms behind my back and drags me away from the altar to an area out of camera shot. 'What the hell do you think you're doing?' he hisses.

I spin around to face him. 'What the hell am I doing? What are you doing, Mark?' I gesture to Deòiridh who has removed the mask. 'That woman was about to stab our son.'

He snorts as he lets me go. 'Don't be ridiculous. Deòiridh wouldn't really stab Ike. What do you take us for?'

'I've no idea, Mark.' I back away. 'I don't know what you're capable of.'

He gestures to the video equipment. 'This is a re-enactment. It's theatrical. Something for the Brethren. It's not real.'

I'm shaking with rage. 'It's real for Ike. What sort of trauma do you think you're subjecting him to?' I point at Ike's tiny pinkie. 'His finger? Christ, Mark.'

Mark's cheeks flush. 'You know that was an accident. It's not like he'll remember anything…'

Deòiridh steps closer. 'You needn't worry, Hanna. Ike is sedated.' She lays a hand on my arm. 'We're broadcasting to over a hundred worldwide followers of Molech. Ike is a celebrity.'

Mark steps forward, hands open as if to reassure me he's not a threat. 'The ritual is all about wealth and success. This is for us. The Brethren pay huge sums to be part of this re-enactment. Our family will be safe and the business secure. Come on, Hanna. Equal partners, what do you say?'

Equal partners in business, a perfect family of four. All I'd ever wanted, but not this way. I find myself backed against a wall. 'You're mad, the whole bloody lot of you.'

Then the fire alarm goes off.

One of the other monks must have approached on my blind side because a sack is forced over my head.

'Ike,' I yell. 'Ike.'

Someone manhandles me to the ladder and positions my hands on the rungs. 'Up you go,' says a gruff voice.

I climb. My shin bashes against the trap hatch and the pain steals my breath. Then I'm dragged and pushed along, before being lowered onto a chair.

Mark's voice. 'Check the control board, it's bound to be a false alarm. Sodding builders probably cut through a cable or something.'

'Mark,' I shout. 'You're in too deep with this lot. Temi wouldn't commit suicide. Someone must have killed him.'

The sack's made of mesh and I can just make out we're in the kitchen. Someone grabs my hands and binds them behind my back.

Another robed monk strides in, removing his hood. Sebastian. He opens a cupboard door and studies the control board. Emerging, he checks the controls on the range before heading back out into the hallway.

Someone's behind me and the sack's tugged from my head. 'Mark,' I yell.

Deòiridh walks in with Ike in her arms, thankfully wrapped in a blanket.

'If you hurt him, I'll kill you,' I scream.

She smiles. 'He's fine.'

I try to stand, but my legs feel like they're made of jelly. 'The police and fire brigade will be on their way,' I say. 'And Mark will have to settle the residents and reset the alarm. There's no way you and your cronies can do whatever you had planned for tonight.'

'And if you don't want to be gagged,' says Deòiridh, 'I suggest that you keep your mouth shut.'

In the hallway, Mark's speaking to someone on his mobile. 'No, there's no fire. Yes, I know we'll be charged...'

I eyeball Deòiridh before throwing back my head and yelling at the top of my lungs. 'Help, help me.'

'Stupid girl. Now we'll have to do things the hard way.' She nods at the monk standing behind me, who thrusts a gag into my mouth and ties it behind my head.

'No, just someone playing silly buggers,' Mark says. 'No, we don't need anyone to come and check. Thank you.'

Deòiridh glares at me.

'Deòiridh,' Mark yells.

She throws me a superior look. 'Excuse me.' She still has Ike in her arms as she heads out to find Mark. I want to scream at her to put him down.

I hear them talking.

'Do we need to go outside?' asks Deòiridh.

Oh no! Jenna took Kwami outside. Suppose they find them?

'No,' says Mark. 'It was definitely a false alarm. Sebastian's disconnecting the system. I'll send Isaac round to reassure the night staff it was just a faulty connection. Isaac?'

The robed monk guarding me heads out to the hall.

Left alone, I wriggle my hands. They must have used duct tape to bind them, because the more I struggle, the tighter the tape cuts into my flesh. I've got to get to Ike. I push down on my feet and try to walk the chair towards the doorway. I've only moved a few inches when I hear someone coming.

Deòiridh's in the doorway. 'You do like to make things difficult, don't you?'

Mark's standing behind her. 'So, do we abort?'

She smiles. 'No way. The Brethren are waiting. A small delay will only enhance the anticipation.'

He gestures to me. 'What about Hanna?'

'Bring her. She can watch.'

Two hooded monks return. Lifting me from the chair, they drag me across the hallway and lower me down to the crypt again, where they secure me with more tape to a hard-backed chair before resuming preparations.

Ike's back on the altar, his blanket discarded on the cold, stone floor. Sebastian's manning the video – I hear him re-establishing a link on the computer. Twisting my neck, I see a screen full of people – a massive Zoom call with all participants masked. I squirm, but they've secured me well. I open and close my mouth, trying to work the gag loose, but it's impossible. All I manage to emit are gurgling noises.

The monks are gowned once more. They assume their positions and begin to chant. Deòiridh is wearing the bull mask.

I moan helplessly, but it does nothing to disrupt the ceremony.

Deòiridh re-lights the candles and wafts incense over Ike's small body. He seems oblivious, but his eyes are wide. I can't imagine how frightened he is. Willing him to look at me, I try to send comforting thoughts by telepathy.

She raises the knife.

I scream, but the sound is muffled by the gag.

Lowering the knife slowly, she rests the tip on Ike's chest.

This doesn't look like a re-enactment to me. I moan as a drop of blood beads on Ike's tiny chest.

Mark's standing to Deòiridh's right. His hand reaches for the knife's handle. 'Careful.'

But even through the mask, Deòiridh's eyes are wild with excitement. 'Trust me,' she whispers.

Mark glances my way. For the first time, his eyes flicker with uncertainty.

I open my eyes wide, willing him to intervene.

He turns back to Deòiridh.

She's playing, rocking the knife gently across Ike's skin. Pinpricks of blood appear while she gazes, transfixed.

Murmurs stir from the ranks of the seated monks. One struggles to his feet. Is it Stefan? 'Wait,' he cries. 'What's going on?'

I turn to look at the screen. Some of the brethren appear agitated but I can't tell if it's with horror or excitement. Sebastian lowers the video camera.

'Keep filming,' yells Deòiridh.

He shakes his head, but refocuses the lens on the altar.

Mark moves his fingers to the tip of the knife, halting the motion. 'You've cut him,' he says.

Deòiridh glares. 'You can't have a sacrifice without spilling blood,' she hisses.

Mark grabs the knife in his fist. There's blood and, for a horrifying moment, I think it's Ike's, but no, the knife has sliced into Mark's palm.

'What are you doing?' screams Deòiridh.

They stagger back from the altar with the knife between them. They're so close they might be embracing. Mark's eyes are wide. Has she stabbed him? No. They separate and I see the knife sticking out of Deòiridh's chest.

Mark backs away.

Deòiridh remains upright. Gripping the knife in both hands, she pulls it out. Blood gushes from the wound and she falls to the floor.

The monks gasp in horror. Sebastian, transfixed, keeps filming.

I feel a hand on my shoulder and turn to see Jenna. She loosens my gag.

'Where's Kwami?' I whisper.

'Hidden under the hydrangeas.' She produces a pair of scissors I recognise from the kitchen and cuts through the tape binding me. 'He'll be fine. He's in his cosy with an extra blanket.'

I rub my wrists. 'I need to get Ike.' I try to stand, but I'm light-headed and I wobble.

Jenna helps me across to the altar.

Isaac lowers his hood. 'We need an ambulance.' He paces up and down, trying to get a signal on his mobile phone.

'Isaac,' I say.

He looks at me.

'It's over,' says Jenna. 'The police are on the way.'

He raises his hands as if we're pointing a gun.

Jenna and I exchange a glance.

I speak calmly. 'I'm taking my son now.' I reach for the blanket and wrap it around Ike before scooping him into my arms.

Isaac makes no move to stop me.

Deòiridh's on the floor. Her mask has slipped and blood pools around her. Mark's gazing at his blood-soaked hands, rubbing them together like Lady Macbeth.

I stare at him in horror. Who is this man? I want to tell him I'm leaving and taking the boys, but even looking at him turns my stomach.

Jenna tugs me. 'Come on.'

She climbs the ladder first. I pass her Ike and clamber up myself. We're almost at the front door when I put a hand on her arm. 'Suppose they follow?'

'I think they're in shock.'

'No, we need another distraction. Take Ike and wait by the car.'

In the kitchen, I rip pages from a copy of *Mother & Baby* and lay the screwed-up paper on top of the range before lighting the gas rings. While they catch, I grab a bottle of cooking oil from the cupboard and douse a couple of tea towels before stepping back and throwing them onto the flames.

Mr Biggles stretches and mews, then jumps from the chair, hurtles between my legs and out through the cat flap.

'You'll have to fend for yourself,' I say, as fire rages and smoke plumes. I run back into the hallway and into the powder room.

Peeking out, I see Mark come rushing up from the crypt with Stefan and Isaac at his heels. 'Damn it,' Mark yells. 'Get the fire extinguisher. The fire brigade won't come. I only just convinced them it was a false alarm. We'll have to deal with this ourselves.'

The hallway is full of smoke. Coughing, I rub my eyes. I'm disorientated and can't even see the door. Then I spot the yellow orb inches from my face. Leaving the men to tackle the mini-inferno, I follow the orb across the smoky hallway and out through the front door.

Outside, I skirt the lawn, heading for Mark's Range Rover. Heavy footsteps are closing in when there's a thud and a cry of pain. Thank goodness Norris never got around to digging up those tree stumps. Reaching the back of Bartholomew block, I press the bleeper on Mark's key fob and the Range Rover lights blink back.

Jenna's behind the vehicle with Ike. She transfers him to my arms. 'I'll get Kwami.'

She disappears under the bushes as Ike stirs. 'It's okay, Mummy's here,' I say.

Jenna re-appears and secures Kwami in his baby seat. How has he slept through the whole drama? Did they drug him, too?

Jenna climbs into the back of the Range Rover and I pass Ike to her. She straps him into the booster seat, tucking the blanket around him, while I scramble into the driver's seat. I start the ignition and swing the Range Rover around, just as a robed man staggers from the path.

I catch Jenna's eye as she fumbles with her seatbelt. 'You okay?'

'Yeah.' She yells. 'Go, go go.'

I hadn't intended looking back and yet, at the last bend, I can't resist glancing in the rear-view mirror. The gothic house stands proud. No sign of the robed men and Mark must be occupied with the fire.

Turning my attention to navigating the iron gates, I'm forced to brake. In the middle of the drive, the headlights pick out two piercing red eyes. A massive dog barring our way.

Jenna leans between the front seats. 'What the hell is that?'

From the back seat, Ike murmurs. 'Gainde.'

The dog stands, ears alert, tail erect. Is it real?

My back is rigid. My fists grip the steering wheel so tightly that I fear my knuckles might break the skin. I press lightly on the throttle – once, twice. The Range Rover responds with a warning rev.

The creature's eyes bore through me as if searching my soul.

Seconds tick by as we hold each other's gaze.

Finally, the dog jerks his head. He offers me a last doleful glance before sloping off into the shadows.

EPILOGUE

Yellow roses lend a splash of brightness to an otherwise sterile room, their fragrance sweet and lemony. In the bed, a young woman smiles in her sleep.

Ike, in the chair beside her, wears a suitably smug expression.

I laugh.

'What?' He runs his fingers through his curly hair, and I wince, noticing the missing digit. It never seems to bother him. He was so young. I wonder how much he remembers of our time at *The Sanctuary*? Sometimes, I find myself about to ask him, but I always catch myself before the words escape. I don't want to undo the years of counselling; to reopen a door to the past that should remain firmly shut – for him, at least.

'You, the proud dad.' I smile. 'It's not as if you contributed much when it came to the hard work.'

When he grins, I experience a warm glow. He's so handsome, the touch of grey at his temples only enhancing his good looks.

The door flies open and my youngest son barges in, arms

laden with helium balloons, a bottle of bubbly and an enormous pink teddy bear. 'So? Where's my niece?'

'Shh.' I frown. 'Sally's asleep.'

Kwami pecks my cheek as he hands me the balloon strings. Setting the champagne and teddy down on a spare chair, he folds Ike into a bear hug. 'Congrats, mate.' He's a couple of inches taller than his elder brother, which has generated much good-natured banter over the years.

I gaze fondly at my two sons, feeling a sense of achievement. The past twenty years have not been easy. After divorcing Mark, I raised the boys alone while he spent six years in a prison cell for manslaughter. He'd have served longer if I'd had a say in the matter, but coercive control – gas-lighting, holding me against my will, trying to convince me I was mad – is harder to prove. And I will never forgive him for what he did to Ike – although the defence lawyer managed to ensure Deòiridh took posthumous blame for all child abuse charges.

Noticing a few greeting cards on the bedside table, I turn to Ike. 'Did you hear from Jenna?'

'She sent a video message.' He pulls an iPhone from his pocket and scrolls down to find it. 'Here.'

Taking the phone, I lower the volume and touch the screen. Jenna and Lou appear, their eyes sparkling. "Congratulations," shouts Lou. "Lots of love from your Aunties," yells Jenna. "We're coming up to see you soon!" they chorus in harmony.

I stifle giggles, not wanting to wake Sally. As I hand the phone back to Ike, a card catches my eye – a beautiful African Hibiscus. I know who that's from. Opening it, I read the message. *"Warmest congratulations, dear Ike and Sally. Felicitations from Auntie Lebe."* Lebe, Jenna and I remained steadfast in our belief that Temi did not take his own life.

Over the years, Lebe and I became regular Skype buddies, with Ike spending six months of his gap year in Lagos as her guest.

'Are you still planning to visit Nigeria once you finish your MA?' I ask Kwami.

'Yes. It's time I went to see where Nduka lived and worked for so many years. Lebe says the hospital named the new training wing after him.'

The boys are proud of their grandfather's work, and rightly so. He set up mentoring programmes for many young doctors, doing much to inspire his proteges. It saddens me that I didn't get the chance to know him. My sons have no living grandparents. Vita passed six months after her stroke. Perhaps a blessing? She wouldn't have wanted to live the way she was.

Sally stirs and Ike plants an affectionate kiss on her forehead. Kwami and I exchange a glance and he winks.

Sally opens her eyes and smiles. 'Have you seen her yet?'

'Not yet,' I say. 'We were waiting for you.'

She pulls herself up to sitting and reaches for the call bell. Minutes later a nurse enters carrying a swaddled child.

Ike gestures to me. 'Granny wants a cuddle.'

The nurse places the baby in my arms.

I loosen her shawl and gaze down at her beautiful face, long eyelashes and pouting lips. 'Oh, I'm in love.'

Kwami looks over my shoulder. 'You did a good job, bro.'

'Hey!' Sally pouts.

He gives an apologetic grin. 'Sorry. You too, Sal.'

The baby squirms. Her arm wriggles free and a star-shaped hand opens and closes. As I take the tiny hand in mine, I feel the raised birthmark just behind her knuckles.

'It's a nevus,' says Ike. 'The doctor says it will fade away naturally by the time she's six.'

'Shame,' says Sally. 'I kinda like it.'

I rub my finger lightly across the heart-shaped birthmark. 'Yes,' I say. 'So do I.'

LULLABY

(to the tune of Rock-A-Bye Baby)

Hush little nightjar,
'Tis time to sleep.
You made a promise,
Secrets to keep.

Heed little owlet,
Tu-whit, tu-whoo.
Think you're so wise.
If only you knew.

Soar away raven,
Spirit and ghoul.
Eerie the portent,
Chills to your soul.

Poor little songbird,
Smothered in bed.
Even a bird song,
Can't wake the dead.

ACKNOWLEDGMENTS

With gratitude to my editor, Claire Chamberlain for feedback, copy editing and proof-reading. Thank you to fellow author, Patricia M Osborne for development editing of the manuscript. Also, a big shout out to my beta readers - Fiona Campbell, Jane Collins, Samantha Froud-Hill and Maureen Utting,

I am grateful to Andy Keylock for the beautiful and enticing cover design. Special thanks to Samantha Rumens at Marketing Pace for marketing my books and providing ongoing advice for Broodleroo's social media platform.

Finally, thanks to my partner, Colin, and my family and friends for their continued encouragement, support and love.

ABOUT THE AUTHOR

Suzi Bamblett lives in Crowborough, East Sussex. In 2019 she graduated with a distinction for her MA in Creative Writing (University of Brighton)

Suzi writes psychological thrillers and suspense. Her *Imagined Dialogue with Daphne* can be found on the Daphne du Maurier website. Suzi's work has been published in literary magazines and academic collections including Shooter Literary Magazine (2020) and Storying the Self - Performance and Communities (2022)

Prescient Spirit is her third novel.

For more information please visit Suzi's website Broodleroo.com where you can sign up to receive news.

ALSO BY SUZI BAMBLETT

The Travelling Philanthropist

Praise for The Travelling Philanthropist:

"Transports you to another time and place"

"A great page-turning read"

"Couldn't wait to find out how it all ended"

Three Faced Doll

Praise for Three Faced Doll:

"Grabbed me from the start"

"Gripping and full of surprises"

"Kept me guessing right to the end"

Printed in Great Britain
by Amazon